A Day and a Night and a Day.

Also by Glen Duncan

Hope

Love Remains

I, Lucifer

Weathercock

Death of an Ordinary Man

The Bloodstone Papers

A Day and
a Night
and a Day

a novel

Glen Duncan

An Imprint of HarperCollins*Publishers*

HarperCollins books may be purchased for educational, business, or
sales promotional use. For information, please write: Special Markets
Department, HarperCollins Publishers, 10 East 53rd Street, New York,
NY 10022.

FIRST EDITION

Designed by Jessica Shatan Heslin/Studio Shatan, Inc.

Library of Congress Cataloging-in-Publication Data

Duncan, Glen
    A day and a night and a day : a novel / Glen Duncan.—1st ed.
        p.   cm.
    ISBN: 978-0-06-123999-1
    I. Title.
    PR6104.U535D39 2009
    823'.92—dc22

                                                    2008026420

08 09 10 11 12   ID/RRD   10 9 8 7 6 5 4 3 2 1

For

Jon and Vicky

A Day and a Night and a Day

The room he wakes up in has the fraught stink of a phone booth, which in spite of everything evokes escort ads and brings a pang of loss, not for sex but for tenderness. The last woman was a young dark-haired prostitute in Barcelona he'd paid extra to lie with him for an hour postcoitally, his nose in her downy nape. Just lie here? Yes, if that's okay. She'd been palpably uneasy, as if affection was an edgy perversion, but what could he tell her? He was astonished himself.

Dry-mouthed, he lifts his head off his chest and feels a granular crunch in his neck. No idea how long he's been out. The handcuffs look brand-new, glamorous against his dark skin. Sikh men wear those steel bangles and often have showgirl eyelashes yet appear superbly masculine. He wouldn't have minded being a Sikh. Selina years ago said the turban had deep phallic allure—which was the sort of thing she came out with apropos of nothing. Naturally non-sequiturial, by the time he met her she was exploiting the trait having learned it charmed people. Their friends regarded her as someone enviably at ease in her own skin. He, privy offstage and after hours, knew her hung about with superstitions and fears, all the trinkets and bogeymen of her half-shucked Catholicism. Nonetheless she glimmered in the crowd: women knew to be at the top of their game, men made adjustments, maximized themselves. Standing at the bar he'd watch her and remind himself he was the one going home with her.

What the women objected to, aside from the standard injustice of random beauty, was her intelligence. Intelligence on top of the long legs and natural blond was sheerly immoral. That and having the guts to do what they stopped short of: publicly date a negro. Or half-negro. Or whatever he was. He'd stand at the bar and let the warmth of sexual ownership flow through him. Harry, languidly drying a highball glass said: You two are a profane enchantment, you know that? He did know it. Manhattan's streets met them with a murmur of outrage. Imperious amusement, Selina said. We return them imperious amusement and benign disdain. That's easy for you to say, he said. You're not the one they're going to beat the shit out of. You're not the one they're going to *lynch*. This was 1967. With her he thought the biggest thing his life could offer had arrived.

And since here he is almost forty years later it turns out he was right.

His wristwatch is gone. They removed it when they brought him in. *Carry nothing of sentimental value*, so he never does. An airport Swatch, $75. He's always loved the harried polyglotism of airports. Transit lounges suggest the great subversion: there aren't countries, only people, the secret everyone suspects and governments live in fear of. He remembers the brownstone doorway of his childhood in East Harlem, darkness framing the blistered stoop, the blinding asphalt, the smell of garbage cans and urine. You stood on the threshold and felt the world right there like the hot flank of an animal. There was one never-repeated visit to his grandfather ten blocks away, a straw-colored Santa Clausy man with a plump nose and huge sour pants who said get that nigger brat out of here.

Which thought turns out to be the last fluttering postponement. He strains against the handcuffs until his skull thuds, stops when the pain gets too much. Any pain now is an outrider for the pain coming. People use the phrase "the worst-case scenario," it's always contextual. Not here: This is *the* worst-case scenario, the Platonic Form, of which all others are imperfect instances.

He can't remember which fake name he's been using, for a yawning second can't remember his *real* name—then it comes to him with his mother's face and a feeling of nearness to her. She was a supple dark-haired woman with green eyes and what he now realizes was a mouth so sensuous as to amount to a destiny. Juliet. The crazy wop broad with the nigger kid. In *Capitals of the Western World* Italy was Saint Peter's Square and the Trevi Fountain, white statues against a blue sky, but she'd never been there, she said. Born here. I'm an American. You're an American. When he took his childhood miseries to her she'd doodle gently on his bare back with her fingernails, her attention somewhere else. Along with the green eyes she gave him English, Italian, a handful of Dutch words and her own wrecked Catholicism, which naturally didn't survive his education's dismantling of dear things. Where the house of many mansions used to be is pointless space, scalloped by physics, not even infinite any more.

Somewhere in this simmer he's busy with the problem of getting out of his body. There's a simple but horribly elusive equation if only he can remember it. Elsewhere he's accepting the room's details as the last of itself the world can give him. You imagine it'll be a lover's face or an evening sky. Instead bare concrete, a shivering fluorescent, four plug sockets, stains on the floor.

The door opens and three men walk in, two olive-skinned in combat fatigues, one white in pastel Gap casuals.

He wishes he still believed in God, checks the pliable air for His presence, but of course there's nothing.

Considering he's Calansay's first black or even semi-black man—an American with jewelish green eye and piratical eye-patch to boot—the islanders have assimilated him without much fuss. A few days of aphasic shock when he walked into the Costcutter, the warmth of stares when his back was turned, then they made the shift. Collective intuition says he's come to die among them so curiosity overrides: they want his story. The teenagers call him Captain Mandela, a handful of enlightened souls Mr. Rose, the majority That Black Chap, a tiny minority matter-of-factly The Nigger or The Coon.

Augustus Rose. His birth name's returned to him like a child he abandoned who against all odds is full of forgiveness.

You must be out yer heed.

I promise you Mr. Maddoch I'm entirely sane.

Mrs. Carr the postmistress had supplied Maddoch's name after Augustus had seen the ruined croft and enquired.

There's nae hot water. Christ man it's not habitable.

I could do a bit of work on it while I'm there.

Visible incredulity from the farmer. The two of them sat face-to-face over pints of Guinness in a snug of the Heathcote Arms. Heads had turned when Augustus thumped in on his stick, the room's dark wood and dull brass livened. It was late autumn and drizzling. The landlord had lit the fire. Augustus felt its heat on his cheekbones. Maddoch's donkey jacket released curls of steam.

Well I don't see why you'd want that when you can just as easy stay at the Belle Vue.

They'd circled this question via the croft's broken boiler and choked chimney, the leaking roof, the mold, the mice, the rot, the fundamental absurdity of the proposition. Maddoch rolled cigarettes with tea-ceremony precision, once reached down to stroke the pub's arthritic Labrador, who'd stood sadly absorbing the affection for a minute before turning and limping away. The animal was dying, Augustus knew, since like spoke to like. It looked lumpily taxidermed already.

I need my own company, Mr. Maddoch. You understand.

Exhaustion ruled Augustus but out of it sprang intuitive certainties: nothing new had entered the farmer's life for a long time. Now the man's curiosity was alert. Ditto the other islanders. They wanted the one-eyed stranger, believed he was something. Feeling this Augustus almost got up and left. The pain in his kneecaps prosaically stopped him; underneath it, a grander inertia. He saw how stupid he'd been to remain among people. Should have crawled into the Sahara or the Alaskan wilderness. Antarctica, the rough honor of being eaten by a polar bear, blood and guts in the snow, red and white, like Christmas.

Maddoch leaned back in his seat and sucked on a roll-up, eyes narrowed against the smoke. Curiosity notwithstanding there remained money-paranoia: a deal this good had to be a trick.

Augustus wanted to rest his head on the pint-ringed table, go out, go out, quite go out. The pub smelled of tobacco, spilled beer, furniture polish, unbeaten carpet all the way back to horse-drawns and powdered wigs.

How long are we talking about? Maddoch asked. I mean assuming it's for rent?

In Augustus's earliest years hat stands or clouds or wallpaper patterns or dogs or mere empty spaces in certain light blurted clues to the world's hidden meaning. He suffered many near-epiphanies. His mother's Catholicism was visceral, sporadic and inaccurate, but sufficient that out of the nebulous mass God, Jesus, Mary and the Devil soon hardened and descended with the grammar and math of sin and atonement. By the time he was four infancy's numinous anarchy had clarified into angels, miracles, souls, prayers and the everlasting horror-barbecue of hell. His mother was part of the cosmogony, though she didn't know it. Practically, her motherhood was unreliable. Augustus often found himself in the grudging care of neighbors, and there was a dark lipstick he didn't like on her, days she couldn't get out of bed but lay on her side with her mouth squashed against the mattress saying *Jesus* every now and again, long periods when they never went anywhere near a church. Still, she was the center of his world. He carried the thought of her into everything he did, and everything he did he did with the passion he'd inherited from her.

You're too fierce, darling, she told him one afternoon, drying his eyes. He was six years old. 128th Street sprang surprises on him. Today a punch in the mouth from an older boy, Clarence Mills, had left him fat lipped and throbbing. *You ain't no nigger, shortstop. Your momma's a wop got kicked outta her house 'counta you.* Augustus hadn't understood. Until this day his brown skin had been the only relevant credential. The Italian and Puerto Rican kids were at war with the blacks (and each other) and wanted nothing to do with him. Clarence's excommunication left him in no-man's-land. *Wop* he understood: his grandmother's country (there were secret rendezvous with this worried-looking lady, candies stuffed into his pockets, her delicate watery-eyed face suddenly close and a hug releasing the scent of her perfume and raincoat) and the language he and his mother slipped into sometimes. The red-white-and-green flag of Italy was on the spaghetti packet, held by a fat-faced chef with a mustache and a big smile. That was *wop*. But kicked out of her house? 'Counta you. How on account of him? He went inside and stood with his cheek against the wardrobe. His mother at the sink with her slender back to him had carried on talking as if nothing was wrong until his subdued replies alerted her.

It's good to have big fierce life in you, Juliet said, but it means when they hurt you it's twice as bad. Come here, let me look. Augustus stood between her bony knees losing himself in her glamour. The older medium, touch, was passing away; now he had to see her, the big-eyed face full of what he didn't know was still her girlhood. She was wearing her dark hair in princessy ringlets then. It means you're going to do something big in life, she said. The people who do something big in life are like you, have a hunger, *passione per la vita*, like a fire inside them, here. *Fuoco dentro di te.* She put her hand over his chest and he imagined a version of the burning oil drum the bums stood around in the vacant lot at the end of the street. She could turn anything into something special. His specialness was a secret between them to be guarded and gloated over. In these moments he passed into her and looked out at the world from safety behind her eyes. He could feel sorry for the other kids, even

Clarence, because whatever they had they didn't have this. On the other hand there was a junk shop a few blocks east displaying in its dusty window a funny little brown plastic doll with a grass skirt and a spear and eyes made from green glass. You wound it up and it did a wobbling dance. That's you, dummy, Clarence had said, and everyone had laughed because of the green eyes.

Okay now give me a kiss, Juliet said. He had to undissolve himself from her to do it, felt his soul reassembling in a rush—then there he was, sufficiently separate to get up on tiptoes and press his lips with passion—*ouch*—against hers.

The man in the Gap casuals—"Harper, by the way, in case you need to ask for me"—is in his mid-thirties and has an American accent even Augustus who's been everywhere can't pin down. Mostly the r's are Manhattan rhotic but occasionally the long *a*—*Haahper*, he said—slides them into pure New England. He's Redfordishly good-looking but that's no surprise to Augustus. Since television all specialists have got better-looking: athletes, classical musicians, politicians. Expertise used to be sufficient, now beauty's criterial. Harper's body says gym work, skin care, manicures, Caligulan excesses ferociously redressed the morning after. The man wants pleasure but he wants to last.

Nothing's happened yet, though the room's packed with dry energy. The two in combat fatigues (Augustus has them as Egyptian though they've yet to speak a word, perhaps have been ordered not to) have gone out and come back in with a folding table and three chairs, also a soft and clanking canvas bag he doesn't want to think about and can't stop thinking about. He's still not sure why they want him—or rather, he's not sure which of the two reasons they might want him is the right one. He's two kinds of terrorist, after all.

"So," Harper says, pulling up a chair opposite Augustus, "what's on your mind?" There's a controlled brightness to the interrogator Augustus knows will mean transcendent implacability. Harper sits hunched forward, elbows on knees, alert, receptive. In the movies a young man arrives before his date's ready and has to pass an awkward ten minutes with her father. This is how he sits. Well sir, I'm thinking of switching my major at the end of the semester . . . Maybe this is the alternative world Augustus will escape to, a TV drama of the young Harper's first love affair. They used to say think of your loved ones but it was a bad technique. You ended up hating your loved ones because they couldn't help you. Pain revealed the paltry dimensions of love. The paltry dimensions of everything, in fact, except pain.

"I was thinking that if I applied for my job today I wouldn't get it," Augustus says.

"Because?"

"Not good-looking enough."

"You've got the Morgan Freeman thing. Gravitas. Gravitas goes a long way."

"Not like beauty." He used to get Selina to lie naked with her wrists crossed above her head then look down at her and say, *A thing of beauty is a joy forever.* Her nude armpits drove him crazy, the rise and fall of her breathing, her deliberate cold stare.

"I wish you were wrong, but you're not. Friend of mine's a publisher. These days they look at the head-shots before the manuscripts. You want a cigarette?"

The cigarette's options along with other things *in potentia* flit about the room like sprites. Something in the ceiling directly above Augustus's head is edging into his consciousness: a pulley, a hook, evoking the waxy headless carcasses of pigs in the open back of a Hell's Kitchen delivery truck set gently swaying by the driver's jump down. You could see the terrible leftovers of their personalities.

"I'd love a cigarette."

The handcuffs are fastened to a steel loop in the chair's seat, the ankle cuffs to a ring in the floor. Harper detaches the handcuffs from the loop but leaves them locked around Augustus's wrists, an intimate manoeuvre: Augustus smells aftershave, freshly laundered clothes, garlicky breath under a layer of peppermint. He could bite a chunk out of the tawny face but it'd come to nothing. That Harper's made the same judgment detonates fraternity when their eyes meet and flick away.

"There you go." Softpack of Winstons from the shirt's top pocket, orange disposable lighter. You're supposed to think of the interrogator as a natural phenomenon, like the weather. Lightning. Nothing you can affect. Training, such as it was, seems a long time ago. He knows he shouldn't have taken the cigarette, let Harper light it for him. Sharing fire goes back too far.

"Even the girls in extreme pornography are beautiful now," Harper says. "Animals, mutilation, feces. Download the other day, one woman shitting into another woman's mouth. Both of them absolutely beautiful. Could've been modeling L'Oréal. Either depravity's losing its clout, or beauty is."

Augustus thinks of Elise Merkete, a colleague he'll never see again. Feminism, she'd said in a conversation more than three years ago, overestimated the power of diagnosis and underestimated the laziness of women. They'd been in a safe house in Washington D.C. drinking tequila, lit only by the lights of passing cars. The full diagnosis never really left academia, Elise said, and even given the bits that did it took only two generations before women couldn't be bothered anymore. She'd been an aid worker in El Salvador in the '80s when Augustus in his journalist incarnation first met her. They'd been harrowed friends for a few months as the bodies piled up under the music of flies, then news of his mother's illness called him home and they lost touch for twenty years—until Barcelona. Elise had begun the life out of disgust. That was the process, she said: One day you realized you were full of disgust. If you were made a certain way disgust spilled into action. Once it had happened there was no going back. Old constraints fell away like a rotten harness. That evening in D.C. the two of them had shared an intimation of death. The safe house boiler wasn't working and seeing their breath indoors brought a kind of despair. If death was your profession that was all it took. They hunted out extra quilts and piled them on the double bed, got in and with sudden miserable urgency made love. Augustus had never slept with her before. She'd been raped by a national guardsman in El Salvador. (What's the matter with you? the soldier had said. You don't like my technique? But I studied in America!) She revisited sex now as a ruined project she couldn't entirely give up on. Augustus hurried because her body's long ago violation rose up as if through her pores to confront him. She didn't come, told him she never did. He tried to hold her but in a few minutes they were awkward again. He got up and made coffee in the dark kitchen. Outside the streets were gashed with frozen slush. When he came back she'd wrapped one quilt round herself and fallen asleep.

"Okay," Harper says, exhaling smoke. "Let's talk about how this is going to work."

On Calansay his resolution is to keep the gun with him at all times. Harper had said: " 'It's better to have a gun and not need it than to need a gun and not have it.' Tarantino. *True Romance*." The reference was lost on Augustus. Its sentiment wasn't. Therefore reinforced inside pockets in his jacket and overcoat. The weapon bumps his ribs when he walks.

The land is three flat acres between a ridge of low hills and the sea, a pan of salt-scoured sedge and gorse dotted with yellow-eyed sheep, several daintily limping with foot rot. Maddoch's croft, or what's left of it, sits a hundred meters from a narrow cove of tarry pebbles and viscous lime-green seaweed. It's a littered beach: dented oil cans, rotting rope, three net floats that would have been bright red in their day now bleached pinkish white. Augustus's prowls have discovered desiccant condoms, beer bottles, a maxi pad, the scars of fires. Eco-death in microcosm. He pictures teenagers coupling here under the stars but the image immediately hauls in the universe's silence and emptiness.

There are birds. Crows lope away from him with a look as if he radiates atrocity. Black-headed gulls wobble midair with sunlit dangling legs. Oystercatchers scrutinize the tide line, beak-stab, generally come up with nothing. Maddoch's farm is on the other side of the ridge so Augustus has the landscape to himself. The place speaks in Spartan declaratives: a blast of raw wind; a sudden stink of dead fish; an abrupt downpour. None of these utterances invites him beyond itself. More familiar landscapes would have persisted in evocation: God, spirits, purpose, meaning. He's done with all that. What's left is the contingent bones and meat and blood of himself, the paltry fact of his skull, the entropic drift of his organs.

Maddoch wasn't exaggerating the croft's dilapidation. There's a hole in the roof big enough for Augustus to stick his head through. Half the bare floorboards are rotting. Bracket fungus is growing in a corner of the kitchen. Damp maps the lime wash. The fireplace is home to a pile of rubble it appears to have vomited. Windowpanes are missing or flimsily boarded up. The three rooms smell variously of cat piss, dog shit, mold, dust, drains, wet earth. Barbed wire erected against teenagers has been cut and shoved aside. More condom remains, torn pages from porn magazines, cigarette butts, broken bottles, beer cans, a bong with the glass bottom smashed. Painstakingly (accrued damage but also ritualistic concentration he can't explain), Augustus has filled three garbage bags and dumped them at the side of the building, where what was once a vegetable garden is now waist-deep in nettles.

He can't face the labor of unblocking the fireplace but there is in any case a miraculously still-functioning wood stove on which he heats up canned soup or fish or beans. Not entirely without shame Maddoch tractored down a supply of logs, told Augustus to give him a shout when he needed more, nae charge. Word of the ludicrous rent has got out, village opprobrium has descended. Maddoch is now the villain of his own piece.

The boiler engineer took two weeks to appear, by which time

he'd achieved mythic status in the exchanges between Augustus and Maddoch. Then he arrived, pronounced half a dozen replacement parts necessary, and left. Parts to be ordered from the mainland: another ten days. Augustus washed in the brown-bottomed tub with freezing water and a bucket, a fierce business that shrank his nipples and balls.

When the parts arrived the engineer returned to install them. Several false starts and adjustments, then *bhup* and the sour smell of ignited gas; eventually a savage expectoration of first warm then scalding water from the kitchen tap. The engineer had manifestly been told to glean what facts he could but went away with not much to report. Most of the time Augustus left him in the croft alone, and when he was there answered monosyllabically. The old one-eyed black Yank was living all alone and doddery and the place stinkin like a toilet and if he didn't get that roof fixed soon it was gonnie come down on his fuckin *heed*.

After his first hot bath in three weeks (he'd filled the tub, eased himself in, let the heat reduce him to animal blankness) Augustus sits wrapped in his overcoat on a rock twenty feet above the sea with a half bottle of Oban whiskey. The bath heat has lasted and these sips go into him with a different heat that joins it in his chest, belly, loins, creeps into his bones. This is good, the warm inside and the cold out. Like God, he sees that a thing is Good, goes into it, lets it be, without thoughts or complications. If nothing else what he's been through has freed sensual pleasure from mental interference.

If one of the islanders should pluck up courage to ask him directly: What the fuck are you doing here?—(imagination puts these words into the mouth of cotton candy-haired Mrs. Carr, who's most likely never said "fuck" in her life)—what would he tell them?

He knows how it's supposed to be, a triumph of the human spirit. He can hear the movie trailer voice-over, picture the blurb on the novel. *The story of a man's spirit destroyed . . . and of the love in which it's reborn.* A shy friendship with the postmistress. Laconic fraternity with Maddoch. *Now, on an island at the edge of the world, he must learn to live again. . . .* What's happened to him hasn't killed him so it must have made him stronger. (Selina said: If you don't believe the Nietzschean maxim when you're eighteen there's probably something wrong with you. If you still believe it when you're twenty-eight there's definitely something wrong with you.) He knows art's job in God's absence, to make beauty out of ugliness, good out of evil, meaning out of chaos. Suffering, yes, brokenness, yes, despair, yes—but survival, healing, hope. The movie trailer will use a sequence of single-shot fades, each accompanied by a heartbeat: a prison door opening; a bare lightbulb; his terrified face covered in sweat; Harper smiling; Selina slipping her robe off; an explosion; a lone figure in silhouette on a darkened beach.

Harper had said: We're suffering representational saturation. We've written too many books, made too many movies. By the time you're eighteen you've already encountered representations of everything important, you already know the scripts. It's no wonder we're so limp. The twenty-first century's the century of the definite article. You don't need to describe or evoke, you just name it and put "the" in front of it. It's like compressed data files: The suburban nightmare. The dirty war. The mom who knew. *The torture victim who* . . . one way or another transcends, finds

15

God or love or the violin or forgiveness of his torturer. That's what art's complacency expects of him, Augustus knows. That's how it's supposed to be but that's not how it is. How it is is an assortment of facts: He wakes up drenched in sweat. He's come here randomly. He has no hunger for life beyond immediacies. He spends hours in the fetal position. He assumes someone's coming for him. He thinks of death constantly. Despite which his own triviality's a perpetual tinnitus. Despite which he suffers stretches of boredom, the image of his life as a heap of dirty clothes that'll never, now, get laundered.

As a child Augustus believed huge revelation awaited him. He and Juliet were the protagonists in a mystery, two adventurers lost in a world of tantalizing clues. But at the same time *she* was the mystery. There was a secret to which he wasn't admitted, the dark lipstick and her going out. This wounded him, but no matter how much he hardened his heart to her she always drew him back. Hey kiddo, what shall we do today? I've got a headache like the end of the world but if you could climb up and reach me that Alka-Seltzer . . . Deep down he believed it was because they weren't the same color. Yes, this is my *son*, he kept hearing above his head. The weary emphasis was damning, gave him a vision of himself and Juliet hand in hand in outer space after death, her suddenly torn from him and pulled upward toward milky light while he drifted on alone. Many nights he fell asleep praying he'd wake up white. Sometimes in his dreams he *was* white; there was his astonished and delighted face in the mirror, same mouth and nose and eyes but with her fair skin and the relief of having come at last into his inheritance. Hope for this transformation drove his relationship with God, Jesus, Mary, even the unnerving Holy Ghost. Water was turned into wine, wine into blood, bread into body. Jesus could miracle anything into anything, so why not a brown boy into a white one? *Ask, and ye shall be given.* Yes, but he knew there was more to it than that. To get what you prayed for you had to be good. *Whomsoever striketh thy left cheek, offer unto him the other also.* This was how God spoke, Juliet explained. It meant if someone hit you on one side of your face, you shouldn't hit them back but let them . . . but instead you should . . . She wavered. I guess it means if you offer them the other side of your face they'll feel lousy and ashamed and you'll have won because they won't want to hit you again. Is it being good? he asked. Juliet chewed her lip a little. Well it's what Jesus did, she told him. Augustus was determined to do whatever it took. He began meticulously behaving himself.

Then, on the summer afternoon Clarence Mills obligingly whacked him across the face with a rolled-up comic book, everything changed.

It had been a lousy day for Augustus from the start. Juliet had left him with Mrs. Garner and wouldn't be back till six. All morning her attention had been elsewhere. It wasn't her going out he hated but her mind giddily on something else before she left. Jeez, kiddo where's my purse? You seen my purse? Her dark ringlets bounced. He was peripheral, something like a cushion or a coat hanger. Nothing crushed him like seeing her not really seeing him. At Mrs. Garner's she'd forgotten to hug him, hurried back, administered a distracted embrace, then gone.

And now Clarence. *Whack.* Fuck are you lookin at, Wogger? (He ain't no wop an he ain't no nigger . . .) Weeks of writhing

17

virtue had made Augustus a neighborhood figure of fun. Secretly he believed he'd amassed an enormous amount of Jesus-like behavior and was close to being granted his desire. Therefore, molten but resolute, he offered Clarence the other cheek. The half-dozen kids went quiet.

Clarence, amazed, *was* shamed. It made him furious. Laughing, he belted Augustus again, harder. The other kids fell about. Augustus turned and walked away, eyes hot crescents. Fuckin *pussy*, Clarence called after him. Fuckin momma's boy *pussy*!

128th Street smelled of stale pee and baking asphalt but grief made it a soft dream. The brownstones loomed over him like consoling uncles. *Love your enemy.* His enemy was Clarence, but *love* was the kisses his mother gave him and his arms around her, which thought provoked an unsettling vision of kissing Clarence that made his scalp shrink and his private parts tighten. That couldn't be it. Jesus couldn't mean *that*.

Disobeying orders he traipsed back to the apartment and tried the door. It wasn't locked. There was the living room, but with a tension in its contained sunlight that made him not call out. Instead, in slow motion, he went on sneakered tiptoes with a feeling of swollenness and gathering recognition (hadn't he dreamed this?) to the bedroom he shared with her.

This door was already wide open. There was the bed and on it was a colored man, naked, with his muscled back to Augustus. He seemed enormous. The sight of his bare butt with the bedclothes pulled down around it hurt Augustus in his heart. He stood very still, the blood in his cheeks singing of Clarence's two whacks and the warm feeling of kissing love when he wrapped his legs around

Juliet and the man's bottom with its awful dark crack which he'd wipe after he went to the bathroom and the tiny yellow flowers of his mother's sheets right there.

All he could see of Juliet was her arm draped over the man, her long fingernails doodling on the bare back. What do you want, mister? she'd say, whenever Augustus flopped down on his belly across her lap to invite this. Oh no, I've got better things to do thank you very much. But she always did it. Two minutes, you hear? I'm timing. Not a second more. You're like one of those Roman emperors, do you know that?

When the man rolled onto his back Juliet came with him, smiling—then saw Augustus. "Oh, no. Baby? Are you all right? What are you *doing* here?"

She was naked too, shoved herself off the man's body and with compressed violence got into her dressing gown. "*Caro mio, stai bene?*"

Augustus felt space filling up around him with a soft invisible force, in spite of which he also felt two hot tears leave his eyes. Ducking Juliet's outstretched arms he darted with raised fists toward the man on the bed, who had a slender long-eyelashed face and prominent cheekbones, fingernails of pearly whiteness, and who caught Augustus's wrists with infuriating giant ease and said, "Whoa, little brother, easy now, *eeezy.*"

"Sweetheart come here, let me talk to you—let him go, Leonard."

That stung additionally, "him," a terrible precise degradation. When the man released his wrists Augustus flung himself past his mother and ran as fast as he could from the apartment.

"There's a big obstacle for you," Harper says. He takes a last drag on the Winston, drops the butt, concentrates on crushing it with the toe of his shoe. "Which is . . ."; he looks up, meets Augustus's eye with the calm friendly alertness, "that we know you have the information we want. Probably all of it."

The eye contact tells Augustus Harper's not afraid of his prisoner's humanity, or is merely curious about it, hasn't yet stopped being pleasantly confounded by not feeling what he's supposed to feel. The guards already have the air of giddy self-distraction and Augustus knows how it'll be with them: They'll require jokes, infantile euphemism. Let's give him the helicopter! Buckle up now. They'll laugh when they gouge his eye out and leave it hanging on its nerve (he feels the sudden hot bloom of urine in his lap) because if they don't laugh how can they have done such a thing? Appeals to their humanity will move them to greater excesses because in here it's their humanity they're afraid of.

Harper's different. "We're often dealing with people who may or may not know what we think they know. Naturally that leaves open the possibility of them convincing us that they actually don't know."

The interrogator's eyes flick down, register that Augustus has wet himself, flick back. Augustus imagines Harper thinking if he shits himself we'll hose him because it'll stink and I don't need that.

"Obviously in your case we know you know."

From which it follows that there's room for resistance but not dissemblance. Either way he'll end up dead. His skin feels the logic of this in a million pinpricks but there's a spark of euphoria at the certainty of death—gone in an instant because it's not death he's afraid of.

"Let's establish the knowns to save time," Harper says. He selects one of two manila folders from the table. "We know there's an international organization that operates under at least a dozen names, Sentinel, Rogue, The Watch, POFV, RJO, Outcast, etc. You'd think we're far enough into self-consciousness to stop naming secret organizations so humorlessly. The po-facedness is one of the things that depresses me about this set-up. They should've called it The Nippy Nubbles, something like that. Think of the intel briefings, everyone trying to keep a straight face. Anyway we know it targets individuals deemed criminal by internal consensus. Vigilante democracy, I love this. We know it has members of the administration on its hit list as well as Third World tyrants and Russian slavers. Good bad guys as well as bad bad guys. We also know that you, a Sentinel operative recruited by Elise Merkete, have, as Yousef Saleem, spent two years forming an attachment to a terrorist cell in Spain. I love this too: because you want the guys behind the Barcelona department store bomb in '02. This is not John Walker Lindh. This is the vendetta script. We like this. This is personal. We see this. Who'd you lose in the explosion?"

Augustus hadn't had much hope they wanted the faux convert. Now he knows they don't. Now he knows the information they want is the information he doesn't want to give them. "Does it matter?" he says.

"No. Just curious. A Loved One, we can assume. Maybe we'll come back to it later."

Augustus's scalp tingles. He hadn't realized he wasn't fully alert. This is what happens: You forget where you are. Despite everything you forget where you are then without warning remember. There are those times driving a car when without realizing your mind's been elsewhere you suddenly come to and wonder how long you've been gone and whether if someone had stepped into the road you'd have hit them.

"Six months ago," Harper says, "we foiled an assassination attempt on the president but the Sentinel operative was killed. That is, we're pretty sure it was Sentinel. Either way Washington's had enough watch-and-wait. A Mugabe that's one thing. The commander in chief? No. Obviously I see where you're coming from. But what I see's irrelevant."

Augustus thinks of his half-dozen fake passports and driver's licenses. You send backups wherever you're going. That's fine until you're smuggled from the country you're picked up in. His genuine passport's with Darlene in New York. The Carl Garvey he flew in on is in a safe house in Rabat. The Yousef Saleem was in the Barcelona apartment but they'll have cleared that. Elise has the Lewis Carlson in Paris.

"I'm not going to insult your intelligence," Harper says. "I'll ask you questions and you'll have the opportunity to answer."

They both know there's no need to expand. Instead Harper gets to his feet and puts his hands in his pockets. The movement again releases the scent of clean cotton. Augustus thinks: Jakartan workers at the Gap factory get a dollar a day—then almost laughs at the smallness of this injustice among the horrors he has to choose from. The thought takes him away for a moment, sends him lightly flying over the headquarters of the World Bank, then a green sunlit river, a forest, the roofs of East Harlem—but most vividly to the hotel room in Barcelona four years ago, Selina saying, Are we really to be given this, now, after all these years? They'd lain for what seemed like days (but was in fact less than forty-eight hours) in the giant bed with a feeling of truancy from the city's bright afternoon. A maid had knocked and Selina had called out: "*Por favor vuelve más tarde,*" Please come back later, and it was only in the foreign language he heard her voice thirty-two years older. You love someone then lose them. Decades pass. You have other lovers, other versions of love. Then one day you're at a kiosk buying cigarettes and a voice beside you says: Oh my God. And you admit in that instant that this is what you've been wait- ing for all along. The lost thing found.

When he comes back everything's acquired a new throb, as if the room's asking him, incredulously: Don't you *get* it? He realizes that as lately as five seconds ago part of him was still thinking of somehow getting himself out of here. You don't believe in the soul until you feel it straining to escape the body. Of the philosophical crowd at Harry's only ex-Catholic Selina skulkingly admitted to Dualism. All those hours of relished argument, cigarettes, booze, reefers, *The Doors* interminably on the jukebox. Into this life we're born, into this world we're thrown. Existential bombast, but true. He remembers the moment he knew she wanted him, was going to have him. With a touch of erotic shame he grasped that the white slave mistress germ was in there for both of them but since they owned up to it in all but words it didn't matter. In his heart he knew she wouldn't have done it if he'd been pure black and this excited him, pulled for the first time on his European blood, said it could be of use. How do you describe yourself, Afro-Italian? I don't describe myself. I just show up. She'd said: Don't pretend you're not working it, those green eyes. Nothing radiates like a guy's happiness with his physical self. It's okay, don't sweat it. Half the girls at Harry's go weak at the knees when you come in. She had a way of flattering him that maintained her wryly above him. It was one of her personae, the girl of jaded omniscience, a line of self-satire. Like most beautiful brainy women she felt compelled to mock the ludicrousness of her advantage. He was so crazy about her he didn't know where to start. It took effort to be cool. She was used to guys seeing her as an unearned gift. He was determined to receive her as an entitlement. But after they went to bed together strategy, for either of them, went out the window.

Harper leafs through the sheets in one of the manila folders. Augustus looks at the two guards. They're smoking and chuckling over a deck of porn playing cards. According to an article he read somewhere young men in the west have stopped ejaculating inside their women, feel unfulfilled if they don't direct their semen onto the face or breasts. The Devil may not exist but if he did this would be the sort of triumphal curlicue he'd go in for, a cheeky twist in the struggle to invert life. *Get laid before the job*, Augustus had been advised in Barcelona. *When your finger's on the trigger you don't want to be distracted by thoughts of what you might have done one last time.* So he'd made the appointment with "Inés"—and been delivered into the irony of reawoken tenderness. They'd had sex missionary style and been brought into awkward intimacy when their eyes met. He had no illusions she got any pleasure out of the act but there had been moments when they'd been revealed to each other as people. What had he seen in her? A tension that was her controlling her fear lest he do violence to her. Beyond that sadness for the younger self she'd betrayed. Beyond that the faintest trace of species benevolence, a concession that connection with each other, however blighted or fleeting, is all we have. He'd left her apartment building knowing his focus had suffered—and within twenty paces found himself smoothly abducted by Harper's people. It occurs to him that she, Inés, was the last representative from the world he'll never see again.

"Let's start with the Barcelona cell," Harper says. "I'll give you the profiles, you tell me everything you know about them."

"Willingly," Augustus says.

"This is the easy part. I need everything you've got on these guys."

Of the twelve names and faces in Harper's folder Augustus knows eight and can provide details of four planned actions in the next six to twelve months. Meeting places, codes, fronts, dummy operations. It had taken two years to get in, almost two years' study before that, the claustrophobia of ostensible conversion. The Koran's lulling music of tautology, then the obsessed bleating of Qutb and Maududi. You don't fake conversion. You sign part of yourself over to it and hope it can be reclaimed. You acquire another optional reality. By the time of his arrest he was three days away from taking out Husain, Masood, Ali and Fawaz, the four behind the Barcelona department store bomb. He's twice been involved in actions himself—abortive since he tipped off the authorities through Elise. This was the tightrope he walked every minute of every day. Elise had said: They're going to kill you. They're going to find out and they're going to kill you. But they hadn't. Three more days and it would've all been over. Then what? Elise had asked. Then nothing. The word "nothing" had emptied him, for maybe the first time showed him there really was nothing beyond killing them. His imagination stopped as if at the edge of a flat earth. There was a life on autopilot in New York: his four restaurants, his proxy, Darlene; an apartment on the Upper East Side, a house in Vermont; people he'd abandoned; a way of life; a world. Elise had said, gently: I don't think you'll be able to go back. You have the disgust now. I had the disgust before, he told her. It's just I was too lazy to do anything with it.

Harper, pacing, makes notes, seems eventually oblivious of the guards, one of whom is soon frankly asleep. Augustus makes the information last because he knows what's coming when it dries up. As kids it was the same with an ice-cream or candy bar: Sooner or later no matter your contortions it was gone.

Harper returns to the chair facing him and places his hands on its back. "I'm a fan of yours," he says. "Narcissistically. You remind me of myself. We've got a lot in common."

"Apart from good looks?" The survival habit says talk, establish reason, humor, a basis for the appeal to compassion.

"Sure," Harper says. "Mixed blood for a start. My father was half-Swiss half-English, my mother second-generation Russian-American. Not quite your cocktail but enough to make me impatient with categories."

One of the guards stretches his legs and his foot nudges the canvas bag. Augustus feels the muffled clink in his teeth, skull, kneecaps, sees televised surgery's clamped open cavity and rubber gloved doctors rootling the organs, shoving a stomach out of the way or holding a satiny heart up to the camera. He wishes he could just for a moment wrap his arms around himself.

"Your mother was Italian," Harper says.

"Italian-American."

"Straighten it out for me."

"Her father was from Dutch immigrants, her mother Italian. I never knew my father but obviously I know what color he was."

"That's some misbehavior for a white girl in the forties."

"She got her marching orders for it."

"But managed."

"She was a resourceful woman," Augustus says. Harper nods, concedes the bad taste of his allusion. Avoiding the hackneyed matters to him, Augustus perceives. The man's been doing this long enough for an aesthetic to emerge.

"So I'm picturing it," Harper says. "You grow up at the black end of East Harlem in the fifties. Next door the Italians are giving way to the Puerto Ricans. You're not really Italian and you're not really black. There's your mother, but she's white. Catholic, presumably."

"Regularly lapsed."

"So that's your shelter for a while until your own intelligence evicts you. You're looking for a home. Passionate half-breeds always are."

Augustus says nothing.

"I speak of home metaphorically," Harper says. "Something abstract to which your concrete self's irrelevant. Anomalous hybrids are acutely susceptible to transcendent systems: creed religions, ideologies, pure logic, mathematics, the occult."

Because he's had these thoughts himself Augustus can't help feeling another surge of kinship with Harper. *Until your own intelligence evicts you.* It was true. He was "smart" by the time he was eight, reading at least two years ahead of his age, the flower in PS 122's desert. By the time he was twelve, church and the Bible were places he fished for contradictions.

Then one summer when he was fourteen Juliet brought home a battered single-volume encyclopedia. She was high on reefers, moved with slow precision and talked in the sleepy voice he'd started to hate. Puberty was upon him, messing everything up. He'd umpteen times fished out her underwear from the laundry hamper and jerked-off with his face pressed into it. Imperfectly erased the memory for days, sometimes weeks, then he was at it again. What he thought of as his degeneracy (contradictions notwithstanding, Sins of the Flesh and Fear of Hell endured) brought him closer to his mother, allowed the beginning of real forgiveness for what she'd let him walk in on all those years ago. They enjoyed periods of being in jaded cahoots, usually when she got a new job. But the jobs never lasted. There was always some stuck-up bitch or bullying asshole. She'd get depressed, go out dolled-up, come back high or drunk, sometimes not at all. Mornings after her excesses she went to church in spiteful penitence. Augustus refused to go with her. Very occasionally men visited the apartment and took her places. Once an Italian sailor moved in for a week and refused to leave, until a tall zoot-suited black man with a reddish conk came and very calmly pulled a gun out and used it to oversee the sailor's departure. Nonetheless through all this she fed Augustus, erratically and indiscriminately, books. *King Lear* or *The Lone Ranger*. If it came within her means she grabbed it and took it home for him. Here, read this. And so the encyclopedia.

"You're probably right," Augustus says. "I always had the feeling of looking for something."

He remembers the afternoon he came across the entry for SYL-LOGISM. He was sitting stewing in the apartment's open window wearing only a pair of knee-length shorts. Practically every word of the explanation was alien to him but there was an example: *All men are mortal. Socrates is a man. Therefore: Socrates is mortal.* The sounds of the kids playing in the street below tickled his bare soles. "Therefore" was a word he'd never considered before but suddenly he felt relieved, as if an inchoate suspicion about the way things were had been confirmed. If all men were mortal and Socrates was a man, then Socrates had to be mortal. There was no argument. That was the thing: *There could be no argument.* He looked up from the book and experienced in addition to the bladder-tingle of the four-story drop an icy rushing outward from himself, though into what he didn't know, hope, maybe. Joy. The street welled with mute encouragement. It meant something that there were things you couldn't argue with. It meant . . . he couldn't say what it meant, but it was as if he'd been given a crucial clue. He felt a great fondness for Socrates, whoever the fuck he was.

"Truth, certainty, first principles, all the big franchises," Harper says. "I was reading a movie review the other day, *Superman Returns*. It had the phrase 'this tired franchise.' Sometimes you get a big articulation from an absurd little context—because that's what the world is now, a tired franchise. The whole business of being born and working and screwing and getting ill and dying. I'm not just talking about the west. Primitives with clay hair and peyote visions are a tired franchise. Plus you look hard enough one of them's wearing a diver's watch or an Adidas shirt. You go to the movies?"

"Hardly ever."

"What was the last thing you saw?"

"I can't remember. *Independence Day*, maybe."

Harper smiles. "One of a whole genre of American movies that spends millions of dollars creating utterly realistic visions of America suffering terrible destruction. *Deep Impact. Armageddon. Godzilla. The Day After Tomorrow.* Someone should be doing a Ph.D. on the number of times we need to see Yellow Cabs flying through the air or the Statue of Liberty falling over. Then Baudrillard says the U.S. secretly wished for 9/11 and everyone jumps on him. It's hardly a stretch. The dominatrix's Rolodex is all bankers and judges. Makes you think the administration knew we were ready for it."

The virus in this conversation for Augustus is that he knows it's going to end. There's a temptation to go with the fantasy that he's got it all wrong, that what he believes is going to happen can't possibly happen if they're going to talk like this, if they're going to get along. But he knows it's pointless. Harper's big enough to contain all the contradictions. As God would have to be.

"Look at the way we consume our science fictions now," Harper says. "We do it with a bored concession that this is most likely the way the future will be. It used to involve quantum imaginative leaps. Now it's just weary logical extension. This is also the tired franchise, the future. You know they're showing this new soap in Brazil, called *America*?"

The sudden shift confuses Augustus. "I haven't heard of it," he says.

"Well it's called *America*. You can imagine. OTM illegals have gone up 400 percent since it started. OTMs—you're familiar?"

"Other Than Mexicans."

"Right. Coyotes are smuggling Brazilians into the U.S. door-to-door for ten thousand dollars. If you don't have the franchise you want it, tired or not."

The adolescent Harper's girl would have been WASP cheerleader to his quarterback, part of the desired franchise, Harper
surprised at the sadness and ferocity of himself when her sweater
comes off over her head with a click of static. From her hot hair
and the smell of her nail polish he's carried back into her childhood's blind exercise of its entitlement to calcium, carbohydrates,
proteins. Privilege is arousing, he discovers, but underneath the
arousal is something dismal: his first acknowledgment of the
contingency of power. She's white, rich, educated, at liberty in
the land her fathers calmed with genocide. Your ability to do what
you want derives from where and when you find yourself. If you're
in the wrong place or time no amount of volition will set you free.
In the back of the fogged Buick she straddles him, kisses him with
a beery flower-soft mouth while he holds her bare waist and feels
the edge of her ribs. Her breath comes through her nose against
his face and lowers them to a new level of intensity. Suddenly it
occurs to him that he likes her—there have been moments when
their eyes have met and he's seen beneath her posture of baroque
boredom a greedy energy and an invitation to allegiance—he
could love her! The realization panics him. His fingers fumble
at the hooks of her bra and she breaks off kissing him to say let
me get that and uglily reaches round with fluid skill and undoes
it and he knows in fact that he hates her. His genuine self rises
up: all his lust has contempt at its core because desire makes him
weak and it's weakness he hates. The finality of this truth detains
him and he knows that if he stays with it he'll lose his erection.
So he begins, internally, as the vinyl gasps under their shifting
weight, *yeah, that's right you fucking whore, now arch your back, that's it.*

A soft hum of mechanization from somewhere in the building reveals itself by stopping. The new silence expands like a gas, which when it reaches the guards brings them alert. Augustus loses the image of Harper and his girl, feels as if he's falling, wonders briefly if he's going to faint. He refocuses to find Harper studying him with a slight smile, as if he's been tracking the line of his thought, as if silence is another medium through which information can be made to seep.

"We get to know each other," Harper says, quietly, and Augustus feels suddenly tired, all but overwhelmed by the desire to capitulate, now, before any of what must happen happens. Years ago, walking Selina home from the antiwar rally in Central Park (to what would be, when they got to her apartment, their first lovemaking) she'd said to him, When I think of the millions of words wasted on the bogus task of working out what the right thing to do is it makes me fucking exhausted. We always know what the right thing to do is. We *always* know. She was full of absolutes she half-believed. Her political anger was really anger at the violence done to her by her own conscience. Secretly Augustus suspected she was waiting for a morally bankrupt man to seduce her completely so she could stop bothering. The great schism was that her older brother Michael had enlisted in the Marines. Lovehate, she'd told Augustus. It's always been that way between us. He's done this to spite me because . . . She'd gone further than she'd intended, now had to decide. I should have let him fuck me, she said. Least that way he wouldn't be going off to get shot.

We always know what the right thing to do is. It's a long time since he's thought of her saying that, though it was with him through the late '60s like a flame in his chest. He knows what the right thing to do is, here, now—or if not that he knows what the old habit dictates.

Drearily enlarged in understanding he feels morality like a presence in the room with him, imagines it as an idiot child he's been conned into looking after all these years. People die without giving up the information because they believe in something, they transcend. Pain is total occlusion yet they see round it. Pain is beyond reason, an obliterating giant stupidity to which all your history of jokes and nuance and ideas and caresses is nothing, simply nothing, yet some people create a space it can't occupy, an alternative dimension where the decision not to talk is held like a pearl in a paperweight beyond reach or harm. Some people you're not one of. You don't have the belief, the big idea, the first principle—only the motive like a word you've made meaningless by repetition. *Vengeance.*

"The information you've given us is going to be a big help," Harper says, tightening out of their reverie. "This is good. Easy for you because these bad guys are your bad guys. The next thing isn't going to be easy because we want your good guys. Your good guys are our bad guys." He pauses, seems about to continue—then changes his mind. Their eyes meet again and Augustus sees how little time there is left. Open your mouth now and you know what'll come out: *Please don't do this I beg you I'll tell you anything you want to know please for God's sake don't hurt me please please please.*

So he jams his teeth together.

After the first frost Maddoch drives over with a builder and spends the day repairing the croft's roof and chimney stack. The rubble in the fireplace *is* the chimney stack, according to Maddoch, kicked in by vandals. About half of it is reusable, the rest goes into tough plastic bags hefted into the back of the builder's van.

"You didn't have to do this," Augustus says. Since waking he's been pleasantly feverish but knows the pleasant phase can't last. The repairs outlay has hurt Maddoch, who occasionally submits to his conscience the way a woman long since disgusted by her husband might occasionally submit to marital sex. The farmer labors in contemptuous silence in the cold, plucking clout nails from his lips and hammering them in with bitter precision. Among other things his face says he's under increased island pressure to find out what in God's name this one-eyed black American's doing here. Augustus nearly tells him: waiting to die. I saw this place in a book once, that's all. It looked like the edge of the world.

It's a windy morning of flaring and subsiding light. Though the effort nearly kills him Augustus sticks around and tries to make himself useful, handing up hip tiles, flashing, batons. In their eyes he's an old man, though he thinks he's probably younger than Maddoch. He registers them selecting only the lighter things for him to handle, registers too the laconic politeness summoned because he's black and has by his extraordinary presence on the island embarrassed a racism that would otherwise have remained barely conscious. The builder's burning question—What happened to your eye?—goes unasked, but Augustus feels it like a smooth pebble pressing the empty socket under the patch. I imagined them doing it and they did it.

Lunch brings awkwardness. The builder, having seen the state of the croft's interior, retires to his van. Augustus understands: Maddoch wants to join him but without offending his tenant, therefore hovers absurdly with Tupperware box, flask and tabloid. TOBY SEARCH: NEW CLUE the headline says. The four-year-old boy who's been missing for almost a year is still missing. The parents have become media staples, assimilated celebrity. Harper had said: Is anyone going to be surprised when they end up on a reality game show? Is anyone going to be surprised when a reality game show devised exclusively for the parents of missing children hits the screen? First prize is investigation funding for another year. Or one where the families of murder victims compete against the convicted murderers? Families win the right to execute, murderers win freedom. Who's going to be surprised? Who's not going to watch?

Augustus takes his stick from behind the door and shrugs his overcoat on. "I've got to go into the village for a while," he tells Maddoch. "You don't need me here. If I'm not back just leave the key . . ." has to think because there's no precedent . . . "on the windowsill round the back."

His conviction, having set off up the track that leads over the ridge, is that he'll have to leave Calansay. People insist on involvement. He's been here six weeks but stand still a moment and there's the soft beat of the island's curiosity, its pulse of demand. A flame of anger wobbles up in him then dies. The fuel system for anger's gone. Like all his remnants it reduces to an aspect of exhaustion. Injustice gathers in his throat, tears well but recede. He has starts of feeling that can't come to anything. Especially injustice. The prevalence and scale of injustice let you dissolve into it anyway. The more you know the less you do. The truth *is* out there, Harper had said, but exposure disempowers it. Suspicion of atrocity is an aphrodisiac to the liberal conscience, proof of atrocity its climax. But the atrocity itself brings a kind of detumescence. It's the nature of horror: you've got to *half*-see it for it to work. In *Jaws* you don't see the shark until the eighty-third minute. Once you've seen it your fear goes flat. You know this is right. It had been one of Harper's catchphrases: You know this is right.

Shivering, Augustus struggles on up the path kept rhythmic company by the pain in his hip and the handle of the stick in his palm. Leaving Calansay's out of the question. He doesn't have the energy.

From the ridge the track runs down through a field of tan bullocks, long-eyelashed creatures with big-boned heads and a malty odor. They amble aside as Augustus passes, averting their eyes. Selina was easily fractured by the beauty of certain animals. There had been a trip upstate to her aunt's vacant summer house in Ghent, Edenic to Augustus, whose experience of greenery began and ended with Central Park. One afternoon he'd found Selina crying, silently, leaning on a fence, watching two horses in the meadow beyond. It's they way they were nuzzling, she said, laughing, when he came close and put his arm round her. I know this is pathetic. I know this is anthropomorphic idiocy but they were being so gentle with each other. Later that night she'd sensed him thinking about it. They were together on the couch, him sitting, her lying with her feet in his lap. They'd lit a fire, sunk into watching the flames. Through the stupor she knew he felt tender toward her. The thing with the horses, she said, out of the silence. (Love showed off with casual telepathy.) Correct, Augustus said. He'd pulled one of her woolen socks off and was massaging her foot. It's sentimentality, Selina said, I'm sentimental. It's a weakness. Augustus looked at her. The couch was dark brown cracked leather. She lay with her hands on her chest and a red corduroy cushion under her head, her blond hair spread glinting around her. She could look at him with a lucid dispassionate intelligence, something old and female and divine, he told himself. He didn't know what to do in the face of it, was genuinely in a state of something like awe. It's no good, she said. I know it looks sweet but sentimentality's the flip side of cruelty. The Nazis for example: inverately sentimental. Don't let it take you in. Augustus waited a moment then said: There's blond hair, and then there's *fire*lit blond hair. (Love showed off with non sequitur and violent tangent.) Selina held her thought then let it go. She had a tense resistance to compliments he loved breaking through. It was an erotic delight to him to watch her yield to indulgence, the warmth of a bath, the first sip of whiskey. They both took intense pleasure in satisfying trivial desires. You know what I want right now? An Entenmann's vanilla doughnut. So he'd go to the deli immediately and come back with a whole box and the two of them would sit gorging in a trance. Augustus stared at her. Fear hovered on the edge of things for both of them that all their gratified greed for each other would have to be paid for somewhere down the line. This is *Porphyria's Lover*, Augustus said. Do you know it? It's one of Browning's dramatic monologues. Porphyria is the gorgeous blonde. The poem's speaker is this guy, her lover. They meet in secret at a cottage by a lake. He hasn't had sex with her yet—but that evening, as he holds her in his arms and she looks into his eyes he realizes she's going to let him. The waiting's over. He can have her. Selina moved her foot so that it rested against his groin, very slightly exerted pressure. Augustus quoted:

> *That moment she was mine, mine, fair,*
> *Perfectly pure and good: I found*

A thing to do, and all her hair
  In one long yellow string I wound
  Three times her little throat around,
And strangled her.

Charming, Selina said. He strangles her? He strangles her.
No sex, just strangling? Just strangling. Wow. I knew there was
a reason I put out on the first date. Maybe I should get a crew cut
just to be on the safe side. Augustus pulled off the other sock,
kissed her bare sole, the soft pads of her toes. (He'd entered the
phase where nothing of her could be allowed to remain alien to
him. I'd eat your shit, he'd told her. Nothing of you isn't sancti-
fied. I know, she said, but let's not, okay? Not until we've absolutely run out of things to do in the sack. Plus think of the sheets.)
The point of the poem isn't the murder, he said. It's the absence
of Divine or Natural justice. After he's strangled her the guy waits
for something to happen, some sort of retribution from above—
but nothing comes.

And thus we sit together now,
  And all night long we have not stirred,
  And yet God has not said a word!

In bed that night she said to him: You don't want to strangle
me, do you? He was on his elbows above her. They'd left the
curtains open because there was a full moon. An oblong of its
light lay on the bedroom's bare floorboards. They'd made each
other take turns standing in it. Augustus was quietly stunned
that these elemental things—firelight, moonlight—were still

around. His world was buildings and leaping ads and the flanks of cars. Meanwhile out here all this weirdly alive indifference reduced civilization to a fleck. Selina's eyes and teeth and earrings glimmered beneath him. No, he said, I don't want to strangle you—why are we whispering? I just mean, she whispered, that I know you probably do want to strangle me, but I'll need some time to work myself around to it. I don't want to strangle you, he repeated. Truly I don't. You don't? I don't think so. He watched her eyes blinking. I think I might like to strangle you, she said. I mean not to death, but there's no doubt it'd be exciting. Anyway we can take some time to work around to that. There's no point pretending about these things. I do want to kill you sometimes, stab you repeatedly or rip your throat out with my teeth That's all right, isn't it? I guess, he said. She kissed his bottom lip. It's fine, she said. I won't kill you and you don't kill me unless I ask you to. Okay? Okay. I love you. Fuck me. Fuck me nice and slow.

Sixty-eight, that would have been, they'd turned twenty-one. She said it was deflating to be legally an adult, your last entitlement to imagination gone. Through the winter they'd marched in Manhattan, scarved and booted, ears and noses raw. Kenneth d'Elia had burned himself to death in protest outside the UN. By the time the lovers slunk north to Ghent, exhausted, neurotic from hash and booze (both of them had had such terrifying hallucinations on their two or three acid trips they'd determined to leave LSD alone) Martin Luther King, Jr., and Robert Kennedy had both been murdered, the Tet Offensive had devastated Saigon and NBC had broadcast footage of General Nguyen Ngoc Loan, chief of the South Vietnamese police, summarily shooting a VC prisoner in the head. Selina had had one of her controlled toxic exchanges with her father over the phone: Did you see that? Did you see it or not? These are our allies in Vietnam. These are the guys on Michael's *side*. Her father was someone important at Northrop Aircraft. Yeah, Selina said, he's the guy who makes the planes and the bombs. I'm the ethical rich girl who'll get bored with politics and take up batik. The book she'd taken to Ghent was Updike's just published *Couples*. Augustus came down one morning to see her toss it on the fire. She was standing on the hearth wearing only a T-shirt, her bare limbs pink from the heat. Two hundred thousand corpses, she said, and I'm reading about bourgeois bed-hopping. She watched the book curl as the flames caught it. Firelight picked out individual golden hairs on her mons. If we're going to have art, she said, let's not have art that's done like a *hobby*. Then the irritation passed and she looked sad. I'm losing my sense of humor, she said. This is what happens when you've got a small mean soul. Never mind all that shit, Augustus said, having learned to handle these plunges brusquely. The main question is: Is there enough bread and eggs for French toast?

She lived resigned to her internal contradictions. To her social and political animal, God was dead. The species had decisions to make, no room for fairy tales and hocus-pocus. In the public arena she was acidly rational, secular, iconoclastic, an existentialist committed with light self-ridicule to progressive liberal democracy. But someone at a party produced a crucifix and said if she really didn't believe in God she'd have no trouble spitting on it. Go on, the guy said, do it right in Jesus's face. Of course she couldn't. Wow, the guy said, guess you won't take a shit on it then. That was going to be my next test. It was laughed off and soon forgotten by the crowd but walking home with Augustus in the small hours she'd said: It's true, I'm hopeless, still riddled with all the rubbish, still scared I'm going to get my comeuppance. Do you know I still think about my guardian angel, and how sad he must be that I sent him away? Augustus laughed, remembering his own childhood belief. The problem with *my* guardian angel, he said, was that he was white, flaxen haired, with a look of slight disappointment that he'd been given a black kid to guard. I always suspected he wanted me to fall off a cliff so he could get reassigned. Eventually we agreed it was best if we went our separate ways. They were walking down Third Avenue in rain so fine it seemed not to be falling but hanging in stasis. When he stopped and kissed her her face was cold and fresh but her mouth tasted sexily of the evening's liquor. His cock stirred. Selina felt it, pressed herself against it, gave him the look of collusion. It was a strange look; she deadened her eyes in some way that drove him crazy. Anyway fuck them all, she said, as they walked on, holding hands in her coat pocket, my soul's none of their business. It's what I vote for that counts.

But she was plagued by nightmares about Hell and the Devil from which she woke on big indrawn breaths, covered in sweat. One in which the Devil had stuffed her and thousands of other people into a glass bottle. The bodies were so tightly and randomly crammed that many had broken legs and arms. Satan, giant, kept peering in, saying, Look, I'm going to squeeze another one in—and he'd shove another person in and the weight and heat and suffocation would get worse. She laughed about it in the morning, but waking from it she'd whimpered and thrown herself off the mattress. You dream about the Devil because you identify with him, Augustus told her. Your essence is rebellion. Look at you: You're against the Church, against your parents, against the government, against convention. He's your guiding archetype. That's sweet of you, she said. But if he's my guiding archetype why's he stuffing me into a fucking jar? I dream about the Devil and going to Hell because I'm terrified of the Devil and going to Hell. Pathetic, but there you are. My soul's stained with sin.

The shadowy sin was hers and Michael's. Augustus never pushed. Whatever there was to tell he'd resolved on letting her decide if and when. He believed he didn't care anyway, told himself all that mattered was whether she was screwing him *now*, which since he was down at Parris Island waiting to get shipped to Vietnam, was moot. Augustus told himself this (adopted a businesslike mental tone and reduced the problem to one of maximizing sexual profit) but his heart or soul or mind or wherever it was love resided hurt with the thought of a competitor. Father-daughter or mother-son couplings were creepy; brother-and-sister affairs had the glitter of doomed romance. He wished Michael had never been born. Sometimes it seemed Selina did too. She'd grown up with—or rather acquired—an abiding fear that Something Bad was waiting to happen to her. I feel like I sold my soul then imperfectly erased it from my memory, she said. I get these intimations. I know Lucifer's coming for me, sooner or later. It's just a matter of time. This is my idiot self talking, by the way. I'm aware of that. Maybe it's just cancer I'm scared of. There's a lot of cancer in my family. I'm just warning you.

By the time Augustus reaches the village he's wincing every step. Despite the cold he's hot, dizzy, wet with sweat. The glands in his armpits and groin are up. He makes it to a bench outside the post office and sits down, breathing hard.

Marle, Calansay's largest village, is one short High Street and less than two hundred homes. Costcutter, the Belle Vue Hotel, the Heathcote Arms, a dozen shops and the ferry port bleeding its odor of diesel and creosote.

At the sound of the post office door opening Augustus looks up. A girl steps out. She has a small flinty face and soft dark eyes, maroonish hair tied back, and is in the process of rolling a cigarette, hampered by a heavy canvas bag that's slipped from her shoulder to her elbow. Mrs. Carr the postmistress appears in the doorway behind her. The girl registers Augustus in a sideways glance, hoists the bag onto her shoulder, turns back to Mrs. Carr.

"So there's nothing else you can think of?" Her accent's Scottish ("think of" is "thankuv") but much diluted.

"Hen look at the place," Mrs.Carr says. "You're better away to the mainland."

"I know. Sort of sick of it over there though." She licks the Rizla, rolls, seals, begins pocket-patting for a light. A man's leather jacket, Augustus decides, too big but maybe that's the fashion.

"Nip over an see the Lockes at the Belle Vue," Mrs. Carr says. "And like I said you can try Ade McCrae at Costcutter just down-aways but a wouldnie hold yer breath."

"Okay. Cheers for the info."

Mrs. Carr stands holding her elbows while the girl crosses the street. Augustus sits still, piping hot and too exhausted to struggle out of his overcoat. The gun's a live coal against his ribs. On the opposite pavement the girl stops, lights her roll-up, turns and waves, half to the postmistress, half to him, then sets off toward the hotel. Mrs. Carr leans out and notices Augustus for the first time.

"Afternoon Mr. Rose. Y'all right there?"

"Just resting," Augustus says. "Long walk."

"Aye an it's bracin today." Mrs. Carr returns to watching the girl, who's stopped to look in the gift shop window. It's new to Augustus to be in the postmistress's presence but not to be the center of her attention. Normally Mrs. Carr's consciousness man-handles him with impunity. The girl walks away up the street, leaning left to counter the weight of the bag. Where the ponytail was gathered up he'd seen the soft hair in her nape. His sexual self's dead but can still be consulted academically: yes, he would have desired her—which is vacuous except for a renewed sense of the hollow where desire used to be. For a while without it he'd been locked in a cycle of mourning and rage, as if the tenderest root of himself had been ripped out. Now like the other losses it's been added to the space inside himself that's sometimes a refuge.

Augustus struggles to his feet, pain sheet-lightning his hip, and has to clamp his jaws together to keep his teeth from chattering. Flu, maybe. And the two-mile walk back to the croft still to come. He imagines lying down at the cliff edge to die, damp turf tickling his nose and fingers, hallucinations swirling in from the sea.

The girl stops outside the Belle Vue Hotel and looks up at its Georgian façade.

"She's after a job," Mrs. Carr says to Augustus. "Not much chance here." In this as in many of the postmistress's remarks is the question of where Augustus's money comes from. Calansay has an HSBC from which he draws cash with an ATM card. Beyond that his financial arrangements are a mystery. Left to him they'll stay that way.

The girl takes a last drag of her roll-up, tosses and stubs it underfoot, then goes up the three steps of the hotel's porch and disappears inside.

"Now what can I do for you Mr. Rose?" Mrs. Carr says.

When there could be no argument that was philosophy. In his early teens he embraced it as if it was a lover from a previous life, acquired concepts—entailment, necessity, contradiction, sufficiency—and with them clarity and impatience. Everyone thought they had an argument for what they believed. But mostly they weren't arguments, just ignorance and chaos and things they'd got into the habit of repeating because someone else had said them. He showed his mother the Socrates example, which she got and which opened a little flower between them, but she couldn't understand why he was so lathered up about it. Don't you see what it *means?* he said. Don't you *get* it? She'd been sitting at the kitchen table peeling him an orange—under normal circumstances something he could watch her do all day. What? she'd asked him. What does it mean? It means you can . . . It means . . . What it means is . . . Jesus! What it means is that there's a way of knowing what's *true*. The unexpected difficulty of getting this out had made him physically squirm and his mother laugh. He laughed too now that he *had* got it out. Well there's a monkey boy in here who hasn't washed his hair in five days, Juliet said. I know *that's* true.

They were becoming people to each other, beyond mother-and-son. Six months after Socrates a little money had come (from her sister, who'd married into it) and they'd moved to a slightly better apartment. She was waitressing at a chichi Italian restaurant, Ferrara, on the Upper East Side and making good tips. There was talk of taking classes. What about bookkeeping? She said. I'm pretty good with numbers. Maybe I'll learn to type. Can't you see me in a big office at the top of a skyscraper?

Augustus had acquaintances but no real friends, lived his life through books. After the first flush of joy—all S's are M's; all M's are P; therefore: all S's are P—he'd begun to see the scale of the effort that would be required. Required for what? He didn't know, but something big still awaited him. The *passione* endured. He read, daydreamed, read, walked the streets, read, became known as The Professor. A shocking discovery was how many fiercely held beliefs he had—that there was a point to being alive; that some things were absolutely right and others absolutely wrong; that he had a soul; that life was a mystery to be solved; that it didn't end with death—shocking because philosophy revealed these as mere articles of faith, assumptions, hunches, instincts. Belief was inferior to knowledge. A truth wasn't something you believed in, it was something you knew, and a truth wasn't a truth unless it could be proved. It astonished him that those around him went about their business as if the world—as if *being alive*—was uncomplicated and unmysterious. An old white-haired black guy went door to door with a little foot-pedaled grinding machine to sharpen knives. How long had he been doing that? What was the point? He looked eighty. Had he ever wondered if his whole life was an illusion created by some wicked scientist, a dream from which he'd one day wake up on an operating table in shock? How could people *not* wonder these things? One evening in the kitchen slicing an apple, Augustus visualized himself turning and sticking the knife through his mother's throat. No reason; they were talking about Cassius Clay. There's something princely about that man, Juliet said. It's like he's embarrassed by his own nobility so has to do all that swaggering and clowning. I'd marry him tomorrow if he asked me. Augustus was seduced by the idea (for him too Cassius Clay rang with the force of The Other Realm) but in the middle of it had this vision of himself turning and knifing her in the neck. What would happen if he did that? Obviously he'd go to jail, but what would it really mean? And why in God's name would he ever *think* of doing something like that? Was he crazy? Where did evil come from?

He read his way through the bulk of the school library in a year. His mother held down the job at Ferrara. Then a big change: She started seeing the restaurant owner, Gianni Cardillo.

"It doesn't have to be like this," Harper says. "And other clichés. But what's the alternative?"

Pain leaves room for nothing other than the wish for it to stop. If Augustus had the information Harper asked for he'd have delivered it. It's absurd that he genuinely doesn't have it. Harper could have started practically anywhere else and got something of what he wanted. Ironic gods are running the show.

"Come on," Harper says. "Get your breath."

Augustus remembers the day he discovered crucifixion had been a common method of execution. *The Illustrated Roman World* in the 112th Street library. What was he, ten or eleven years old? In his chest he'd felt the expanding heat of injustice; he had a vision of all the people who'd been crucified before Christ had made it famous. Naked, they thronged a hellish landscape, wailing and holding their wounds. It was as if he was the first person who'd noticed them and now that he had they were demanding something of him.

Harper uncouples the cuffs from the loop in the chair again, lights another Winston and passes it to Augustus. Augustus thinks he'll vomit if he tries to smoke but it'll mean respite the length of a burning cigarette. The first drag tells him his mouth's swollen. He has to deduce and infer since discrete neural signals are lost in the conflagration.

"What's your method?" Harper asks, resuming his seat opposite Augustus.

"What?"

"What you hold onto for this."

"I'm not holding on to anything," Augustus slurs. "I just don't know the answers to those questions."

Harper pushes his shoulders back, holds them for a moment as if to ease tension, then slumps forward. "I imagine going the Hemingway route," he says. "The old man and the sea. Hold on for just five more seconds, then five more, then five more and so on. Break it down further—one second, half a second, quarter of a second—eventually you get to the Zen thing of inhabiting the now. Get that down and there's neither the pain you just felt nor the pain you're going to feel."

"Just the pain you're feeling."

"No, you slip it. Pain's a reaction, every reaction takes time. Eliminate time, you eliminate the reaction. Remember the Buddhist who set fire to himself in Saigon, burned to death without making a sound? He wasn't feeling any pain. It's the only explanation."

Irony, Augustus knows, refuses to lie down and die. His instructor at the first *halaqah*, Saeed, had been obsessed (erotically, Augustus thought) with the likelihood of torture and death in the prosecution of *jihad*.

"I'll bear it in mind," he says to Harper. "Don't think I'm there yet." He hasn't taken more than three drags but already the cigarette's halfway to the filter. Harper leans back in his chair and laces his fingers behind his head. In the movies this calm would have rage just beneath it. Modernity demands such psychologies derive from breakage, trauma, delusion. The closest Augustus can get is imagining Harper feeling a slightly above average level of irritation when browsing in a microelectronics store and finding two models of something both of which do almost all the things he wants but neither of which does all. (In Augustus's vision Harper's accompanied by an equinely beautiful young woman who with constant low-level annoyance is one of his mistresses. Though mildly aphrodisiacal the experience depresses her these days since like everything else it's become self-conscious, situated, ironic. It reminds her that she sits on a nest of things she knows about herself—the exact formidable degree of her beauty, the exact formidable degree of her intellect, the exact formidable degree of her corruption—and isn't likely to shift from it now. Shopping, with the ample resources she has, outlines the dimensions of her unsatisfactory life, alternatives to which she knows she'll never explore.) Augustus sees all this because a version of Harper's consumer irritation is familiar to him. He lived for years in Manhattan with the urban malaria of precision dissatisfactions. But whereas for Harper the condition segues into a feeling of well-being, for Augustus it was always a failure, proof of vague yet giant loss. The part of him in mourning for all that was gone required ceaseless distraction: television; work; doomed affairs; fine-tuned consumer preferences—despite which the mourning went on, in dreams, in the small hours, sitting on the can or waiting for the kettle to boil. At moments his own face in the bathroom mirror conceded the worst, that he was still suffering from the loss of the old gods and stories, that he was still, with the confused center of himself, looking back. Harper doesn't look back. He's something different, a new type that can turn nihilism into buoyancy. As he moves forward the past drops away behind him like a crumbling bridge.

"Listen," Harper says, leaning forward to reforge the earlier intimacy. "You're still a man. Don't make me take that away from you."

The sincerity and reason of this hurt Augustus in his heart. Tears well and fall, which he knows is the first hairline fracture. He thinks again of all the people crucified before Christ. The demand they'd made was for his recognition of how alone they'd been. Any second this interlude with Harper will end and he'll be alone again. He starts to construct a comfort—that the murdered millions of history will be with him—but it dissolves into nothing.

Because he can't face Maddoch and the builder Augustus kills daylight in Marle. In Costcutter he picks up supplies he doesn't need—soap, toothpaste, a can of tuna, a small packet of rice, disposable razors and at the checkout ambushed by a sugar-craving a bar of Galaxy milk chocolate—then spends two hours over three large whiskies in the Heathcote Arms, shivering between swallows, some sort of blood noise bothering not just his ears but his teeth as well, as if his fillings are picking up radio. The dog lies by the fire, raises its head from time to time but doesn't get up. At the bar someone's showing Eddie the landlord the latest thing, an i-phone. Not on sale here yet; this one's from America, retails at $600. It does everything. Augustus's skin prickles: Harper had one, demonstrated it during the hours in the medical unit. You see what this means, right? he'd said in a tone of neutral enquiry. Augustus's morphine was wearing off. They'd had him swimming in drugs, all fathom of hours and days gone. It means not having information on demand's no longer acceptable, Harper continued. There's no standing on the street wondering what year Kevin Spacey won the Oscar, it's there in your hand, instantly. It's going to shut down a big neural chunk. Memory'll go. The optimists' corollary will be that it'll free up the brain à la Einstein never memorizing anything so as not to take up space. Maybe we'll all become geniuses. What do you think? Augustus couldn't answer. The remnants of the drugs and his mouth plump from the beating. Some of his teeth were gone; his tongue had given up confirming their absence. It was no surprise to him that he didn't hate Harper. Once you saw there was no escaping the relationship you brought to it whatever gave it bearable shape. At moments Harper had been a father he'd disappointed or a lover he'd betrayed, once or twice a primitive deity seeking vengeance for all the gods abandoned by history. Imagination was condemned to make something of things. There was a narrow strip of barred glass just below the room's ceiling letting in what Augustus believed was natural light, the first he'd seen in a long time, which soothed him, or rather which had been soothing him until he began to feel the morphine wearing off. These days, Harper said, unwrapping a peppermint and popping it into his mouth, technology's realized it can't surprise us any more. When a woman realizes she's given you all the sex tricks in her repertoire and now it's only ever going to be more of the same, panic sets in. All she's got left is quantity so she throws more and more at you knowing it's diminishing returns. Technology's got the same problem. It's getting desperate. There's the fusion of hardware and organic life coming but that's not going to surprise anyone. We're there already with pacemakers and all the optical stuff for the limbless. He held up the i-phone for Augustus to see, dexterously with the lightest touch of thumb and forefinger drag-enlarged a photo of a smiling blond girl on the little screen. You show teenagers one of these gizmos and they go, Yeah, does it come in any other colors? Microelectronics was the last revolution and we're antsy for the next one. Mass clairvoyance maybe, alien invasion. It's hard to imagine. This is why we're crazy for climate change: Give us something new and big. Melting ice caps, Biblical floods, anything as long as we haven't seen it before. Genetics is the thing, I guess.

Eddie the landlord, having worked out the punter is trying to *sell* him this device, is shaking his head and laughing. Och no I've had mine from MI5 a week ago. Jesus Christ. Charlie, c'meer an look at this wee gadget.

Augustus swallows the last of the whiskey, grips the head of his stick and pushes himself to his feet, feels the gun swing and bump like a giant pocket watch. There's a dip in the pub's murmur to accompany his exit. He's on nodding terms with Eddie, who this time incorporates a give-me-strength eye-roll to mark the hopelessness of the i-phone pitch. The landlord's one of the few islanders who's accepted the black chap's story's not for sale. It's established something between them which in Augustus's old life might have become friendship.

Outside, surprised by a lash of cold rain and a sky darker than he'd expected he stops to button his coat. Street lamps are on in their first peach phase. The air tastes of the just gone ferry's steel handrails and diesel. He thinks of all the silvery fish that have been hauled out of these waters, creatures wrenched from their element suddenly naked under the sky. Vikings raided here, a thought which evokes a world so much less cluttered with people. Buttoning takes a long time. His hands aren't on form and his face feels as if it's wearing a beard of bees. A droplet of water falls from the pub sign and spends its little personality in a trickle down his neck. He decides the Costcutter carrier bag's redundant, transfers the items to his pockets. *Not the gun pocket. Only the gun in the gun pocket.* Safety's on but there's a recurring vision of accidentally shooting himself in the foot or shin. Whether his life will flash before his eyes is one of the things he still wonders about, though he tells himself that even if it does it's just the brain superheroically rifling its files for anything that might help.

The fever's no joke now. He's let it romance him among the whiskey blooms for two hours but out in the cold and these skirls of rain he can't imagine it allowing him home without trouble. The sky's low and soft and the hills beyond the village are dark. Black water *chock*s at the jetty. The road back follows the coast before turning inland. Two miles and most of it uphill. Some miscellany to be found dead with: soap, toothpaste, tuna, rice, razors, a gun. He realizes he needn't have waited so long: the rain would have sent Maddoch and the builder back to the farm.

Marle's ferry port is also its bus terminus, a tarmac turning circle called for a reason he can't be bothered to discover "the banjo." Buses on Marle are erratic and he's never inquired which one, if any, goes his way. There's a timetable in the bus shelter.

"Fuck!"

The girl's in there and he startles her—disproportionately it seems to him until she plucks her earphones out. The light in the shelter's broken. She'd been sitting in the dark bent forward with her head bowed.

"God almighty."

"Sorry. I didn't mean to startle you."

One hand's spread over her heart. In her young face he sees shock at how lost in herself she'd been but also light-speed threat assessment that takes in everything from his possibly bogus bad leg to the nearness of Costcutter's lights and the half-dozen fishermen seeing to their boats in a dour trance. Factors flare around the core calculation—black man; eye-patch; not local—but she keeps them out until the priority work's done: no immediate danger. Her shoulders relax—then tense again: she mistrusts all her conclusions. The world shows you *okay* then lashes out.

"No, it's me," she says, laughing not genuinely. "Miles away."

"Just wanted to check the schedule," Augustus says. "I'm sorry."

Consulting the timetable's impossible without the light, and in any case someone's sprayed graffiti over half of it. The girl stuffs the earphones in a pocket. Used to be if someone had gadgets they weren't homeless or broke. Now anyone can be anything. Impatient with categories, Harper had said. Augustus billows and shrinks hot and cold, wrists maddeningly sensitive to the coat's cuffs. The thought of all the land between here and the croft empties his legs. The track down'll be waterlogged. Maybe just curl up on the bench here. Go out, go out, quite go out.

"Can't see a damn thing," he says. "Guess I'll walk."

"You American are you?"

The "guess I'll walk" was so he could turn and do just that but she got the question in. Nothing to stop him ignoring it except he finds himself wondering what "American" means to her, supposes rippling stars-and-stripes, limousines, Coke, the prongs of Lady Liberty's crown. He thinks of these images as a layer of cellophane spread over a dark sea.

"Yeah, I'm American," he says.

"The accent," she says. " 'S great. Anyway sorry, sticking my nose in."

His concentration goes, reeled back in by the fever. Peripherally he's aware of her consciousness settled on him. Their little contact demands a phatic exit line but he can't think of anything. He turns his back and takes two unsteady steps into the blowing rain.

Headlights dazzle him and he stops. A bus pulls up at the shelter. Its doors gasp open and passengers one by one alight with a processional quality that mesmerizes him. Time seems to stand still. The brightly lit bus remains stationary, doors open, engine running. The driver looks down at Augustus, nods, then turns his attention to a newspaper folded against the steering wheel. For a few moments this stasis feels dreamily hellish to Augustus, as if he's died and been assigned a mild damnation. Then he understands: This is the terminus; the driver goes by the clock.

"You go up near Maddoch's farm?" Augustus asks.

"Up to Marsh Hill," the driver says. "You can swim across from there."

Augustus's left hand in his pocket feels as if it's melting. Swim? What the fuck? Then he gets it: a joke; the rain. He knows where Marsh Hill is. From there a mile on foot back to the croft. This mile fever-filled with mischievous presences. He sees himself, clothes sodden, flailing at shadows. So be it. He has his stick. He glances at the girl, who's made no move toward the bus, finds her intent upon the rolling of a cigarette, which he reads as a little self-consolation for their abortive exchange. In the back of his mind, habit's been intuiting her history: too full of life, an indiscriminate force that should have been trained into athletics or math or the cello instead left to drive her into wrong adventures. Consciousness without structure, energy without direction. She's many times found herself sitting amid wreckage trying to understand how such good impulses and generous hungers bring down such catastrophe. Lonely, he thinks; still carrying the ruby of her genuine self no one wants—then feels lonely himself since such thinking's only habit and leads nowhere.

She looks up with a smile, which he after a moment of dizziness returns. It's obvious she's not getting on this bus, or any other bus. He plants his stick on the step, grabs the handrail and hauls himself onboard.

You hold out for a length of time so disinformation will feel like a genuine yield. That you can hold out for a length of time is the central humorless assumption. Augustus doesn't know how long he's been holding out, or, with certainty, *that* he's been holding out. Time's been showing a schizophrenic side, rushing, stretching, pooling, freezing, doing the opposite of whatever he wants. He's kept trying to make out the hands on Harper's wristwatch (the guards have removed theirs and left them on the table) but it's no use. In any case what good would it do? If the watch said ten o'clock he wouldn't know if it was night on the first day or morning on the third.

"I don't think you've been honest with me," Harper says, easing himself onto his haunches and bobbing there for a moment until one of his knees ticks. "You've got the detachment method down." The guards have been nodded back to their corner. One of them mops his face with a pale blue hanky so large it's hard to believe it fitted in his pocket. The other guard whispers something Augustus is convinced is a joke about the size of the hanky and which evokes for him a vision of the man at home with his wife and noisy indulged young sons, a ceiling fan above the dining table, bowls of spicy stew, large rosemary-flecked breads, a wall calendar, a TV with satellite channels. This is the betrayal: you want them to be other, monstrous, in forfeiture of love and humor, but commonality persists. The people who do this are people. Which truth is like a spirit of boredom in the room. Harper straightens up. "You make yourself the object of your own study," he says. "As with meditation employ value-neutral awareness: now I'm breathing in, now I'm breathing out, now here's distraction—an ad jingle, a sexual image—now a pain in my left side, now the resonance of pain, now pain subsiding, now fear of more pain etc., keeping all the while separate from yourself."

Augustus remains silent only because it's all he can do to breathe. He's hanging from the ceiling hook, shackled ankles dangling. His wrists are on fire. A film of wet heat clings to his face. The waistband of his trousers has slipped down to expose his pelvis and the sensitive zone above his pubes Selina used to deliberately dawdle over. That they haven't touched him there yet makes the area a screaming invitation. The predictability of his future adds to the room's bulk of warmth. He imagines a camera zooming out from him suspended here—room, building, desert, city, country, world—how quickly the details of his situation would get lost. Millions of television news reports: political reshuffles; sports results; quirky or heartwarming codas; the weather. Not long ago an item about a woman who prayed nightly to David Beckham.

"But if you know the technique you know its limitations," Harper says. "Generally effective while the subject knows the injury's recuperable."

Then why bother with the recuperable injury phase at all? As if telepathically tuned Harper says: "On the other hand escalation teaches nuance, and the longer this goes on the more important nuance gets. I need to be able to read you properly."

The information Harper wants isn't—Harper believes—time-sensitive. He wants names, places, the infrastructure, the *how*. There's no hurry. Augustus has been fighting this thought since they brought him in but now without warning his resistance goes, a tiny violence like a loose tooth tweaked free. When he closes his eyes his body knows what a drop into darkness sleep would be. Lying with Inés after sex he'd felt himself drifting off, it was so quiet and still; resisted because her waking him would have brought transaction back. If Harper lets him fall asleep now (he pictures his head's galaxies and nebulae going out as if their plugs are being pulled) he'll never wake up again.

"Tell me something," Harper says. "Have you ever been in love?"

Augustus opens his eyes. Harper smiles and says, "Academic interest only. Here, rest a minute." He slides the chair back under Augustus's feet so he can stand and take the strain out of his arms. The blood in his shoulders begins unpacking itself, draining joy into him. Harper sits down, puts his hands in his pockets, stretches his legs. Come on, seriously, if you talk I'll listen. Augustus doesn't doubt it. This is the other thought he's been avoiding, that Harper wants more than just the information, that his life's gone a certain way and he can't resist the opportunity to test the choices he's made. The man knows himself but rarely gets the chance to take a sounding. By now Augustus knows he's one such chance. Knows too that if he wants this over as quickly as possible he should keep his mouth shut or tell Harper to go fuck himself. He sees the sort of courage that would take, the cleanliness of it, could laugh at how filthy he is with fear.

"When I was young," Augustus says.

"White girl."

"You know all about it already."

"You're black, you grow up with a white girl myth. You're too smart and handsome not to have got one. How old were you when you met her?"

"Nineteen. Same as her."

"Was she beautiful?"

"Yes."

"And you were full of what, brilliant shame?"

Augustus hears the question but is detained by the previous one. That rat-faced little bitch, his mother had called Selina once, suddenly revealing the jewel of jealousy having until then inveigled her into wry sorority in the matter of their shared burden, namely him, His Smartass Highness Who Always Had To Be Right. *Rat-faced* showed him for the first time it was partly the hint of meanness in Selina's sharp nose and chin that drove him crazy. As a little girl she'd tripped running with a glass jar of pennies and nickels. The accident left her with a scar like a sickle under her bottom lip. Your sexy scar, he said, which annoyed her at first because she assumed he was performing the standard romantic inversion, force-loving the bit of her he hated. Then she saw the cruel white woman was part of his fantasy and subsided, enriched. Augustus remembers going to bed with her that first time. She shared a sixth-floor walk-up in the East Village with Vera, a bony white girl with small face and a mass of dark hair like a Cossack's fur hat who wrote songs and worked at the ACLU and chain-smoked Virginia Slims. The apartment, on Eleventh Street between Second and Third, was a mess. Television said nice white girls were clean and tidy but the chaos and dirt here looked feral. Certainly both girls hated their parents but what might have started as juvenile rebellion had revealed innate laziness. Augustus, stunned, wondered if they were going to do it standing up, since there was no visible room to lie down, until Selina began slinging things off what turned out to be her bed, a mattress on the floor under the window. She went to the record player—then as if she'd caught his thought that this was too big for musical accompaniment changed her mind. The Harry's consensus was you fucked without batting an eyelid but there was no fooling themselves: they were full of catastrophic potential. The months of flirting and fencing suddenly fell away, left them a nude insistent reality. In reverential silence they went to the bed. For a long time kissing was a way of avoiding looking at each other since their eyes when they did gleamed with fear. Augustus was so preoccupied by the fact of having got her that he found himself trying to pretend she was someone else so he could get hard. For the first few minutes both of them faked hunger out of terror that their instincts had been wrong. It was nearly a disaster. But between them they got her blouse buttons open and the exposure of her breasts stilled him for a moment. He lifted himself to look at them, then at her. For a second or two he thought she was going to cover herself or roll away. But she calmed and looked back at him with something like amoral curiosity, and that was that. There was no going back. Once he was inside her it was a terrible effort to slow himself down, and every time he did there was her stare of collusion.

"You were nineteen," Harper says. "So we're talking Sixty . . . what? Seven?"

The arithmetic's beyond Augustus. His face prickles, his feet are bags of blood. "Sixty-seven," he says. "Yeah."

"Now they're saying the sixties only happened in Haight-Ashbury and the King's Road. The rest's just wishful revisionism."

Harper closes his eyes for a moment and Augustus risks a glance at the guards. They're actually *playing* cards with the porn deck, which presumably requires a weird concentration. He gets his eyes back on Harper just in time. Don't suggest these interludes are wasted. "Well there was a lot going on in New York," he says.

"The Vietnam party and the miracle of contraception. Must have been something to be able to fuck strangers without wondering if you were signing your own death warrant. Don't you think it's laughable there's only been one window in history from the 'thirties to the 'eighties when sex wasn't a potentially lethal activity? Syphilis at one end and AIDS at the other and between them fifty golden years of trouble-free fucking. You were lucky."

Selina dug out a bottle of Jack Daniel's from somewhere and rolled them a joint. It was March, Manhattan's nothing season, everyone reluctant to uncurl from winter's searing. While they lay together talking about the world the apartment's radiators hissed and tonked. Augustus, trying and failing to hold the feeling of cunning conquest, was in shock. For the first time since *therefore Socrates is mortal* a new reality raised itself into view and he realized it had been embedded all along, waiting for him to be ready to see it so it could shiver free. You saw the word *love* all over the place then suddenly got your license for it. A delicious panic filled him. He daren't wonder if it filled her too. Maybe it did: there was something displaced about their conversation now—the latest bombing campaign; the absurdity of Ronald Reagan becoming governor of California; Jack Ruby's death and the reawoken migraine of the Kennedy assassination—this was their métier but the new reality (once the word *love* was in there was no getting it out) was a pulse of mockery behind it all. They'd done this thing—after weeks of mutual stalking and the building expectation of the Harry's clique—fucked each other, and what emerged from it shrank everything else. Ludicrous that a whole world could be washed away like that, but here it was, a new heaven and a new earth. He imagined the ten-thousand-strong rally crowd standing in stunned silence having watched the two of them at it on the mattress. You go to bed together and discover disloyalty to everything else. Except—he caught himself—hers to her brother. *He did it to spite me.* No doubt she'd done this to spite him in return. Her eyes had had plenty going on. She'd wrapped her legs round him and pushed her breasts up for his mouth but he knew she was moving dreamily between motives. Even without the shadowy presence of Michael there was the giant fact of her father and fucking Northrop Aircraft. Earlier, when Augustus had walked her to her door and she'd slipped her hand into his and looked at him in the way that meant yes she'd said: I should warn you, I'm trouble. So am I, he'd said, the kind of trouble that eats trouble like you for breakfast.

"It was a good time," Augustus says, seemingly involuntarily since the sound of his own voice surprises him. "We thought we were shining."

"But you're not using it now. The memory of love."

Augustus coughs up something ironish and pulpy, retains it on his tongue for the moment it takes Harper to say with a nod he can get rid of it, then turns his head and spits it into the corner.

"Wouldn't be any point," Augustus says. "You need something that hasn't already failed." Telling this lie feels sacramental, a small victory. In Barcelona just before the bombing Selina had said: Everything's better now. Coffee tastes better. Breathing feels better. Talking, waking up, watching a movie. *Peeing* feels better. Her body had kept its shape though naturally not its tension. That first hot afternoon she'd been nervous, closed the hotel room's leaden drapes. Three decades take their toll on a gal, she'd said. You'd better prepare yourself. They'd stood face to face. He'd opened her robe and slowly covered her with kisses. He wanted to get down on his knees and thank the Lord. In fact he got down on his knees and tenderly kissed her cunt. On the morning of their second day, after they'd made love and were lying together she'd said: Are we really to be given this, so late in the day? And in a state of complete muscular and skeletal peace he'd smiled and said: Yes, we are. God's got a romantic streak after all. She slid her leg over his, nuzzled his chest, pinched the soft flesh under his ribs (as if every moment required its own proof that yes, here they were, after all these years together again) and said, If He's responsible for this I might consider giving the old bastard a second chance. How do you feel about ordering up a couple of Long Island Iced Teas, by the way?

"This is the crux," Harper says. "The failure of the scripts. Love, justice, equality, salvation. There's a script here and now failing, right? Several scripts. The conversion script. The epiphany script. The reversal script, in which by interrogating you I end up interrogating myself."

"I was hoping for the rescue script," Augustus slurs—and after a pause Harper chuckles, their eyes meet, the connection's sweet, demands acknowledgment.

"The humanist script says humor trumps everything," Harper says. "You go with that?"

Augustus has acute pins and needles down his left side. The body persists in such things regardless, which consistency is the real horror, not Sartre's Nature-gone-crazy and people's tongues turning into centipedes. "No," he says. "We're past fairy stories."

"Hollywood's pushed us past them, ironically. On-screen psychopaths now are Wildean wits, charismatic wisecrackers, above all empathic: They *get* it. We're over the delusion that if only these people could share a joke with us they'd be incapable of doing what they do. Now it seems incredible we held on to that delusion so long."

Laughter was absent from the *halaqah* meetings in Barcelona. Jokes were tacitly taboo. The cell's culture was one of fierce po-facedness and cocked anger. In the first weeks and months it wasn't a problem for Augustus, since in the wake of the bombing he'd lost his ability to laugh anyway. But as time passed the capacity for seeing the funny side began to reassert itself. There were moments of terrible temptation, rich ironies and juicy puns the act of resistance made doubly delicious. Several times he had to pretend visits to the bathroom so he could sit with his shirt stuffed into his mouth to smother the sound of his laughter. Eventually he understood. Humor destroyed literalism. The *halaqah*'s silent proscription made perfect sense.

"Humor's the gap between what we are and what we'd like to be," Augustus says. "Same gap conscience operates in."

Nodding, Harper gets to his feet, paces away, reaches up and squeezes his left trapezoid with his right hand. It's not the first of these tension-easing gestures and in spite of himself Augustus grasps at the theory of imperfectly suppressed compassion surfacing in another form, like referred pain.

Presumably at a signal from Harper the guards put down their cards and get to their feet. Everything goes from Augustus except the knowledge that he won't be able to stand any more. He realizes he should have spent the interlude readying disinformation. Fear comes up so fast from soles through knees belly chest and there it is filling the back of your throat and the space behind your brain so you can't talk, no room for anything.

At Marsh Hill Augustus gets off the bus into the night's soft tumult. He's sorry to see the vehicle pull away. In the few minutes from Marle its bright interior befriended him with local ads and the muted conversation of the three lady passengers at the back. Trundling through the dark it had had the feel of a last unit of civilization. He'd sat sweating and shivering and being in ten thousand spider bites eaten by the fever but also knowing the bliss of having his fate in the driver's hands. A great nobility attached to drivers if you were in a bad way. Declining celebrities presumably fell for theirs, the silent pilot, the dependable silhouette. Take me home, oh please just take me home.

Augustus watches the taillights disappear. Certain reflexes of the imagination still fire—the wind is God moving His hands—but come to nothing. The world's emphatically literal. Appositely literal since he's leaving it soon. You know where you're goin' now, Mr. Rose? the driver had asked as Augustus alighted. Yeah, I've got it, thanks. But alone in the billowing rain he's not so sure. Without the bus his sense of direction dissolves; he feels it going—then it's gone. Is the lane on his left or his right? He takes a few steps up the hill—then catches himself, shocked at how crazily the fever's working him: The road hugs the coast; for Christ's sake there's only *water* on your left. The lane's across the road on the right. Follow for a quarter of a mile, then the stile on the right, dry stone wall, footpath, another stile and you're on Maddoch's land. Come to the croft from the opposite side. Go now before . . . go now and get the stove—or even light the fire if they've finished the . . . go now.

The wet road passes under him in many more steps than he

would've thought necessary, but still, there's the lane in front of him where the trees meet overhead (mourners consoling each other, Selina said in the preliteral days) or so he thought but is wrong because with no idea how such a thing could be possible finds himself pitching forward in what feels like slow motion (he has time to equivocate between reason's *ditch* and the fever's *portal to another dimension*) before sudden contact—a terrible flash of pain in his left knee and right shin—brings physics back.

At his first convulsive reflex—to get to his feet—the pain sears, yanks a cry from him, a pure sound of himself he hasn't heard since Harper, who for a split second he expects to see standing over him. Don't try to get onto your knees because the knee and the shin are pressed against something sharp and can't take any weight. The knee and the shin now have the luminous importance. Despite the pain he has to think the maneuver through. Use your hand to feel where the edge of whatever it is is. Farm tool or car part. Some sort of blade. There. That's the edge. So now you roll, take the weight on your elbows.

The ditch bottom's flooded but for a few moments he has no choice but to lie with his right side partially submerged. No idea how he could have gone so wrong. And so many more opportunities for going wrong between here and the croft. Is this it? Found dead in a ditch? Why not? Why's he come here if not to discover the manner of his dying? Isn't this earth and water, iron and stone? What other graces was he expecting? He imagines Maddoch's black-and-white collie tomorrow morning drawn by its nose, never smelled a dead man before, then Maddoch coming up, *get ewt there Sam* assuming fox or sheep or badger or whatever. The dog not sure how to be, what signal to give, circling away and back as Maddoch's long owl face registers. Fuck me it's the *coon*, which he'll pronounce *khun*. And there the farmer will stand in the silvery morning amid the sunlit puddles, breath visible, hands hot in his pockets, already around the core shock the vague fear that this, whatever the explanation, won't be good for him, for his scheme of things. Christ almighty. Christ al*mighty*.

Augustus breathes easier, locates his stick. No denying the temptation to lie still, close his eyes, go out, go out, quite go out. The ditch smells of waterlogged earth, an unbankruptable freshness, the planet's thrusting monomania for renewal. If the dead weren't dead this is the force they'd feel pushing through eye sockets, ribs, jaws, the upheaving freight of microbes and nitrates. Sorry, can't stop: life.

Suddenly the rain comes down harder. He rolls onto his side, gets up on one elbow, shivering. Footage of the sun reveals fire tearing itself off in giant strips; this is the fever now, agitated and profligate. He's not, apparently, to be given peace. The pain in his knee and shin is as if the blade or whatever it is is *stuck* in there but when he reaches down feels only a small tear in his soaked trousers. Lean forward and grab a fistful of grass, haul and use the stick to take as much weight off the legs as possible, but even so it's going to hurt—

With a twist he rights himself flush to the bank that slopes down from the roadside. Possible fracture of the shin, possible chipped bone in the knee, nothing broken but enough damage to double the distance home. There are times when the islanders send out their collective spirit to harass him. Look at you: old one-eyed black man lying in a ditch at the edge of the world. *What the fuck are you doing here?* Tell us or die but for God's sake put an end to this.

A sodden fox trots past, a vision of urgent purpose from tail-tip to snout that hasn't changed since the species arrived. Without God there's only the richness of the accident and it makes no sense to praise accident; still, creatures have the beauty of being undividedly themselves. The restaurateur, Gianni Cardillo, who fell in love with Juliet, and who was a very peripheral Mafioso, had a passion for animals, and for wild animals an infantile rapture. This is the glory of God, he'd say, watching television lions strolling the savannah. How can anyone say there's no God when you see somethin' like that? Jesus, people are fuckin' *blind*. Augustus had of course begun with and for many years maintained a hatred of the man whose money supplemented him through college (my mother's *ass* is putting me through college, he told Selina, in a tone that conceded his own disgusted willingness to take the arrangement if the alternative was having no life on a scholarship) and whose connections after college spared him the draft. But eventually in spite of himself came to see there was more to it than that. Cardillo went to women for the answer to the question of his secret worth, to be told whether, apart from the knack for getting on in the world, he was any good. Once she'd given him that, there was nothing he wouldn't do for her or those she loved. In his honorable moments Augustus knew casting his mother as whoring strategist was bogus. She was genuinely drawn to Cardillo, who had warmth, quick understanding of people, delight in the world's contradictions and a doglike nose for pleasure. Augustus could see the change in his mother, that for the first time in his life she wasn't worried. I know this is going to be hard for you, baby, she said, once it was apparent Cardillo wasn't going away, but all I'm asking is that you give the guy a chance. You want him to be a lousy bastard, I know, but remember just because you want something to be true doesn't mean it is. He wants you to be a lousy bastard. Doesn't mean you have to be. Augustus had had a dreary feeling she was right, that his soul was being confronted with a signal to grow, and, with bizarre clarity, that Cardillo's was too. Still it took years for both men to see the war between them was a reaction to the shock of having liked each other from the start.

The fox is gone by the time Augustus drags himself up the bank onto the road and struggles to his feet. *And miles to go before I sleep.* Or one mile, but there remains the question of what just happened. The lane's ten feet to his right. How did he go so astray? The rain hammers down with continuous urgency. The downpour's added twenty pounds to his clothes. He suddenly realizes he's unbearably hot and begins wrestling his overcoat off, imagining himself seen through a thermal imaging camera, the observer going, *Jesus this guy's on fire.*

At his second attempt the lane really is the lane, overarched with black mourning trees just the way the illusory version had been. The darkness at least is a comfort. His time with Harper had been brutal with light. You'd never think you could feel such grief for the loss of darkness. He'd thought of it then as a lovely young goddess who used to come and lie on him but never would again. Sometimes woken in the night by a dream (the same dream, always, that he's back in the interrogation room) he wraps himself in his sleeping bag and steps outside. Darkness now is pure phenomenon, nothing to do with him. This is the final relationship with the universe: you find solace only in things that offer none.

But his current state makes the darkness unpredictable, gives it an occasional twist or flake of light. The two new injuries, knee and shin, are rich power sources for the fever. At one point he wakes up on the cratered tarmac with no memory of passing out. His teeth and scalp are full of prickling confusion. When he reaches what he thinks is the second stile (in fact it's the wrong stile altogether) he's shivering so violently it takes him several attempts to grab the post and pull himself onto the step. Mud clutches and sucks, he twice loses his stick, falls, vaguely recognizes beguilement but wills himself down to a deep geography that corrects his errors and brings him as the last of his strength goes to within sight of the croft.

A hundred meters, he thinks, no more. That poor bastard who collapsed just before the marathon finish line and got helped up, made it, then got disqualified because of the help. What a dream the stadium must have been when he waltzed in, a softly roaring otherworld. These are gorse bushes. Those grayish masses sheep. And Maddoch leaves the key on the windowsill round the back. What happened to your eye? Well, son it's like this: I imagined them doing it and they did it.

The last thing he remembers before he collapses is Harper's voice in his head saying: The world's not what we thought it was, the world's what it's always been.

He wakes to the sound, smell and light-flicker of fire. For a moment he lies still—on his back, dry, warm, with aching skin—knowing nothing, where he is, what happened, *who* he is even. His mouth's parched. He turns his head on the pillow, an animal looking for water.

"Well then."

It takes a second for recognition to gather (with it the rushed reassembly of his history) then he has the face and the name: Maddoch. The farmer stands in the doorway, rolling a cigarette. Beyond him blue-gray fleecy light that could be dusk or dawn. Dawn, Augustus thinks; there's a hint of burgeoning. The rain's stopped.

"How're you feelin'?"

Augustus swallows, tastes bile. He remembers seeing the croft pale and distinct against the dark hill and being surprised he'd thought *home*. "Thirsty," he says, swinging one leg down off the cot. Bare leg: he's been undressed and put in dry underwear and a clean sweater, imagines the horror that would've been to Maddoch and the wealth of gossip the scars will provide. Scars like you wouldnie be*lieve*. Aye, *all over*. There's a wad of toilet roll tied over his kneecap, same arrangement for the shin.

"Hold your horses, man," Maddoch says, moving forward. "Stay put fra minute."

"Just need some water."

"Stay put, I'll get it."

Maddoch goes to the sink, picks out and rinses the tin mug (part of the camping set Augustus has relied on since coming here) then fills it with water. Augustus remains half up, sleeping bag clutched over his loins. The drink, when Maddoch passes him the mug, gives him a joy so simple and pure he could weep.

"Another? Give it here. I'll ring the doctor's in a minute. Surgery doesnie open till—"

A shift in the light makes them both look to the doorway, where the girl from the bus shelter appears, peering in, one hand on the door frame, the other in the leather jacket pocket.

"Oh, sorry," she says.

Maddoch hands Augustus the refilled mug. Augustus stares at the girl.

"'S'yer guardian angel there," Maddoch says. Which doesn't move them forward. Despite everything Augustus is aware of the fire shimmying in the hearth, its claim on a radius of domestic life from a contract forged half a million years ago amid a ring of red-lit moist faces. The change it makes to the croft's interior hurts his feelings, as if he's been cheated: a transformation like this should have been his decision.

"What happened?" Augustus says. "Where are my clothes?" He's seen his mud-spattered trousers draped steaming over a chair near the fire, his filthy overcoat on the back of the door the gun the gun the gun—but neither Maddoch's face nor the girl's says they know about it.

"She found you," Maddoch says. "Pole-axed, legs stickin out the door. Thought you were deed!"

The girl takes a step inside. "Only for a sec when I first saw you lying there," she says. Her eyes flick from him to Maddoch and back again.

"Let me get dressed," Augustus says. "No need to call the doctor. I'm fine."

"Take it easy, Mr. Rose. You've had a bad turn there and a nasty knock. You seen the state of your legs, man?"

People here, the fire's transformation of the room, his feeling of overfullness—the world's done all this behind his back. He forces himself to speak calmly. "I'm sorry. I'm grateful for your help. Mr.

Maddoch, if you could just pass me my bag there I can put something on." Pointing, he realizes he's still visibly, comically, shivering.

"Hen, just give us a minute will you?" Maddoch says.

"Oh aye, sorry."

When the girl withdraws Maddoch slides the rucksack over to Augustus then turns his back and busies himself with the unfinished roll-up. "I'll tell you what," Maddoch says. "You're lucky she came along there."

"What time is it?"

"Around eight."

"What's she doing out here at this time?"

"Lookin for work if you can believe it. Lassie's half cracked if y'ask me. Anyway we've nothing. Christ knows why she's not away to the mainland."

Putting the clothes on hurts. Augustus clamps his jaws to stop his chattering teeth. By the time he's got the sneakers on he's faint, knows if he tries to get up he's asking for trouble. He sits holding the edge of the cot. Give her something. The figure fifty pounds suggests itself. He has a fifty, unbroken from God knows when, in his wallet. Assuming the wallet's still in the coat. And the gun, Jesus he could have dropped it anywhere. There'll be the tedious clambering of her saying no no I don't want that and him having to persist. He could get Maddoch to do it if he didn't see the farmer pocketing the cash.

"You'll need a whatsit jab," Maddoch says. "Quack doesnie come out now that I think of it, but I can run you in later."

"It's fine," Augustus says. "Don't worry. Tell me what happened?"

"Best ask herself," Maddoch says, going to the door and opening it.

The girl's not, Augustus decides, "half cracked," but something's not right. Too much energy and not enough education, yes, but also a flipping between awakeness and abstraction. How old is she? Nineteen? Sixteen? He infers prematurely swallowed chunks of experience. The pull on his dead interest's like the itch in a phantom limb. He could groan and roll away.

"Prob'ly shouldna been walkin down here but I just thought there was something funny—you know how you get a feelin? Anyway sorry." She says "sorry" a lot. She's got instinctive generous curiosity but there's some painfully ingested knowledge that checks it. "Recognized you from yesterday at the bus stop when you gimmie that fright." Pronounced *freight*. She laughs easily but it's always partly a plea not to be hurt. She can't stop looking at him but looks away if he looks back. After dead loss in the village Maddoch's was the first farm she tried for work. On her way to the next she'd seen the croft and wandered down to take a look. Augustus, unconscious, soaking, had been sprawled across the threshold, legs bleeding. She'd run back and got Maddoch.

"Lucky for you, Mr. Rose," Maddoch says. "I was just about to go in for the wife's prescription." Throughout he's avoided Augustus's eye. The scars have unbalanced him, confirmed the croft arrangement's a mistake. Augustus foresees the clipped attempt at eviction, the thought of which, the effort it'll require to talk Maddoch down, makes him dizzy.

"I came here f'ra holiday when I was little," the girl says. "Always thought I'd come back one day."

"I've told her," Maddoch says. "There's no work. Summer, maybe, but not now."

"Best be off anyways," she says, standing suddenly. "Just wanted to make sure you were okay, you know?" This is her catching herself. She relaxes into things, makes quick friends—then snaps awake, remembering you don't relax into things, the friends turn out to be not friends. Best be off anyways.

Augustus knows the timing for the fifty pounds has to be right if he doesn't want Maddoch interfering. He waits till they're both out of the door then gets up and, after a moment's adjustment to the floor's pitch and swing, goes after them. Moving's a succession of cattle-wire shocks, dull bites in the bones. The wallet's in the overcoat where it should be, as is the gun. At the croft's threshold cold air surprises his face, neck and hands, sets the fever's pins-and-needles off again.

"Just a second, Miss."

Her face when she turns shows a reflex fear that she's to be called to account, smothered quickly in a smile. Augustus beckons her, aware as he does so not just of Maddoch observing, realizing he's missing something, but of the wet land and low gray sky, the sheep nibbling the hill. This place avers the planet going on without people, the giant facts of rain and sunlight, the sculpted bulk of deserts, fish-heavy oceans, a wealth of spectacle for no one and nothing.

"Have a drink on me, okay?"

"Och don't be daft," she says. It's her natural attitude but there's no disguising the double take and scurry for adjustment when she sees it's a fifty. Suddenly Augustus knows she spent last night not in a hotel. All these things he knows and doesn't want to, survival's gift of vacuous penetration. He shivers.

"Go ahead, take it. I insist."

She shakes her head but her hands sing from the jacket pockets. He wonders if she's on drugs. Doesn't look like a user but you can't tell these days. "If it makes you feel better," he says, "I'm loaded." A gust of wind whips her ponytail forward and what feels like a wet bedsheet against him. He sways, rights himself. Her head's down, shoulders up.

"Miss?"

She lets out a laugh then sniffs and he wonders if she's crying. It only lasts a couple of seconds but in that time he suffers a surge of claustrophobia, caught between the hot room and her bowed head.

"You don't look loaded," she says, not looking up.

Whatever's trying to form Augustus doesn't want it. The room's heat presses his back. Everything has to stop and he has to put the fire out and lie down and them not be here.

Maddoch cranes his neck, owl eyebrows raised.

"Here," Augustus says. He takes her hand (the cold knuckles are prominent) and forces her fingers around the crumpled note.

He doesn't want to look at her but she says, "Okay, thanks," and lifts her head so he gets one glimpse of her face that suddenly looks exhausted before she turns and walks away.

They've left him alone. Harper sent the guards out for a break, followed them to the door but hung back. For a moment it was just him and Augustus. "Information's the map," Harper said. "Disinformation's a tracing of the map held over it in the wrong place. Right picture, wrong coordinates. You think I don't know the difference?" Augustus couldn't answer. He was still in the pain furnace where there was nothing but the paradox of knowing you couldn't stand it and standing it, the extremity from which either annihilation or transcendence must follow yet neither did; only your loop of incredulity and no scream loud enough. "You're a mystery," Harper said, smiling. "I'll give you that. I don't know what you're holding on to but whatever it is you're going to let go. You know this is right." No rancor, just the limber body calmly alert. After the cheerleader Augustus imagined Harper would have switched to less cooperative girls, since seduction better served contempt. There was a narrow rich margin of things girls didn't want to do that you could with relentless coercion get them to do. The prize was their awkward mastery of disgust or fear. Someone Augustus couldn't see came to the doorway, exchanged a few quiet words with Harper, then Harper left, closing the door behind him.

Augustus lies on his side on the floor, hog-tied, his bare feet in a congealing puddle of blood. Pain sends its giant repeated signal from his beaten soles up through his shins and thighs and chest into his head where he can't stop the futile frenzied attempt to make it something he can sidestep or shuck. A scream's an attempt to open yourself wide enough to accommodate what's happening. He remembers the day Clarence Mills got knocked off his bike and broke his arm. The snapped bone came through. There it was: *bone*, the thing dogs gnawed, in case you'd ever been in any doubt, your inside bits only God knew all about. Clarence screamed, but every few seconds stopped screaming and stared at his injury. The anesthesia of disbelief. Fleeting. These moments are just pain adjusting its grip.

He feels sorry for his body that's served him so well all his life. You forget the personality of your thumb, kneecap, ankle, until someone has them at his mercy. At the same time rage because what can a thumb or kneecap or ankle do but force on you in exhaustive detail the report of what's happening to them? This is the soul's bargain with the flesh: for kisses and handshakes, the taste of fresh strawberries, hot sand underfoot or a snowflake on the tongue it risks the worst that can be imagined. Does everyone, he wonders, feel the way he does now that this has happened, that he's always known it would? The moment they laid hands on him in Barcelona (it was just that: one hand on his shoulder, one on his wrist, a dark car liquidly materializing alongside) his first thought was that the thing he'd been expecting all his life had finally come around. He'd known it would find him in the way he'd known someone like Selina would find him. Harper even looked familiar. He recognized him as he'd recognized Selina the first time he walked into Harry's and saw her holding a drink and laughing sly-eyed at someone's joke. You had these shadowy certainties from before birth, the dark inhabitants of Wordsworth's clouds of glory. Your body arrived with its strands of DNA, your soul with its strands of myth. Or so he might have put it in the days when he believed in the soul.

Lovers don't finally meet somewhere, Rumi said. *They're in each other all along.* When he'd first embarked on his fake conversion Augustus had looked forward to revisiting Rumi as a friendly face in a dour crowd—

I am ashamed
to call this love human

79

*and afraid of God
to call it divine.*

He did revisit him, but in secret. His Islamist brothers had as much contempt for The Mevlana's poetry as they had for Playboy bunnies and The Rolling Stones. Heretical Sufi delusions of becoming one with God, rampantly erotic language, music, dance, contemplation—nothing but insidious distraction from the real job in hand: militant revolution and the establishment of Islamism worldwide. Love (like humor, like art, like sex) fed imagination, induced play, swelled ambiguity. To Husain and the literalist crew it was worse than useless, it was subversive.

What are you thinking? Selina had asked him one night in the small hours. They were at her apartment, in bed. It was winter and the city was under three feet of snow. The building's thermostats were awry; it was too hot to cover even with a sheet. Augustus had got up and opened the window. Now puffs of snow-flavored air came in. Earlier that evening Selina had heard from her mother who'd had a call from Michael. He was in a military hospital with a broken leg. One of his buddies had snatched his helmet and thrown it up into a tree, where it had stuck. They'd tried everything, including shooting, to bring it down. In the end Michael had climbed up. A branch snapped and he fell. Selina was high on relief. On the phone with her mother she'd laughed—oh thank God, Mom, thank *God* (it was the first time Augustus had ever heard her address her mother with anything other than suppressed contempt)—then when she'd put the phone down stood with her arms wrapped around herself. When he moved toward her she waved him away. Go and get some champagne. I want to celebrate. No let's go out. Let's go to Harry's and get wasted. How long does a broken leg last?

They'd gone out, spent the evening in the bar with most of the usuals then sobered up with cheeseburgers, fries and vanilla shakes at the Cooper Square Diner. The snow and cold air had reinvented the city as an innocent thing. Selina bought the early edition of the *New York Times* on the way home. We'll just read the sports and the books. Just for one day we'll pretend everything's okay—okay?

What are you thinking? She was lying on her belly perusing the paper by the light of the bedside lamp. Augustus lay halfway down the bed, propped up on one elbow, caressing her ass, occasionally bending to kiss the sweat in the small of her back. In the eight months they'd been together he'd discovered the insufficiency of the flesh. Love demanded expression and the flesh did everything it could but it wasn't enough. Naturally: the flesh was of this world whereas the current that connected them came from whatever was beyond this world, flowed through them and back to its mysterious source. He'd stopped being surprised that he thought in these terms. They were ludicrous and inevitable. Love turned out to be the thing his life had been waiting for, the place for the *fuoco* to rage. It had taken them five or six encounters after that first day of the Central Park rally to step forward and accept the intensity. An alternative would have been to step slightly to one side of it, this remarkable phenomenon of being in love, to walk it among their friends like a pet panther in a diamond collar. They were both furnished superficially with enough precocious cynicism. But more compellingly they were cursed with a sense of entitlement—not to wealth or power but to epic experience—and the sort of elitism that in the end asked what, if people like *them* weren't going to wreck themselves on it, was the *point* of love? So they'd given themselves to it, begun within days to enjoy casual telepathy, exclusively erotic at first but soon serviceable beyond the bedroom. And to both of them even this seemed a preliminary stage. Called alert clairvoyantly he'd turn to see her looking at him across a crowded room and both of them would feel beyond the thrill dread because however much of this they had they'd always want more and love being love would always give them more in strange and dangerous ways.

"What are you thinking?"

He was thinking, as he kissed her buttocks and stroked her thighs, that the world was the kind of place where while one person was doing this another person somewhere else would be having his fingers cut off or his eye gouged out or his daughter raped and mutilated in front of him.

"Muhammad Ali," he lied. In this they were older than their years. For Christ's sake let's not tell each other the truth the whole time, Selina had said. Beauty trumps truth sometimes, that's just the deal. We've got good enough instincts to know when, and if we haven't we don't deserve each other.

"About the conviction?"

Muhammad Ali had been indicted for draft evasion in May. Augustus was an English and philosophy freshman at NYU and as a student in pursuit of a degree qualified for draft deferral until his studies were over. A feast of guilt for him and Selina. Though she wrapped her arms and legs around him and said they'll have to fucking kill me before I let them take you, he knew his being safe made her fear for her brother more acute. It won't come to that, Augustus had said. I don't graduate till 'seventy-one for Christ's sake. That's a whole different decade. The war'll be over by then.

"About my mother's take on him, aside from that she'd marry him if he asked her." He had to ration mentions of his mother when they were intimate like this. Selina knew it served him as a mild blasphemous aphrodisiac (even now he couldn't resist running his tongue gently over her anus) which was fine with her as long as it didn't begin to feel like a fetish. I'll do anything you like in the sack, she'd told him, as long as it's part of everything else. Do you understand? Anything as long as it doesn't become monolithic.

"And her take is? Other than her availability for marriage to him?"

"That his nobility embarrasses him into larger-than-lifeness."

"You think this is a stunt?"

"No, I think it's for real. But he's jumping with a net. The lawyers know if it goes to the Supreme Court they'll rule in his favor. I think this is the Nation asking its highest-profile son to give whitey the finger on the big stage."

She thought about it, turned a page of the *Times*.

"Maybe," she said. "God bless him anyway. I'd marry him myself, incidentally, so don't get complacent. That air coming in is like an angel."

Augustus was only half paying attention. The thought of what some other person somewhere else was going though while he was lying here sipping from the cup of bliss not only wouldn't leave him alone but was stirring the blood in his cock. Somewhere back down his sexual line he'd discovered—with a feeling of coming deflatedly into his share of species inheritance—the link between cruelty and arousal. God's lousy wiring or the Devil sneaking a hand in during a Divine nap.

"How come you never joined?" Selina asked him.

"The Nation?"

"Yeah."

He laughed. "Oh, man."

"What?"

"I'll tell you something. I was there the night they arrested Johnson Hinton."

"Get out of here."

"I was maybe nine or ten. You know the story, right?"

Selina twisted onto her side and got up on one elbow to look at him. "I know Malcolm X helped the guy sue the city for police brutality. Are you shitting me?"

"I was out on the street with three or four other kids, just mooching around doing nothing useful. Anyway there was a fight between a bunch of guys, God knows how it started, but two white cops broke it up and made a big deal of getting the bystanders to move on. Except some of the bystanders couldn't move on because they *lived* there, right? Which left the cops feeling stupid. So they start getting heavy and this guy Hinton gets whacked over the head with a nightstick and taken away in a squad car. Turns out he's one of the Fruit of Islam. Word gets back to Temple Seven and half an hour later there's fifty of these motherfuckers soldiered up outside the police station."

"Including Malcolm X."

"Including Malcolm X. Us kids had followed the crowd that had drifted up to the precinct house. It was amazing. The cops were scared shitless. And Malcolm *demands* to see the prisoner then *demands* he gets proper medical care, and lo and fucking behold an ambulance comes and takes brother Hinton away!"

"And you were there?"

"I was there. We traipsed up to Harlem Hospital, too, all the way up Lenox Avenue. People came out of their houses and out of bars and joined the march. I'd never seen anything like it. There was a pretty big crowd by the time we got to the hospital. More police arrived and told Malcolm to break it up, and Malcolm cool as a fucking cucumber says he'll cooperate when he's confident brother Hinton's getting proper medical attention. In the end they had to go and get the fucking *doctor* to come out and put his mind at ease."

"You're amazing. I can't believe you never told me that."

Augustus lifted her thigh and kissed her cunt, gently. (Each time he did something like this he knew he was taking a coin from their almost inexhaustible hoard of wealth.) In the whole time he'd known her he'd never seen her so at ease. Normally even stoned part of her kept vigil for her brother. But Michael had broken his leg and was not, for a while, going to get shot and killed. God bless the joker who tossed up the helmet.

"So how come it didn't inspire you to become a member?" she asked. "Seeing Black Power in action."

"Well I was only ten years old. But actually it must have put a seed in there because a few years later I went to hear Elijah Muhammad speak. I was still only in my teens."

"But you weren't convinced?"

"I wasn't *black*. Not properly. I got some looks from the regulars—"

"Your beautiful magician's eyes."

"But in any case they kept talking about The White Man. Separating from the white man. My grandfather's the white man. My grandmother's the white man. My *mother's* the goddamned white man."

"And now your bitch is the white man. Come here."

After they'd made love, Selina said: "We *could* marry him now."

"What?"

"Me and your mother. Me *or* your mother I mean. Could marry Muhammad Ali now. In a storm of publicity."

Now because the U.S. Supreme Court had that year ruled that any extant antimiscegenation law contravened the Fourteenth Amendment and thus subverted the Constitution. Harry had framed a newspaper picture of the groundbreaking couple from Virginia—the aptly named Perry Loving and his beloved, Mildred Jeter (he was white, she was mixed African and American Indian)—and hung it above the bar. Until the ruling interracial marriage had been illegal in seventeen states, though New York wasn't one of them.

"You think he'd marry a skinny-legged thang like you?" Augustus said.

"Poor Seaborn must be turning in his grave," Selina said. "Seaborn" was Seaborn Roddenberry, a Georgian Democrat in the House of Representatives in 1913 whose proposed bill against mixed marriage had been dug up and much quoted in the press during *Loving v. Virginia*. Selina had learned bits by heart. " 'Intermarriage between whites and blacks is repulsive,' " she recited now, in an approximate southern accent, " 'and averse to every sentiment of pure American spirit. It is abhorrent and repugnant to the very principles of Saxon government.' " Augustus kissed her bare armpits. " 'It is subversive of social peace. It is destructive of moral supremacy, and ultimately this slavery of white women to black beasts—' " Augustus kissed down the length of her, lingered between her legs—" 'will bring . . .' umm ' . . . this nation a conflict . . . a conflict as fatal as ever reddened the soil of Virginia or crimsoned the mountain paths of Pennsylvania. Let us—' slower. Yes, like that—'uproot and exterminate now this debasing, ultra-demoralizing, un-American and inhuman leprosy . . .' Oh that's nice. That's really very nice."

The door opens and Harper walks in, alone, carrying a plastic bottle of Evian, which he puts on the table. Its condensation says *cold*. He rights the chair next to Augustus then unfastens the cable between the two sets of cuffs. Augustus straightens his legs; jammed blood loosens, hurries into his thighs and calves. He thinks of a crowd pouring through a broken barrier.

"I'll help you into the chair."

During the interrogation Harper hasn't touched him but now he puts his hands under Augustus's arms from behind and with one smooth hike (so powerful it brings Augustus's infancy back for a moment) has him seated.

"Oh," Harper says. "Wait."

The soles of the feet. You wouldn't think it. But if you reflect there's really only one context in which you hear the phrase. Augustus sits with his legs lifted, as if (the mind goes about its associative business regardless) Harper's about to run a vacuum cleaner over the place. As a child Augustus couldn't bear it if he had to do this when his mother vacuumed, there was something in the gesture that made him feel corrupt, as if he were laughing at her, as if she were his slave!

Harper fetches one of the guards' chairs. "Stretch your legs out."

Not easy, a surge of sweat and despair, but Harper slides the seat under his calves and Augustus lets himself go limp. Harper brings the Evian, opens it and hands it to him. It's cold enough to hurt, lightnings where the teeth are missing, goes down his throat in knots. Harper holds the bottle's plastic cap up.

"People hear that little hymeneal snap of the seal breaking on a bottle they feel safe. That's something, isn't it? Packaging as retroactive terrorism. A guy buys a bottle of Coke for his daughter turns out to be poisoned. She drinks it and dies. But it turns out too that the seal had been broken and he didn't check. What do people think? Guy *deserved* it. Idiot."

Augustus finishes the water, wants more, much more though it's frozen his palate. The small refreshment makes him tearful, his body's readiness to go on, biology's dumb dedication. *Red blood cells rush to the site of injury.* As a kid he'd imagined them as fire trucks: sirens, manful determination, teamwork, sacrifice.

"Let me ask you something," Harper says. "Does it seem crazy to you now that you thought you'd be able to do this?"

For Augustus the water's brought back the horror of hope. Before they'd broken off he'd been close to something, a space just before unconsciousness or insensibility in which, as Harper had said, there was pure awareness, observation without investment or concern. They can't let you enter that state. In that state you don't care, and if you don't care they've got nothing to work with. So they pause. Give you water. The body recouples itself to the soul.

Tears hurry out of his eyes then stop abruptly.

"To plan it," Harper says. "To make the plan work. Feeling of absurdity never crept in?"

"No."

"I'm glad you say that. It's one of the things I'm attracted to in you, this understanding of how easily within reach the extraordinary is, this faith in your own powers of execution. It happens we got the intelligence. We might just as easily not have. Next time maybe we won't. These things hang on threads. Hell of a way to make a living."

"It's not how I make a living."

"Right, I forgot. Front-line journalist turned chef."

Augustus wants to correct him—*restaurateur, not chef*—but is forced by the idiom "to make a living" into a compressed vision, a split-second glimpse of a thousand human labors, from naked hominids loping with spears to lab-coated scientists at the Large Hadron Collider. History happened so fast and pointlessly, he thinks. And if the planet doesn't give up on us before we find a way of doing without, it will go on happening forever, one way or another. The hardest myth to let go of is the myth of ending.

"Do you think of it as capitulation?" Harper asks. For a moment Augustus thinks he means leaving journalism for the restaurant business—but Harper adds, "The embrace of violence?"

Augustus closes his eyes and again feels the dark curtain ready to drop. Knights wore armor so heavy that if knocked to the ground they couldn't get up. He tries to imagine getting up himself, tests his limbs for readiness but gets no response. The effort makes him want to vomit. He does in fact heave, but nothing comes up. The plastic bottle falls from his hand and rolls away across the floor.

"I don't think about it," he says.

"Sure you do. Come on."

"If the law goes, it's not capitulation," Augustus says. "It's all that's left."

"And you think the law's gone?"

"At the highest levels."

"You were in Central America in the 'eighties, right?"

"El Salvador. The highest levels have always operated above the law. It's just that now it's open."

"It's been open for years. The Nicaragua ruling was a public turning point, a coming to full self-consciousness; not just the administration, the whole country. An idea whose time had come, that the United States would judge all and be judged by none. The last inevitable flowering of manifest destiny."

"I have to move," Augustus says.

"Go ahead."

With another queasy effort Augustus maneuvers himself partly onto his side in the chair, in careful increments gets his weight rearranged. The pain hierarchy's established; he knows what to favor, where pressure can be borne. Still the room spins for a moment.

"It's a real shame your guy's hit on Bush failed," Harper says. "I'd love to have seen it. There's boredom gathered around the man now, that feeling of playing it out because there's still time on the clock. He's done what he's going to do, don't you think?"

"I'm not an optimist," Augustus says. "There's plenty of time for more."

"He's fascinating at close quarters."

"I'll take your word for it."

"There's an autism that comes with invulnerability."

"I thought you said these things hung on threads?"

"They do, but he doesn't know that. The invulnerability's a delusion but you can't blame him for it. All the skeletons are out—imbecility, greed, corruption, hypocrisy, criminality, contempt for thinking—and yet the sun still shines and water comes out the tap when he turns it."

Augustus wants to ask for more water (partially slaked thirst is worse, gives righteous anger to what's left) but the risk of upsetting this balance holds him back.

"I would, actually, have liked to see it," Harper repeats. "I've nothing against him except the obtuseness and the look like a huffy chimp. All my objections are aesthetic. But I'd have been curious to see what Americans would have done with the event."

"It's not too late," Augustus says. "You can shoot him yourself."

Harper's smile is bright, concedes deep recognition. "Maybe I will," he says. "I'm vulnerable to boredom."

Augustus feels the subject in danger of closing, forces himself wider awake. "Can I ask you something?" he says.

"Anything."

"What will you do if I don't have the information you want?"

"If you have it you'll give it. You know this is right. And you do have it. Or at least I believe you have it, which comes to the same thing."

"Hypothetically. Say I die of a heart attack right now."

"Hypothetically? If I didn't have the information I'd make it up. Which in the movie would be your cue to say: 'Make it up anyway. I won't tell.'"

"You should work in Hollywood."

"It's on the cards. Entertainment's the natural complement but very few make the transition. The really strong appeal for me right now is in icon management. You know about this?"

For a second Augustus thinks desktop icons—knows it can't be. Then sees: "As in Madonna?"

"Yeah, but not just a pop star or a movie star or a sports star, although you'd want some of them to do those things. What we're looking at is the creation of icons, manufactured characters eventually forming a pantheon like the gods of antiquity. The product content is their traits, their maxims, their loves and hates—everything you get with current stars in an incidental way, except in this case it won't be incidental, it'll be designed and presented from the outset. Neopolytheism. You see it, right? Temples, symbols, rites, initiates. Merchandise across the spectrum."

"There's a woman who prays to David Beckham."

"I know! I saw that. The potential's there. Obviously you're not going to touch the existing religions, but what about the millions who don't have divinity in their life but want it? There's an immense opportunity but it requires a grasp of how needy and dumb people really are. So far we've only scratched the surface. Think of David Beckham if we'd got in on the ground floor. Kate Moss. *Britney* for Christ's sake. People need gods. Postmodern pluralism and the pick-and-mix mindset makes polytheism the obvious revival. Popular culture's been screaming for a new pantheon for decades."

"You can't manufacture divinity like that."

"We couldn't manufacture celebrity like that either in the past but we can now. This is *American Idol*. The transition between obscurity and fame used to be mysterious. Now it's transparent. The message is there's nothing special about this person but we're going to tell you there is and you're going to respond as if there is. Cut to a billion dollars later."

Augustus knows Harper's right and it gives him a feeling of muscular relief to be leaving the world. His body gets a premonitory sense of itself shed like an overcoat. The people he loved are gone anyway. God's been burned up but the habit of imagining meeting the dead persists. A pleasant place of white stone floors and flowering jasmine, blue sky, the crowds of history milling as in a Roman forum, his mother somewhere among them. He knows it's a fantasy, which at this moment pierces him because it means never Selina again either. You live for years with beliefs you'd deny having then the end comes and takes even them away. For a second he doesn't care if the conversation dies—then does. Riddled with life though you can barely move.

"I see you in P.R.," Augustus says. "Illegal wars need good image-makers."

"Right," Harper says. "But I'm tired of dealing with the suits. These guys don't know how to relax. There's not enough music and dancing in my life."

"Inside you're dancing."

Harper chuckles, giddily. "It's a real shame we didn't meet under different circumstances," he says. "You're a person of quality. We could have done good things together I think."

"We don't see things the same way."

"Sure we do. No God, life's meaningless, religions are fairy stories, morality's an illusion, political ideologies are the front men for brute force . . ." Delivered as lilting recitation. "It's all force in the end. The most refined justice system on the planet's underwritten by force. You say if the law goes all there is left is violence. The law's just the violence of the weak majority. We're all the children of Achilles. You know this is right."

"Okay let me go and I'll join you in the icon business."

Harper laughs, again with genuine spontaneity. "Oh man, wish I could. But come on. This stuff you can't even have the conversation. Morality, meaning, truth, the terms are embarrassments. They're like bloated old aunts who should shuffle off and die. The prerequisite for intellectuals now is the acknowledgment of the absurdity of the intellectual life. Philosophy is to politics what boxing is to total war."

It's so long since Augustus thought or spoke in these terms he can't hold them. He's desperate to ask for more water but the risk of checking Harper's flow outweighs his thirst.

"Without God or some other Absolute it doesn't matter what you do, except consequentially, strategically. You know this. People know this, they just can't stand it. Instead they go backward—backward into religion or backward into progressive humanism, which is just as much a myth as Christianity and the rest. Religion's doing so well these days—why do you think that is? It's because it's taken this long for Nietzsche to sink in. God's been dead since *The Gay Science* but the collective psyche's only just got the news. People are flocking to Islam and Christianity in the biggest act of denied epiphany in history—believing because they finally know it's not true. I have this vision of Jack Nicholson from *A Few Good Men*, a huge hologram of his head floating in the sky looking down at the world and going *The truth? You can't hairndle the truth!*"

The Barcelona hotel got British newspapers, erratically: an *Independent* the morning he and Selina had breakfast in bed. She'd read him the headlines. *Climate Change Sceptics Point to New Data.* Jesus, she'd said, who'd be young in this century? At least when we were kids we thought however much bullshit there was there was also really a way things were. Now there's no way things are, only claims about the way things are. For every position a counter-position and the positions themselves nothing to do with the way things are but with the way it's advantageous to say things are. There's information everywhere. It's like some godawful ubiquitous schizophrenia. I met a cosmologist the other week who told me it's statistically as likely that the universe is a computer simulation as that it's real.

"Don't you agree?" Harper says.

"Yes, I agree."

"And yet here we are. You're holding out on me. You're protecting people."

"It seems so."

"Why?"

"I can't help it."

"Without first principles."

"I can't help it."

Harper nods, lowers his eyelids: He's seen this before, understands. He fishes out the soft pack of Winstons. Maybe seven or eight left. Augustus supposes he, Augustus, will be dead before they've all been smoked, gets a foreboding of the world exactly the same but for the presence of his consciousness, knows too that lighting up—again Harper leans close—will set the clock ticking. Nonetheless he inhales deeply. Cigarettes, kisses, cups of coffee, fucks, candy bars, apologies, birthdays, dreams—a certain number of each gone like motes passing through a shaft of sunlight. His mother said angels with ledgers kept track of these details but has gone herself now through the incinerator into nothingness.

"You have feelings," Harper says.

The nicotine's making Augustus dizzy. He wonders again how long he's been here, tries to remember the last thing he ate. Someone on the plane before it landed gave him a cellophaned samosa. Inés's junk email box will have something from Amnesty about western governments outsourcing interrogation. Occasionally she opens and skims these things but feels only another addition to the numberless messages adrift from their moorings. Outsourcing means call centers in Bangladesh.

"Can't seem to shake them."

"I see this. You've left the path of reason."

"You find that you do."

Again Harper acknowledges with a nod. He blows a shuddering smoke ring both of them watch to see how long it holds its form. Longer than Augustus thought it would but still in only a few seconds it's gone. Which is his life and most likely Life. We love watching animals because they're constitutionally incapable of metaphor.

"Or that you really don't," Harper says. "Maybe you still believe there's a reward for self-sacrifice? Greater love hath no man. In which case obviously this is a golden opportunity."

Augustus shakes his head, no, out of habit, but at the same time knows there remain moments of eclipse, intimations of being the object of something's gaze, something that presents a surface of pure indifference but conceals a palpitating kernel of justice. When it happens he tells himself it's just his consciousness compelled like everyone else's to try to wriggle out of its own contingency. *All good children go to heaven.* Somewhere in the crenulations of his brain he knows this deep neural groove endures, but knows too that it was put there and might just as easily not have been. Whoever it was put God in your head it wasn't God. And yet, as Harper says, here they are. With an inner start Augustus realizes it's the first time he's asked himself why he's resisting—and in the asking simultaneously answers. The answer's been with him the whole time but given so often it's become like a word made meaningless by repetition. It would seem a laughably poor answer to Harper. It seems a laughably poor answer to Augustus too, since it's no less absurd than the idea of piling up brownie points for the heaven that doesn't exist.

One cold gray afternoon in November 1969 Augustus and Selina stood watching the ice skaters at the Wollman Rink in Central Park. The burgeoning commercial spirit of Christmas was a soft atmospheric murmur, storefronts beginning to glimmer, kids collectively coming awake. He stood behind her with his hands in the front pockets of her jeans, holding her pelvis. They'd been together more than two years and his thrill at proprietorially putting his hands on her was undiminished. Absurd to take the city's cold air and concrete edges as wistful homage to her suppleness and warmth, but that's what he'd been doing. No quarrel with absurdity if it gave him love. Held by him her hips whispered their bone-cradled secret, the potential for life like the flicker of a tiny fish. Since summer he'd known he wanted her to have his child, though he'd said nothing about it.

I really despise people, she said. Her left eye watered. Humans, I mean. Actual human beings in front of me. This woman took off her shoe on the subway the other day and started massaging her toes. Humanity in the abstract I'll fight for, but actual people . . . Depressing, right? The fascist heart bound and gagged with liberal principles. But maybe if I wasn't a monster at heart I wouldn't do any good in the world? That's somehow right isn't it, that if the best people didn't know the worthlessness of their own hearts they wouldn't be the best people? In fact they'd be the worst people. Augustus said nothing. You could feel such collusion with someone it bordered disgust. Most of the rink spectators were watching them instead of the skaters, imagining, he thought, the profanity of him inside her; her sucking his cock. Might as well have been sodomizing Jesus. They were both used to it; if they stood still long enough hatred and fascination massed around them. At such moments the white faces acquired a look of gradual coming-to, a fresh perception that the times had cheated them of something. How had they let it happen? Woodstock, that nigger with the guitar profaning the national anthem, white girls with their tits out in the crowd, the whole lot stoned out of their minds. The fatalists turned away with happy disgust, content to have the degeneracy of the age confirmed. The rest began to look to one another with wounded urgency. At which moments he'd whisper in her ear, I hear the hoofbeats of the Klansman's horse. . . .

He held her hips tighter and pulled her close against him. It was a thrilling new open space to step into, this certainty that he wanted to have a child with her. Now that he knew it he realized he'd been waiting for the knowledge for some time. Inglorious biology was the poetic contrast to the rarefied stuff of spirit; tubes and eggs and wriggling sperm, the monstrous umbilicus and the gory porn of delivery all to heave a new consciousness up into the world. *Inter faeces et urinem nascimur* it said on the wall in the john at Harry's. Selina reluctantly translated: *between shit and piss are we born.* This was God's aesthetic, Augustus saw, plaited polarities, divinity in a cowshed, new souls amid sewage. He'd let God go pretty much by the time his mother married Cardillo but Selina's Catholicism (a mausoleum, she said, with satirical melodrama; I wander around it, visit the lovely sepulchres and the lovely dead) had brought some of his own back. As a myth only, he told himself, as an artwork, as a *reading.* He'd had two years of English and philosophy at NYU, long enough to have swallowed most of the postmodern pills. It's like synthetic food, Selina said. It'll keep you alive but it tastes like shit. That July Neil Armstrong had walked on the moon. An artist friend of Selina's had thrown a "Landing Party" at a basement gallery in Soho for the televised event, half the guests dressed as aliens or astronauts. Despite grass and acid and booze the historic moment gathered them around the tube and for a few minutes gave them their childhoods back. Afterward Augustus and Selina admitted to each other that the renewed perception of the planet, the solar system, all those spheres clockworkishly revolving around one another had made them think, briefly, of God in the most ludicrously traditional way: genial old white-bearded überdesigner surrounded by star charts and astrolabes. But back at her apartment later that night when they lay in each other's arms she'd said: There's nothing. It's just a massive accidental extravagance. The Apollo mission had sidelined the war in Vietnam, made negligible its tally of burned and mutilated and missing and dead. Augustus knew it felt to her as if Michael had been cut adrift. There was moon*light*, astonishingly, on her bare shoulder and blond hair, which gave Augustus an intimate feeling of connection to the spacemen a quarter of a million miles away. As she floated nearer to sleep she said: I don't like to think of how cold it is out there . . . the *cold* of space . . . She was disgusted with herself for getting a lump in her throat when Armstrong had uttered his " . . . one giant leap for mankind" line. Augustus had noticed. She'd looked at him and lit a joint and said, See? See what a fucking *moron* I am? Ten-cent grandeur. *Mankind*. Jesus, hit me will you? Hit me in the *face*. It filled him with urgent love for her, this war she had with what she thought of as the sentimental side of herself, reminded him of the effort she had to make to play by the head's rules instead of the heart's. By nature she was everything she'd nurtured herself to disavow: elitist, individualist, dualist, theist, emotionalist, capitalist, narcissist, absolutist. I'm a goddamned sadist, too, she'd said, whiskey-drunk one night, and the admission had ravished him. He'd felt the current of cruelty in her from time to time, a different strain of arousal, a deadness in her blue eyes and just before she came a look of barely mastered disgust. (At the Catholic school there had been a fat ugly girl whose life she and two of her friends made hell. They'd nicknamed her NOFAM, which stood for Not For Any Money, as in not for any money would a boy fuck her. The memory still tormented her now.) It excited him, and though he plucked up the courage to tell her they had it in common he did it under the shelter of a generalization. Come on baby, everybody's got this shit in them. It's as old as the species. He didn't want to dwell on it because the difference between him and her was that she'd rejected it as a source of knowledge and he hadn't, quite. She'd rejected it but talked as if she hadn't. She told him her sexual fantasies made her ashamed but that she knew a time was coming when they wouldn't. Outgrowing shame's what we do, she said. Adam and Eve, look at them, the shame didn't last. They wept as they walked away from Eden but within half a mile they were holding hands and thinking about a new place to live. They farmed and had kids and got on with it. God overestimated shame. That was God's big mistake. She had these talismanic insights but suspected herself of sophistry, couldn't look long in a mirror without pulling a mocking face. Augustus knew all this about her and that there was always more to know. No amount of her was enough. It gave him a foretaste of satiation that sickened him without stopping him wanting it. He could kill her. Not in any metaphorical sense, but literally, put an end to having to know her by putting an end to *her*. This was love, of which you had no idea until you were in it.

Now he wanted her to have his baby. He felt this too had been precipitated by the moon landing. Armstrong's "mankind" had heightened everyone's sense of species membership. That long look back at suddenly poignant Earth—"the Earth is a beautiful blue!"—evoking for Augustus geological time, dinosaurs, the systole and diastole of coming into being and passing away, had released in him the basic male seed-scattering imperative and a fascination with physical creation. He'd lain awake long after Selina had fallen asleep imagining her pregnant. It was revolting (a fetal version of himself in her womb, red-lit, claustrophobic, an eggy odor and warm blood feeding him the ghost flavors of her lunch) but beneath the revulsion were calm and certainty: this was what we did, why we were the envy of angels. The revelation matter-of-factly closed his adolescence and opened his manhood. It was a curious thrill to realize you were a man, that you could legitimately add your portion to the world's clamor. Almost a disappointment, how easily you made the transition.

He wanted to tell her but couldn't. She wasn't allowing herself the idea of the future while Michael was still in Vietnam. Once he was home intact she could return to her journey away from him but while death hung over him she felt entitled to nothing. Being in love with Augustus was already a concussive wrong under which she staggered and crawled, sick with guilt half the time. Michael never wrote to her. Does he even know about us? Augustus asked. Oh yeah, she said. My mom'll have poured it all over him like a liqueur. That's *why* he doesn't write me.

There had been two encounters with Selina's parents. The first was accidental and brief. Selina and Augustus were on their way to a meeting of the SDS (Students for a Democratic Society) and her parents were on their way to an evening show of *Funny Girl*. Selina's father wrong-footed Augustus by shaking hands and saying it was a pleasure to meet him at last. Selina got them away but not before her father had invited them to dinner the following weekend. There's no way, she said as they hurried down Broadway. It's a scheme. We're not going. But they did go. Augustus's curiosity and her own compulsive combativeness made it irresistible. The evening, at the five-floor house in Gramercy Park (the official family seat—The Confected Mansion, as Selina called it—was an hour upstate) was surreally volatile. Oh, Mom you've given Ruthie the night off, Selina said, when a pretty Latina maid came to take their coats. What a shame! She and Augustus could've Lindy Hopped or sung the blues after dinner. Ruthie's the regular maid, she told Augustus in an exaggerated aside, but she's cata*strophically* negro. It would've been indelicate. Mom you didn't *fire* her just so we could come to dinner did you? Selina's mother, Meredith, a striking blonde in her mid-forties with Selina's sly eyes and high cheekbones, lifted her chin and addressed Augustus across her daughter: Our housekeeper, Ruthie, has been off all week because her grandson's ill with glandular fever. Darling you're not going to succumb to predictability by making tonight unpleasant are you? Selina breezed away, saying I doubt tonight'll need any help from me. Augustus entered the sitting room (modern Italian furniture presided over by an asymmetrical chandelier of buttery yellow orbs that pulsed as if with jovial awareness) wishing he'd had the sense to smoke a joint in preparation. Selina's father, Jack, officiated at the room's wet bar. Augustus, what's your poison? He was a tall dark-eyed man whose close-cropped silver curls you could picture a laurel wreath on. Oh I guess bourbon, thanks, Augustus said, just ice. That was the last of the evening's uncomplicated exchanges. Laughably benign remarks led in seconds to trouble, though Jack had a marvelous facility for defusing them with a joke or funny story. By dessert Selina was drunk and dangerous. Give up, Dad, she said. I already warned him you'd be charming. You're wasting your time. Your baby girl's banging a jigaboo and the entire Trent ancestry's turning in its overornamented grave. You're homicidal when you think about it so let's not have *charm*, shall we? Augustus, half-drunk himself, felt the room fill with ironish energy. Meredith closed her eyes and clamped her jaws together. It was apparent to Augustus that despite their consumption Jack still glittered with sobriety. Selina got up from the table. I'm going to the Mario Bellini, she said. The Mario Bellini's got my name on it. One of the elephantine red leather armchairs. She crossed the floor with immense high-heels concentration then collapsed into it and glared back at them all. Augustus felt the room revolving: Jack's generous bourbons, white wine with the meal (tiny soufflés, a beetroot salad, sea bream with saffron sauce, profiteroles), port with the cheese and now a balloon of brandy. He had to stop drinking *right now*. Maybe Augustus would like to see the space stuff, Meredith said to her husband. Hon? Augustus had imagined there might be something like this, a quiet word. He glanced at Selina but she'd closed her eyes.

"The space stuff" was Jack's collection of antique astronomical instruments housed on the top floor. I won't give you any bullshit, Jack said to him when they were up there. You know the score. It's not going to happen. Augustus had determined to say as little as possible. Jack leaned against a long table housing a dozen astrolabes. There were many other devices and instruments that did God only knew what, lots of glowing brass, iron, copper. You're manifestly a man of quality, Jack said, then paused to light his and Augustus's cigarettes. Not to mention physical glamour. Selina's more trouble than any man should have to put up with but she's got taste, she's got the eye. Be that as it may you know it's not going to happen. In the end it's not going to happen. I want us to understand each other. Do we? Augustus wished he was leaning against something himself. He said: I think I understand you pretty clearly, Jack. That's half your desired equation—maybe you should settle for that? Jack smiled, nodded, accepted all the relevant information was in. He looked around at the instruments. You interested in any of this shit? he asked Augustus. As a matter of fact I am, Augustus said, but I think it's time we made tracks. Walking home, Selina threw up in the gutter. Augustus had to carry her up the building's last two flights. That was six months ago.

"You're an unbelievably beautiful woman," he said to her as she leaned back into him and over her shoulder he watched a teenage girl who'd obviously only very recently got the knack of skating backward tentatively moving across the ice with a face of anxious concentration and delight in herself.

"Not without you," Selina said. "Without you I'm a mean-faced miserable poisonous witch."

"Not mean-faced."

"Yeah well without me you're an Oedipal train-wreck. A spooked dog snapping at the legs on Madison Avenue."

"Lucky your legs came along."

"Damn right."

Her mood had darkened, he knew, the combination of affection and the laughing skaters saying the world was okay, the pleasure of having a cashmere scarf around her neck and thin suede gloves on her hands. She had to snap herself out of the good moments in case their price was Michael's arms or legs or life. It made Augustus feel like a lousy Satanic tempter. In moments of clarity he wished Michael would just step on a mine and have done with it. It would put an end to this never being able to enjoy anything cleanly, and solve the problem of having to deal with him when the war was over. It's a fucking ménage à trois, Augustus had complained to Harry, who in the manner of bartenders through history soaked up his customers' traumas and triumphs—like God, Selina said, but without the judgment. I swear one day I'm going to go down on her and find he's there already, in full fucking combat uniform. Whatever their fights were ostensibly about they were always somewhat about (they'd uppercased it) the Meaning Of Michael, or MOM for short. Give me a break, Augustus had said. I'm the sin your brother won't be able to forgive, soiling yourself with a nigger. Otherwise he'll have you for the rest of his life, assuming he doesn't get his head blown off. This last remark had been purely to force her to imagine the violence of it. That day the Chappaquiddick story had broken and bled out, making everyone feel dismal. Yeah, she said, you're right. So what? We're all someone's love for some fucked-up reason. You think you're immune? You're hilarious, getting a hard-on every time your mother mispronounces a word in front of me. Thank Christ she's not Jewish. You'd have me in a fucking SS uniform.

He loved her for cutting to the core. Underneath every fight between them was the deeper fight to be the best at telling the truth. Invariably the fights segued into heightened sex, staring at each other with what to an observer would've looked like focused hatred but was both of them trying to burn themselves out in each other, without success. Harry said to Augustus: You guys are a grand passion, man. You know how rare that is? I'm here and I can see it, people want to get close enough to catch a bit of that heat from you. It's beautiful. Most bizarrely, Augustus had begun to see that his mother and Cardillo had something of the same heat, drew people the same way. We can see everything, Selina said, if we're willing to look. Not that most of us are willing. You can tell with kids from infancy: some have to look, others have to look away. The more you look and see the colder you get. Artists with big eyes have small hearts and vice versa. She joked about the great injustice of her having no artistic talent. *If you take the actual writing out of the equation I'm probably the greatest writer since Shakespeare.* She'd once started a novel, soon stalled, defeated not by how little she could see but how much. Art lied by omission, she said, got its glowing portion by ignoring the whole. What, so only *God* should write novels? someone at Harry's asked. Nov*el*, singular, Selina said. There's only one and He's already written it. You're reading it with every breath. The rest's just noble beautiful fraud. Obviously this was to stir the crowd, half of whom were aspiring artists of one stripe or another. The real explanation was that she'd seen what literary greatness would require, knew she didn't have it and, since nothing but greatness would do, stopped right there.

They wandered away from the rink, back out onto Fifth Avenue where three horse-drawn carriages stood waiting for tourists. Look at *horses* for Christ's sake, Cardillo had said. Look at horses and tell me there's no God. Listen, Augustus had replied once, quietly, while his mother's shoulders visibly tightened, listen to me, will you for just a few moments? There's this thing called The Design Argument, okay? Now every time you come out with some crap about horses or lions or fucking chimps you're espousing— claiming, *making* this argument. . . . In the new generosity of his latent fatherhood Augustus felt sorry for the restaurateur. He surprised himself by thinking he ought to be kinder to the man who so crazily loved his mother, who had in effect taken his probably soon to be difficult mother off his hands. It was only thinking this that he realized his own loyalty had shifted: he loved Selina more than he loved his mother. If he could put only one of them in the lifeboat he'd let his mother drown. This was visceral and elating but carried the imprimatur of his own mortality, of the reassuring ephemerality of everything, in fact. He glanced at Selina, the hard little face and pale blond hair, felt renewed excitement at her imperfections, everything from her fucked-up love affair with Michael to the misangled canine tooth that gave her a slight sneer in repose. He knew he'd remember this moment for the rest of his life: the big steaming horses and the buzz of Christmas, the long avenue and subdued sentience of the park, her chilled face and force field of trouble and hunger.

"What?" Selina asked, seeing his look.

"Nothing."

"Nothing?"

"Nothing you don't already know."

Which was enough, because she did know, could see it in his face. He watched her absorb it as if swallowing a drop of something delicious. She had to look away, squeeze his hand. Though she craved—demanded, if she was truthful—love from the world getting it at random moments in pure portions left her rosy with shame. It lifted her mood again.

There had been another march yesterday and the sparkling sidewalk was littered with bits of discarded banners and leaflets. Augustus wondered what energy he'd have for protesting the war if Selina dropped it. They'd started the year with a trip to Washington to decry Nixon's inauguration and ended it with a wrecking raid on the Army and Air Force's ROTC offices. They'd been tear-gassed at Fort Dix when they'd gone out there to support the thirty-eight soldiers under political arrest and narrowly missed arrest themselves in the Weathermen's Chicago action. Governor Reagan in California was calling for the cessation of federal funding to "rioting students." Augustus had been first courted then spurned as a white-lovin' chickenshit by the Black Panthers when he declined membership on the grounds that it was too late for him to start feeling black brotherhood. Go look in the mirror, asshole, Ronnie said. You think some white pig's gonna ask you if you feel black brotherhood before he shoots your fuckin knees out?

"We're not going to this thing tonight, right?" Augustus said, as one of the horses tossed its head and made its harness bells jingle. A little sound brought Switzerland or the steppes with such immediacy you thought maybe you'd had a past life.

"*God* no. You don't want to, do you?"

"I don't have the energy."

"Neither do I."

There was a "freak-in" in the Loeb student building scheduled for that night. Or possibly a "happening"; the nomenclature hadn't settled. Through the year these things had made the news under the umbrella of the antiwar movement, though by now neither Selina nor Augustus saw them as anything more than a chance to get wasted and fuck people you wouldn't normally fuck. Vietnam's gift to the Dumb and the Ugly, she'd labeled them.

"Let's go get a drink," she said. "Couldn't you use a drink right now?"

"Sure. Harry's?"

"No, let's go somewhere else. I'm sick of Harry's."

They ended up in a bar on East 40th Street, a long low-ceilinged place with leatherette booths and despite the low ceiling two large chandeliers. Selina was in a phase of never knowing what she wanted to drink, ordered a Long Island Iced Tea. Augustus had a scotch on the rocks. There was a copy of the day's *New York Times* on the table open at the sports. Sports near the back so that after you waded through all the reasons for despair there was something to imply continuity and optimism. Athletes in motion had moral innocence. The year before, Cardillo had brought in a color TV for the Mexico Games and Augustus had discovered the therapeutic relief of dissolving into the runner's purity of purpose. The prelapsarian state would've been like that, undivided, eternally in the moment. It was like the Fall all over again when they crossed the finish line and their personalities flooded back in and they started crying and giving interviews. He began leafing through the broadsheet, not really reading anything.

"When I was a kid," Selina said, "I had this obsession with being kind to animals."

"You? No."

"It wasn't noble, just an extension of superstition, like not stepping on the sidewalk cracks. Anyway one day in the bathroom I stepped on an ant."

In the time it had taken them to come in here, order a drink and sit down it had gone dark outside. Suddenly the bar was a cozy secret haven.

"I was sitting on the toilet and I noticed this ant crawling around on the floor. Okay, *don't step on it.* But by the time I'd got up and washed my hands and looked at myself in the mirror and gone on various fantastic mental journeys I'd forgotten about it—weirdly until just the split second before I stepped on it, when I kind of half saw it but it was too late to avoid."

Augustus had seen photographs of Selina as a child. One in

particular stuck, her maybe five years old on a white porch in a pale blue sundress, half-smiling half-frowning; he imagined picking her up, feeling the fidgety life of her, the skinny legs and little rib cage. He had an image of her now talking very seriously and calmly to their own future daughter, explaining why something was wrong.

"It didn't die. When I lifted my foot up there it was, still running around, seemingly fine. I was such a moron, I got it onto my finger and tried to kiss it—and swallowed it!"

He looked up from the paper and laughed but in his peripheral vision caught the word "Atrocities."

"You can imagine the state *that* put me into—What's wrong?"

"Nothing."

"What is it?"

Too late. This was the downside of approximate telepathy. Augustus felt the goodness of the moment—the secret chandelier-lit bar rocking on the city's dark water, the whiskey's smoky amber, her mood of indulgence—teeter, then fall. What the fuck did he open the newspaper for?

"Show me," she said.

"Leave it."

Alleged U.S. Atrocities at My Lai.

"Give it here."

"Goddamn it."

He relinquished the paper and leaned back in his seat.

Augustus twitches and opens his eyes, knows that for perhaps five or ten seconds he's been asleep. His legs are still resting on the chair, Harper still sits facing him. For a moment there's free fall through the horror of a squandered opportunity but Harper's slight smile says no, this conversation was coming to an end anyway, don't give yourself a hard time. Says too he knows that's no comfort. How can it be?

"Do you know the movie *Soldier Blue*?" Harper asks.

There are erratic flares of clairvoyance: Augustus senses activity outside the room, looks at the door, tries to open his ears. Another part of his brain drags up because it has no choice his memory of *Soldier Blue*. He and Selina went with a group of friends for whom the purpose of seeing a film was so you could make the definitive pronouncement on it as soon as you were out the auditorium doors. It drove Selina crazy. She used to cover her ears until they were clear of the crowds and there was no chance of her overhearing someone begin, *I thought it was kinda* ... Yet they'd suffered their crowd that night, having sensed this was a movie they shouldn't see as a couple alone. Augustus would've been happier not seeing it all, but the controversy had made it a moral obligation.

"Yeah, I saw it," he says. There had been unmentionable group recognition that Candice Bergen looked a little like Selina.

"I'll tell you what that movie did," Harper says, stretching. "It put Godlessness onscreen for the first time. I'm not talking about the behavior of the cavalry. I'm talking about the sun and the clear blue sky. It's not that a woman's raped and has her breasts cut off, it's that she's raped and has her breasts cut off in beautiful broad Technicolor daylight. Remember how blue and *empty* that sky is above the village?"

To his surprise Augustus does remember. At the time he'd thought not of the Christian God but the Indians' Great Spirit, also rendered nonexistent by the film's brilliant sunlight and aquamarine sky.

"This is the modern story," Harper says. "You look up and no one's there. Have you noticed what a lot of torture movies there are now? No, wait, you don't go to the movies."

Again because he can't help it Augustus searches and finds vague concession: increasingly film posters promise hopeless suffering, usually in a single word—*Saw. Hostel. Captivity.*

"I pointed this out the other day to someone in your position. He said: 'If they knew what was really going on they wouldn't make stupid movies.' Don't you think that's completely wrong?"

Augustus is still registering a disturbance on the ether from beyond the room. He can't stop imagining the guards, voluptuous after lunch, step by step descending into the requisite state of roving irritation. They don't need giddiness now boredom's set in.

"I don't know," he says.

"It's completely wrong," Harper says. "The movies are coming *because* we know what's going on. We have knowledge we don't want, so we send it to the movies. Hollywood's the transformation chamber where unpleasant truths get turned into consumable fictions. You know what the top priority for the administration should be right now?"

Augustus can't concentrate. A hardwired defense mechanism stops him fully replaying his own footage. He gets fragments: the thick porous nose and too-small nostrils of the guard without the mustache; a thread hanging from the seam of a truncheon; the mustached one selecting an angle for a blow with a slight tilt of his head—which last brings nausea and a shock of pity for himself and the unique treasure of his life they're despoiling, like a rape.

"The top priority should be getting the conspiracy 9/11 story out as a movie. Are you LIHOP or MIHOP, by the way?"

"What?"

"Do you subscribe to the theory that the government *Let* It Happen On Purpose, or the theory that the government *Made* It Happen On Purpose?"

The will to acronym goes on, LIHOP, MIHOP, the impatience to get a handle on things. (Plus IHOP, the pancake chain not surprisingly asserts itself.) For Augustus acronyms had their negligible share in the disgust that had spilled over into action.

"Let," he says.

"Okay. Smart money. We need a movie that delivers the strongest version of the conspiracy theory right now. The conspiracy theory says, Look: neocon America wants global dominance, which means control of oil territories and the superlative weaponization of space. For the first you need a pretext for invading key oil countries and for the second massive Congress-approved funding, which you won't get unless something terrible comes along to change the spending mindset."

" 'A catastrophic and catalyzing event,' " Augustus says.

Harper raises his eyebrows. "Is that from something?"

There's a peak in Augustus's certainty of movement outside the cell door, a hallucination of the wall bulging inward as if it's thin rubber and a fat man's leaning on it. For so long now he's wanted to wrap his arms round himself but the cuffs prevent him. Instead he presses his hands against his chest. It's some comfort. Vestigial, from holding a teddy . . . and the teddy used to be a breast. . . . All these things we know about ourselves. It's like standing in the middle of a depressing crowd. Your life has a quota of comfort you burn through not knowing you're doing it. Shshsh. Don't cry. There there. It's okay. Hush. Then one day it's gone.

"Rebuilding America's Defenses," Augustus says, though until he opened his mouth he thought he was going to scream. "A document put out by the Project for the New American Century a year before 9/11. Wolfowitz, Cheney, Rumsfeld, Podhoretz, Libby, Perle, you know the people. Twenty-five founding members half of whom are in with the big three defense contractors."

"See?" Harper says. "We could've cowritten the script. The script's *there*. Nerdy Goldblum engineer to get us through the anti-physics of the towers' collapse and an idealistic young female journalist Jennifer Connelly they try to silence but can't. FAA whistleblower I go against type with Sam Jackson. Gene Hackman in the Rumsfeld role. Who's not going to see it?"

Quoting the PNAC document and pronouncing the familiar names has made it worse for Augustus, reminds him facts are a lifestyle option. Exasperated with Jesus, Pilate barked out: What is truth? American teenagers know: The truth is whatever. Not that he cares about the facts either. Since he quit journalism he only knows what he knows through Elise's insistence. The United States could have carried on racking up atrocities till doomsday and he wouldn't have stirred. It's no surprise to him what any government does, least of all his own. He spent a year recording American-funded massacre in El Salvador. He'd gone there in the hope moral outrage would fill the gap left by Selina. It didn't.

"Thing is get the information out as entertainment," Harper says. "Conspiracy theory's doomed if it's been preempted by a brilliant conspiracy theory movie."

With a quivering effort Augustus says: "Facts are already coming out."

"That's my point. They're *late* with the movie. They're on it with *Rendition*, thank God. Nothing's going to protect extraordinary rendition like *Rendition*."

The door opens and the mustached guard puts his head around it.

"Yeah," Harper says. "Okay."

You think you're already as afraid as you can be. You think you're *filled with fear*. Then you do fill, flood, choke. There can't be any more. You can't support any more fear. But there will and must be more.

The guard enters followed by his colleague holding a box unit with a length of wire and a plug, a fistful of extensions that end in connection clips. So many because some are faulty, like Christmas tree lights. Already Augustus is hunting frantically in himself for somewhere to hide. You close your eyes and open them hoping you won't be there any more. With them closed it seems so feasible.

The guards betray the canteen's torpor but begin the business of lifting him and reattaching his wrists to the hook. Their odor of sweat, canvas, fried food and tobacco has been replenished. Leave the chair, Harper says. Which would allow Augustus to stand if it wasn't for the condition of his feet. The left heel he can put a fraction on. The outside edge of his right foot another fraction. The rest has to go into his arms where the blood's already starting to pack. It's loud and dark red inside himself where he's busy with the problem not of getting out of his body but of making himself so small within it that surface events will be far-off weather. Find a buried gland or dead lymph node and think yourself into it. But electricity. To seek out Jonah even in the belly of the whale.

"Please don't," Augustus hears himself say, very quietly.

"Something," Harper says, standing up. To consider, he means, to chew on. Single words do a lot of work between them now. Augustus turns through ninety degrees, has to be turned back by the mustached guard. "You read the testimonies of people who've survived torture," Harper says, "they're affectless. They tell you what was done to them but never what it did to them. Why is that?" The guard tweaks the cable to correct Augustus's spin, steps back, makes a "stay" gesture, then turns and mooches over to his colleague, who's setting up the electrodes. Augustus is left face-to-face with Harper. Yes, I can look at you, no dissonance, no conflict. It's Augustus who shuts his eyes again, throws the minute version of himself back into the red-lit labyrinths of his body. He still has his appendix. Visualize it, it'll let you in.

"The historian's truism is that the only thing you can do with atrocity is chronicle it," Harper says. "Question is is there a psychological parallel in the individual? I think the torturee can't bring language to it because language humanizes by definition. To talk about atrocity is to make it less atrocious. Conrad knew this, which is why Kurtz's rites remain 'unspeakable.' You speak the thing you allow it in; you allow it in you allow for its understanding; you allow for its understanding you allow for its forgiveness, and that the victim—unless he's a Christlike prodigy—has to refuse. So he never speaks beyond the affectless event. Shocks were applied to my genitals and mouth. He leaves his soul out of it because let in the soul's duties are more than he can bear. What do you think?"

The girl comes back later that afternoon, or he hallucinates she does. The hours have contained marvels. He knows he's got up several times with purposes, lost track, found his way back to the camp-bed and the damp covers. This is the confusion you don't want if you're dying. There's no one to ask but he's asked anyway for clarity before he goes. Just so he knows it's happening.

"Sorry," she says, standing over him. "Saw you through the window. What's happened?"

So he had heard knocking. He's on the floor near the stove. There was a project that got away from him. The fire's out.

"Nothing," he says. "I was doing something. I don't know."

"You'd best get back in bed," she says, getting down on her haunches next to him. She smells of the day's wet weather and the big leather jacket. Also something strawberry-flavored. "I got you some stuff."

"What're you doing here?"

"Sorry. I got you a bandage and disinfectant."

"What time is it?"

"Dunno. Five maybe. Should've kept that going. It's freezing in here." The fire. His bit of floor's floating ice, tilts when he moves. "Y'all right there?" Her hands don't touch but superintend him hauling himself upright against the stove. She rises with him. Her smell's a startling intrusion by the fresh outside world, real time. He imagines the croft's interior as a snow globe. But who *is* the old black man in there, Mommy?

She sees his stick lying nearby, grabs it and offers it to him. For a moment when he feels its head in his hand, things cohere— but have come gently apart again by the time he's sitting on the edge of the bed. He can't believe she's standing there. She wants something. What? It doesn't matter. Whatever it is he hasn't got it. With the landscape it's just been him and it, two parallel phenomena, no interference. He sits trying to find the most succinct and least ambiguous dismissal. Go away. Doesn't sound like you mean it. *Get the fuck away from me right now.*

He finds he's lying down on his side with his knees drawn up. Everything has a whispering pixilated quality.

"You're pissed off. I shouldna come. Sorry."

"Something's supposed to happen. This is that story. It won't."

Not sure whether he said that aloud but there's her small cold face trying to unpack something so presumably he did. The visible effort of the not very bright. One hand clutches the mouth of her bag shut. She's the type for terminally broken zippers. There's a thing she does when her thinking dead-ends, flicks her head as if to get her fringe out of her eyes. She moves on quickly from these failures, pretends they never happened, though every time she looks back there they are in her wake.

"Let me get the fire goin at least," she says. "You're gonnie catch pneumonia. Here." From the shoulder bag a paper bag bearing the pharmacist's green cross. Green someone'll have decided to connote however distantly healing plants. Commercial design's endless refinement of basic drivers. Which was one of the things that led to the disgust that spilled into action. He used to try the stupid experiment of trying to get through a single day without seeing an advertisement.

"What do you want?" he says.

"Nothing. I just thought . . . You know, you could do with the stuff. There's all sorts in there, plasters and ointment an' a wee pair of scissors."

He takes the proffered paper bag and holds it as if he still doesn't understand. She slides the shoulder bag off with a muffled jingle and puts it on the chair. "I'll light the fire, okay?"

Augustus is very close to leaping up and physically forcing her out the door. He's ahead of it, whatever this is, whoever's sent her in with whatever craziness he's supposed to latch onto. Get up and frighten her away. But his legs are empty. One or two neural detonations like very distant fireworks.

"I don't need any help," he says. "Please."

"Okay, sorry. I'll light this and go. You've got to keep warm if nothing else."

He decides to accept this since it means only a few minutes. The wounds are hot. In fact a body alarm's been ringing for some time: infection. He'll have to deal with it. All these accumulating inconveniences like planes stacking over a blocked airport.

"How come you're here, anyway?" she asks.

"I live here."

"I know but how come?"

He doesn't answer. Rain starts to fleck the windows.

"Oh, right. None of my beeswax."

He sinks deep into watching her at the fireplace. She snaps already small enough bits of kindling he thinks for the pleasure of the sound and feel. Two split logs tilted one against the other and twists of newspaper that leave print on her fingers. All done with glazed prehistoric concentration. Purple throwaway cigarette lighter, *shick, shick*, then the room's gathered molecular reverence as the first flame catches, shivers up the newspaper, buckles, limbos at the kindling then with a *crack* unlocks itself and in two seconds has the whole brittle nest burning bright yellow and orange. She moves from her haunches onto her knees though the floor's dirty, stretches her hands out to warm them. He thinks: one of the last old magics. She stares, emptied. He closes his eyes.

When he opens them she's at the half-open door with her back to him and the gun hanging from her hand. Outside it's completely dark, still raining.

"What the fuck are you doing?"

She starts—then freezes. Firelight plays on the leather jacket's fractured back, makes him think of shields hung in a medieval banquet hall. He can't believe he fell asleep. He feels refreshed but the two injuries are filled with cellular gossip.

"Take your finger off the trigger and turn around slowly." He speaks as if he's the one with the weapon, it's so obvious she's terrified. "Don't panic. Just turn around slowly. It's okay."

She lowers her shoulders and turns around. Her eyes are wide, her mouth slightly open.

"Take your finger out of the trigger guard. Just hold it by the barrel and put it on the floor. Pointing away. I don't want it to go off, that's all."

"I've no touched your wallet," she says. "Honest to God I've no touched your wallet."

"I believe you. It's okay." He keeps still and continues in the tone of gentle authority. "That's it, easy onto the floor. Pointing away. Good. Okay."

She straightens, staring at the gun—now with a twinge of

loss, he thinks. Whatever else it's power and she's relinquishing it. A gun in your hand even for a few seconds denudes the mystery of killing. You see a new no-nonsense version of history.

"I'm just going to sit up," he says. "That's all. So I can talk to you. Everything's okay. Do you want to sit down?"

"I've no robbed you," she says. "Check your wallet if you don't believe me. I've no touched your money."

"I told you I believe you. Why do you want the gun?"

She doesn't answer; not strategically, but because her incredible actions are just catching up with her.

"If you're not going to sit down then promise me you'll leave the gun alone."

She puts the gun hand in her jacket pocket. The other hand's gone reflexively to clutch the shoulder bag shut. "Don't tell anyone," she says.

"I won't."

"No but I mean really."

"I really won't tell anyone."

"You promise?"

"I promise."

"Swear?"

"Look who would I tell? I'm not supposed to have a gun either."

"I haven't done anything, you know. I haven't done anything wrong. You'll no believe that."

"I do believe it."

"You're just saying that."

"No, I'm not."

The flow of this exchange surprises them into silence. But that forces a worse intimacy.

"What do you want it for?" he says. She looks at the floor. He waits, then asks, "Protection?"

He can feel disappointment coming off her. Familiar disappointment: her ideas never work out. This is another stalled point from which she can fall back into herself, where it would be better to stay if it weren't for things from the world rousing her impulses. This is what happens: she acts, gets ahead of herself, fucks it up. She's been getting things wrong as long as she can remember.

"Well whatever," he says. "I'm guessing it wasn't for a bank job."

Tiniest move of the head to acknowledge he's trying to be nice about it. (But behind that the older wiser tireder version of herself saying aye but there'll be a catch there's always a catch. This older wiser tireder version is the thing her impulses get ahead of, then have to stand there over the mess they've made, waiting.)

"You a crim then, are you?" she says, looking up.

"What?"

"Only crims and coppers have guns."

Crim is criminal. The difficulty wasn't getting a firearm. The difficulty was getting one from someone you could trust. It had taken a three-day trawl through the pubs of South London. You got a beef wiv me? You lookin like you got a beef wiv me guy which for a ole man iz not a good plan y'get me?

"Neither," he says. "Don't you know in America everyone has guns? Look can I get a drink of water? I'm thirsty as hell."

She's not sure, looks down, takes her hand out of her pocket.

"I'm not going to do anything. You can stay right there next to it. I just need some water."

She probably thinks he's feigning (he imagines) hobbling on his stick to the cluttered sink with his tin cup, but he's not. The shin and the knee he doesn't want to look at because they're on fire. Infection means you either ignore it and get septicemia or gangrene or you go to the hospital or you do it yourself. Sutures he doesn't have. He needs antibiotics. He closes his eyes against the weight of all this practical shit. Plus her. It's as if the croft's filling with clutter. All at the behest of the fire like a little grinning god.

He drinks three tin-flavored cups. The clarity with which he feels the wounds in his legs says the rest of the confusion's cleared.

"What're you gonnie do about your legs?"

He fills the cup and goes back to the cot, by degrees sits down on its edge. "I don't know. Get them looked at, I guess." With a *pop* the fire spits out a tiny glowing shard. He catches himself sketching her past, sees her in a city, hours on the streets because she doesn't want to go back to where she's staying. He can't help it, it's in her face. The big leather jacket's a friend to her, as is the shoulder bag. These are small forces at work on him, a feeling like injured flesh knitting but speeded up. He's tempted to laugh. *That I may not weep*, he thinks, remembering one of Selina's habitual quotes.

"Why'd you give me that fifty quid?" Fefty kwed.

"Thought you could use it."

"You really loaded then?"

Now thirst's out of the way there's hunger. Can't remember the last time he ate. Yesterday there were items: rice, a can of tuna. He wonders if they made it home with him. In any case there are soups and if he's not mistaken a can of creamed chicken.

Wind pulls the croft's flimsy front door shut, at which she jumps again, laughs once then stops as if the laugh was a mistake. "Put it this way," Augustus says. "I've got more than enough money to last me the rest of my life." He's surprising himself, talking, all the while knowing it's pointless, a reversion to habit. But at the same time he's impressed—it's as if there's an orchestrating presence in the room to whom he's conceding a point—by the unexpectedness of her and the gun, the vivid image of her wandering city streets confiding in her brotherly jacket. That sudden nearness to laughter just now was like one of those invisible road dips that catch you mid-sentence. Can't recall the last time he laughed, either. Meanwhile the thought of creamed chicken's going to work on him. His stomach yowls.

"Whatsisname took your coat off," she says. "Passed it to me to hang up. He didn't notice the gun."

"You sure?"

"Pretty sure."

"Otherwise I'm out on my ear."

"What're you gonnie do?"

"About what?"

"You gonnie report me?"

"I already told you I won't say anything. Stop worrying."

The rain comes down harder, calypso on the assortment of bits outside.

"Sorry," she says.

"What?"

"It's still stealin. Still wrong."

She looks at him and suddenly he knows he has to get her out of here, but when he opens his mouth to tell her suffers a feeling of prosaic lousiness because it's sheeting down out there and manifestly she's on foot. Another image of her, head down, hair plastered, shoulder bag clutched tightly.

"You can wait till the rain eases off," he says. "But then I think you should go."

Michael, who'd been nowhere near My Lai, came home on leave that Christmas and refused to meet Augustus. It was a wall between Augustus and Selina, who of course had to see him.

"What do you expect me to do?" she asked. "Boycott my own brother?"

Augustus sat very still on the floor of the apartment, rolling a joint. "I expect you to boycott your own *racist* brother, yes."

She'd been kneeling opposite him. Now she sat back on her heels neatly with her hands flat on her thighs. She was wearing a plaid pinafore minidress, black turtleneck top and black woolen tights. This was the morning after a much worse argument the night before (from which he'd stormed out and gone back to his room at his mother's and Cardillo's) and he could see she'd made a special effort. In the apartment's shaft of sun her feline face looked glamorous, which naturally made him angry all over again.

"You're doing it," she said, calmly. "You know you're doing it."

"Doing what?"

"Making this worse than it is. Making him sound like a *Klansman*, which you know he isn't."

"Yeah I forget this oversensitivity I've developed."

"We both know you're *comfortably* bigger than this."

Augustus lit the joint and inhaled deeply. Too early to smoke but fuck it. She'd had breakfast with her family at the Gramercy Park house and retained he thought the glister of renewed identity: healthy, wealthy, white, Their Daughter, His Sister. He imagined the family around the table of blinding linen and silver cutlery; if not Ruthie then some other white-gloved black maid (Yessum Mister Trent); Michael, who from photos Augustus knew had Selina's blond hair and fine bones, though with his father's sleepy brown eyes instead of Selina's complex blue, possessed of a new quiet masculinity. Selina had felt it, Augustus could tell, thrummed guiltily from it. Turned out Michael was just the type to be made a man by the Marines. With some guys it worked: The brutality of training reduced them to an essence from which surprising strengths grew. Whatever you thought of war, soldiers in it became the bearers of the world's strange tidings. Among which was the news from My Lai. America faced a tumorous question about itself from its own sons. Haeberle's color photographs of the massacre had been splashed all over *Life* magazine. Eyewitness accounts said bayoneting of women and children, rapes, indiscriminate butchery and shooting. The Inspector General had turned the case over to the Criminal Investigation Division and the Secretary of Defense had said anyone involved in the killings would be prosecuted. So far only a Lieutenant, William Calley, had been charged. Selina said it was there in the house with them at home; Michael's uniform, cleaned and pressed, hung on the back of his bedroom door like a sentient thing, a smirking intelligence. She made him hang it in the wardrobe out of sight. After her brother's denunciation of Charlie Company—If that's what they did then they need to face criminal prosecution—her father had declared the subject off-limits, the whole subject of the war, in fact, if Selina was in the house. Then stay out of the house, Augustus had said, along with many other dumb or ungenerous things. Selina just said, quietly: He's my brother and I might never see him again. That's the reality. That's the personal reality I can't get beyond. If that means I'm a moral failure in your eyes I'm sorry. I don't have what it takes. Besides which neither do you. Your objection to me seeing Michael isn't political, it's personal in the most obvious way. It's about *him*. You're right, Augustus had said. He's got the drop on me because he objects to *all* niggers. At least it's a principle, at least it's not just about *me*.

"Would it help if you fucked me?" Selina said. They'd been silent for a few moments, working out what was going on in each other. Now Augustus couldn't meet her eye because yes of course that was among other things what he wanted. Perhaps not even among other things, perhaps *only* that, animal ownership of her. She knew and was prepared to act on the knowledge. It was what the prim parentally approved clothes were for, so she could give him, as well as the version of herself he already had, Mom and Dad's Golden Girl. "Give me a hit of that," she said, taking the joint from him. She took three quick pulls then handed it back. "I know you hate me right now," she said. "It's okay. I'm not crazy about you either. Come on." She got up and went to the mattress, knelt down on it with her back to him. Businesslike, she pulled her tights and panties down, hiked her dress up and dropped onto all fours. Augustus watched, for a moment didn't move and in that moment saw she was at the very edge of herself, conducting what might turn out to be a decisive experiment. He stubbed out the joint and shuffled on his knees to get behind her. Through everything else in his head the sight of her fully clothed but for her bare ass presented in contemptuous submission made him quickly hard, the thought of the cold weather out there and her supple softness kept warm by these clothes. "Go on," she said.

Augustus didn't let himself think, just went into her quickly. To his surprise she was wet, presumably because she'd been playing this out in her head in the silence. Worried he'd come before her he worked her clit with his fingers. The whole thing would be wrong if he came first, which she, after a moment's resistance, seemed to concede. She could have three, four, five orgasms before she'd had enough. After her second she reached around and guided his cock to her asshole. They'd done this before but the challenge now was to dispense with all occlusion or denial. She lay on her side with him behind her, concentrated through the initial discomfort, then when he was fully in twisted and looked at him. This was new, her calmly and in full clarity accepting his hatred. It made him feel psychically smaller than her, exposed as if to a giant intelligence. She just stared and moved cooperatively against him, the slightest affirmatory lift of her eyebrows when he came, violently. He realized he was like Cardillo, went to a woman for the answer to the question of whether he was acceptable.

"Michael and I slept together the summer I was fifteen," Selina said, when they lay together afterward. "We knew it was going to happen. You reach a point of inevitability. It went on all through the vacation. I wish I could tell you it felt momentously disgusting but it didn't."

"Was it your first time?" Augustus asked.

"Yes—Jesus what kind of child slut do you think I was?"

"Hey, you were the one told me you'd been diddling yourself since you were three."

"Five—and that's nothing for heaven's sake, a little girl finding solace in her clitoris. Are you made of stone?"

Augustus could feel what a relief it was to her to have delivered the central dark fact and here he still was. He rubbed the top of his foot against the soft sole of hers. But they both knew the central dark fact alone wasn't enough.

"I knew it was a mess," Selina said. "But you have to understand I had to dig very deep to find the little fleck of wrongness. I don't know that I ever really did find it. It's like imagine you're eating this huge delicious cake and someone tells you that somewhere in it there's a spot of mold, that it's started to go bad. You can't taste it but you know it's there. You find yourself chewing every mouthful forensically. That was an unpremeditated metaphor, by the way."

Augustus pushed upward with his foot against her sole. He liked to feel the force communicated through the ankle, knee, femur, hip. He liked the feeling of lifting her weight slightly with just his foot. "I see it," he said, though he wished he didn't. *Delicious* cake, she'd said. And what was *every mouthful* other than the obvious?

"Eventually I couldn't stand it," Selina said. "I don't want to lie to you. I never quite found the wrongness. It was just that compulsive searching for it began to feel claustrophobic. That and the secrecy, which of course is enriching to start with but becomes toxic. Also, Michael has this insistence, this will. He makes you feel nothing's enough, even everything's not enough. He could kill you and eat your remains and it wouldn't be enough. I began to see it, the giantness of his demand. I began to feel something of how furious he was with everything. I think that's why the army's been good for him, weirdly. The fury's gone into the discipline. Plus I think he's been looking for something bigger than being in love with his sister."

"There isn't anything bigger than being in love with his sister," Augustus said. Among many other things he was wondering if Michael had fucked her in the ass. Possibly this was what her look had been trying to tell him, that if he needed something of her Michael hadn't had, it was this.

"Well, maybe killing and risking being killed," Selina said. "I'm a tough act to follow but I imagine seeing your buddy step on a mine or cutting off a Vietcong's head would do it."

Which images cost her, Augustus knew. Once you force yourself into saying a difficult thing many other difficult things become sayable.

"Anyway," she said, "I stopped it. For a while I thought he was going to kill me, or himself. You break up with someone you don't have to see them. You break up with your brother he's right there across the landing. I don't want you to think this was me suddenly discovering it was wrong. It wasn't. It was me understanding what a mess it was going to be if we didn't stop. Michael made it easier by being ugly to me. It was a horrible time, wake up feeling sick, go to bed feeling sick, every day the same carnage to stare at. But we ground out the weeks and months and eventually a year had passed and it was time for him to go to Brown."

They lay still and listened to someone down the hall taking a UPS delivery, then the delivery guy's footsteps down the stairs, then the building's main door opening and closing. It gave Augustus the feeling of precarious truancy. The world eventually nosed you out and started making demands.

"I don't want you to have any illusions. I'll never sleep with Michael again. That's over for me. But it was a huge thing in my life and it's probably sown the seeds of craziness. Also, I'm in love with you so much it hurts my heart. Also, I feel cursed and on borrowed time and full of lousy karma. Anyway that's what you wanted to know so I've told you."

What *she* wanted to know, he now understood, was whether it made a difference to him. It did: it made him want her more. Partly, stupidly, because he saw it as a project of heroic reclamation, an attempt to get her back to who she'd been before it happened, and partly because her survival of it proved her strength. Like her, he didn't buy the Nietzschean line that whatever didn't kill you made you stronger. Sometimes whatever didn't kill you disfigured and debilitated you for the rest of your life instead of killing you. Mere survival was neither here nor there. It was the manner of survival, what you *did* with whatever it was that didn't kill you. She'd taken her relationship with Michael as inoculation against human strangeness, made it the source of her compassion.

"I want to ask you something," he said. They were lying side by side, not touching, his brown arm next to her white one. There was an aesthetic wrongness to the heating being on while there was so much sunlight in the apartment, further dissonance when he thought of how crisply cold it was outside. He wanted coffee and a chocolate doughnut.

"What?" she said.

He got up on one elbow to look at her. She kept her eyes closed.

With her hands still and one knee very slightly bent she looked like someone tanning. For a moment he had a profound sense of her corporeality, felt a tenderness for her hair follicles, teeth, knees, arteries, her guts snugly hidden under all that beauty. He asked himself if he wanted her for the rest of his life, a question from which his mind ran forward some way, ten years, twenty, then flagged into an enticing desert darkness.

"Will you marry me?" he said.

Harper's cell phone rings and seduces Augustus out of semi-consciousness. You struggle up from under heavy soft folds and too late realize you should have stayed where you were. Same trickery every time. His memory's in chaos. He knows he's given up information but can't remember what. Instead other bits of his past are vivid, as if his life's been exploded and all its moments surround him in floating fragments.

He doesn't hear what Harper says, indeed slaloms in and out of deafness. The mustached guard's absent but his colleague's on the chair in the corner, cigarette in one hand, the other hand massaging his neck. The guard eases his head forward, turns it slowly as if searching for a particular alignment. Augustus imagines the wife at home later with her fingers on him in the dark, pressing and asking: There? Is that it?

The room's wadded with heat. Inés had kept saying: It's not too cold for you, is it? Because there was his thin-skinned chest and scribble of gray hair. Poor thing, she couldn't disguise what an old man she thought him!

Harper gets off the phone, pockets it, approaches the guard

and speaks quietly to him. Augustus goes under again, resurfaces. It's as if a hand gently pushes his bobbing consciousness under dark water, holds it, lets it up. He's come to see it as a last beneficence, this force that gently dunks him out of time. But here's Harper's face again, close. Somewhere in the darkness they lowered him back into the chair only now his hands are cuffed behind him.

"I'm genuinely curious," Harper says. "What are you holding out for?"

Augustus can't sit up. The guard has him by the shoulder to keep him face to face with Harper. Pain's no longer something that happens to him; it's a dense mass in which what's left of him forms a small suffocated kernel. Individual pains need distinctive personalities to make it through. A punch now would be like someone knocking on a door half a dozen rooms away.

"Didn't think I was," Augustus says, but his speech is full of interference.

"What?" Harper says. "Say again?"

"Not. Holding. Out."

"Elise Merkete," Harper says, lifting up the headshot. "*Elise Merkete*. Come on."

When Elise walked up to him on Las Ramblas in Barcelona he hadn't seen her in twenty years. It was two weeks after the department store bombing. He'd spent the days since it happened wandering the city or lying curled up on the floor of the hotel room. He drank himself into warm numbness, a salving inability to form thoughts. Then in the shade of a beech tree on the street's pedestrian spine a shadow falling on him and Elise saying, in a surreal echo of Selina: My God, I thought it was you. (It was a measure of his derailment that this second synchronicity didn't register. He'd entered a continuum of absurdity. It wasn't that the bizarre was more likely, it was that the bizarre had taken over.) He told her everything that had happened and she stayed with him that night. There was no desire between them, not even the kind that rises as an amoral palliative to grief. They lay in silence and she stroked his hair until he fell asleep. In the morning she said: Last night you said you couldn't stand to do nothing. If you still feel that way in a month, call me at this number. There are things you can do. Not overnight, but eventually. He hadn't imagined he would, not because he doubted the durability of his feelings but because he doubted there was anything he *could* do. But the month passed, and he called her. I belong to an organization, Elise had said. We can't discuss it over the phone. I'll leave a message for you at the hotel desk. Go down and pick it up in twenty minutes.

They'd met in a bar converted from a wine cellar, oak casks, candled alcoves, bare brick, cool to the touch. *I belong to an organization that believes in justice.* It was what she was doing in Barcelona in the wake of the bombing. *When something like this happens the people closest to it see the world afresh, what it's become, what's not being done, what needs to be.* She said it without passion, as if continuous exposure to the truth of the proposition had exhausted her. Through the deadening blaze of his purpose Augustus saw she'd acquired a patina of ghoulishness, recruiting from carnage, turning trauma into agency, saw too that this was the latest mutation of the rape, the shape it had long-windedly assumed. He didn't care, or at any rate could ignore the remnant of himself that did.

"Look at the picture," Harper says. "Elise Merkete. You're saying you don't know this woman?"

Augustus is very tired. Selina said that when she was about thirteen the Crucifixion acquired in her imagination an awful realism, the length and heat of the afternoon, the accrual of seconds to minutes, minutes to hours, a centurion removing his hot helmet, the static sky, the relentless sordid violence from which at any moment the victim could have extricated himself. She said it was around then she started to be disgusted by it.

"Don't know her," he slurs. All he wants now is the benevolent hand to dunk him under again. The night in the safe house in Washington, D.C., Elise had talked in her sleep. She'd sat up in the dark and said, quite seriously: "Future generations will thank the elephant," then lain back down in silence. He'd had to stifle his laughter not to wake her; but also it brought her loneliness home to him. She was dreaming, and as far as she knew that was reality. It was awful for him to know she'd have to wake up, that *this* was reality. Hearing her talk in her sleep he'd wanted to put his arms around her, cherish her however clumsily, but he was afraid of waking her. She murmured, turned over and slept deeply again.

He senses rather than sees Harper make a quick gesture to the guard—then suddenly there's cold metal pressing the corner of his left eye.

Augustus had two theories about Selina's pregnancy. The first was romantic: she'd felt greedy love demanding it of them, more life through which it, greedy love, could maraud. The second was pragmatic: it was the last act in the drama of cutting loose from

Michael. Either way it was officially "an accident," a phrase neither of them could utter without subliminally conceding its falsehood. Selina had "forgotten" to take her pill. She and Augustus went through the disaster motions—What the fuck are we going to do? What about school? Your parents are going to fucking *freak*—but caught themselves exchanging looks of reckless delight. It *was* a disaster, but it was also their generation wrenching the future away from their parents. There were moments—opportunities— for forcing the world forward quicker than it would otherwise go. But more than that a new version of themselves, a thing of weird unignorable authenticity, had established itself. Now it was in them—now it *was* them—there was no going back. They were calm, euphoric, scared and certain. They were going to disastrously have a disastrous baby and make a sort of glorious calm disaster and in spite of everything the world would make room for it. None of this was spoken aloud. They were still getting used to it as the truth, as the way things were going to be.

Selina said: "My dad'll want me to get an abortion." The word had to be admitted and got out of the way. She and Augustus were sitting opposite each other at a table in the window of a Second Avenue coffee shop. Winter sunlight bounced off the morning traffic, giving Augustus a feeling of the world's hurry and himself a part of it. The coffee shop too was full of urgency, chrome and Formica and the doorbell *tang*ing and people getting things to go. The espresso machine sounded like a thing being throttled. Selina's eyes had met his for "abortion" then flicked away. Her hair was pulled back into a high ponytail, which revealed the delicacy of her skull and jaw. A capillary showed faintly at her temple. Augustus felt for the first time the precise degree of her strength, the finite wealth of weapons, defenses, energies, strategies with which she could go up against the world. She was great but not indestructible and since she had a child growing inside her now that fact introduced a new level of realism and fear. He was afraid too, but thrilled at the change in her, the sudden different womanhood, her mix of embarrassment and pride. He studied her as she stared out of the window and felt the familiar inarticulable urgency and desperation—for what? For her. There was no other way of saying it. He wanted her without reservation, would forgo everything and endure anything. He had these moments of romantic overflow, was capable of recognizing the absurdity of his own excess but powerless to avoid it. Do you love me? she'd ask him sometimes, when out of nowhere fear of losing him gripped her. The genuineness of her uncertainty gave him a feeling of sweet panic that she should have to ask. He had to control himself, make a joke of it: I love you *madly*. But she'd make him look at her, force him to see she was really crazily afraid—which frightened *him*. You're my life, he said to her once, surprised at the vast simple truth of this.

She turned back to him. He could see her forcing herself to keep a little doubt in reserve in case he agreed with her father about an abortion. He noticed the fine silver chain she wore around her neck had broken and was lying on her scarf. Its pendant was a single pearl. She'd had it since she was twelve, never took it off: one of her superstitions. If he hadn't spotted it, it would probably have later fallen off undetected and she would have been upset. It was a pleasure to him that he could spare her that little loss.

"I'll tell you something," he said. "This kid's going to be fucking beautiful."

The rain doesn't ease off. Eventually Augustus knows he has to eat, which means either forcing the girl out into the elements or offering her something too. Not offering isn't an option. An annoying surprise, the durability of manners. There are these perversions, the survival of negligible things. She's remained on the floor by the fire, legs tucked under her, hands in the leather jacket's pockets. It must be hurting her knees and shins but she seems oblivious.

"I have to eat," Augustus says. "Do you want something?"

She looks up at him out of a fire trance. There's a smudge of smut on her chin. Her face is small, he sees as if for the first time. Young. No more than twenty, he's sure. Again he feels the slight force trying to knit between them. The force is a habit of mind. Instantly he burns through it to emptiness and just the facts of the room.

"You're gonnie cook something?"

"No, I'm going to open a can. Do you want some?"

She takes her hands out of her pockets, rests them on her thighs. "I've still got some of that money," she says.

"What money?"

"That fifty pound."

"Look forget the money, will you? I don't need it. Now do you want something or not?"

"No, I'm okay thanks. D'you not care I was gonnie thieve your gun?"

"Apparently not."

His stick's by the stove but he doesn't want to ask her to pass it to him. Instead he grits his teeth and struggles up from the bed unaided then limps to the doorless cupboard next to the sink. Heinz ravioli. Heinz baked beans. Heinz scotch broth. John West yellowfin tuna chunks in brine. Plumrose hot dog sausages. Must have eaten the creamed chicken. A small disappointment reveals another perversion: your animal heart still sets itself on things. In a knotted Costcutter carrier bag are four wrinkling apples and half a stale sliced white loaf. His chefs would shudder. Augustus stokes the wood burner, adds two logs, opens the beans and the ravioli and tips them into the pan. Out of the corner of his eye he sees her wince slightly.

"What's the matter?"

"Eh?"

"Are you in pain?"

She shakes her head, no. "Need the loo. Sorry."

"It's through there. Don't expect the Ritz." Woeful understatement. By some miracle the toilet's survived the croft's vandalization with only seat and cistern lid missing. It flushes, but the little room's icy and stinking, its one narrow window long since smashed and only half boarded up. Augustus sits on the rim without the seat, it's nothing to him, but when she closes the door behind her he realizes she'll have to squat and feels a twinge of pity for her at the image it conjures, her bent awkwardly trying to hold her skirt and underwear clear of the floor, trying not to touch anything.

She's in there a while. He wonders if she's got her period. Thinking of a woman getting her period gives me a funny feeling in my own insides, he'd said to Selina, as if I had a womb in a former life. Maybe you did, she said. What kind of funny feeling? Like a bud being snapped from a stem, a small weird pain that can make you double up or puke if you think about it too long. It's not like that, Selina told him. Buds and stems, that'd be nice. Try *like being slowly bayoneted*.

By the time the girl comes out he's washed the tin plate and the tin bowl and his one spoon and one fork. The stale loaf's on the table. She emerges drying her hands on a wad of toilet roll, looks around for a bin, tosses it on the fire instead where it blooms brilliant yellow for a moment then disappears. Selina used to say: Metaphors for brevity are everywhere. It's not like God's not dropping plenty of hints.

"It's up to you," Augustus says, "but there's enough if you want some." The croft smells of the heated food. Now he's faced with it Augustus isn't sure he can eat. His leg wounds are full of tiny movements. The heat suddenly gets to him. He goes to the door, opens it, looks out. Cold steady rain and the fresh smell of waterlogged turf, one fishy waft from the beach. Maddoch or the boy must have been down with the dog to move the sheep. The land's empty. He turns back to see she's taken a seat on the upturned crate, leaving the chair for him. When he sits down and begins serving himself from the pan he feels embarrassed. After two or three mouthfuls he stops eating.

"What's your name?" he asks her.

"Morwenna," she says. "It's not Scottish. It's Welsh. My mum."

Augustus nods, slowly, fearing a rapid unraveling of information he doesn't want—but it doesn't come.

"You're Mr. Rose?"

"Augustus."

"Okay, right."

"Who's after you?"

"What?"

"You wanted the gun. Who's the enemy?"

She looks down at her hands. Opens her mouth but doesn't speak.

"I don't actually care," Augustus says. "I'm just . . . In fact never mind. Maybe it's time you left." These seem the first unthought-out words he's spoken in a long time. Some quick current's shot him into them. It brings him out in a sweat. She reaches down and slowly lifts her shoulder bag onto her lap, waits a moment, gets to her feet. Slowly, he supposes, to give him time to change his mind. Or maybe she's worried sudden movement will trip his lunatic switch irreversibly. He forces down another mouthful of food. There's an increasing claustrophobic irritation, as if he's just realizing that all day he's been wearing a too tight shoe.

"Sorry," she says. "I thought you—"

"Jesus what is it you *want*?" His aggression surprises him—and her. She flinches as if there's a blow coming. He's between her and the door, feels the space between them filling with her calculated bolt. He forces himself to untighten, puts his fork down, leans back in his chair. "Sorry," he says.

" 'S all right. Best be off anyways."

"It's okay, forget it. Sit down. It's still pouring."

"Yeah, but you said—"

"I know but forget what I said. Sorry."

The shock of his outburst resonates but a practical part of him nonetheless notes the timeliness of Maddoch's roof repairs. They'd be afloat by now otherwise. As it is he wonders how long the water will take to climb the shallow front step and creep like an eclipse across the floor. Has it been raining for two whole days? His education's wrecked matrix endures, erratic synaptic firings that right now give him among other things *antediluvian deluge flood ark new covenant water baptism water water everywhere he blesses the water snakes and the albatross drops from his neck and suddenly he can pray this* if she's the water snake is the opportunity to bless or would have been but that's what would be what's supposed to happen. Thinking like this the old thing of making connections only connect is again like the phantom limb reaching out because of course under all the connections is nothing.

"You sure?"

"I'm sure. It's fine."

She remains on her feet, uncertain.

"Now I've made this I can't eat it," he says.

Slowly she resumes her seat on the crate, slides the bag off, lowers it to the floor. She bends, searches in it a moment, straightens up with rolling tobacco and lighter in hand.

"I'll go outside," she says.

"No need."

" 'S no bother for me."

"No I mean there's no need because I smoke. I'm out though."

He watches her unpack the idiom. He's out: He's none left.

"Will you have one of these?"

It's a long time since he's rolled a cigarette. He doesn't want to lean close for a light but it's unavoidable. You're still a man. Don't make me take that away from you. Harper's a disease he's got for the rest of his life. Harper *flares up*. You lean close to share a light and there he is, as if in an instant your body's web of veins burns and shows.

"Hang on." Augustus gets up and brings a bottle from by the stove, Glenfiddich, half full. But only the one tin mug. His scalp prickles again. As soon as you start having dealings with—then he sees a solution. He pours half the scotch into the mug and gives that to her. He can drink the rest straight from the bottle.

"Could you not have poured me a large one?" she says when she sees how much is in the mug. "There's enough f'ra week in there."

"Just drink what you want," Augustus says.

After the loss of his eye he tells Harper everything. You think you know the universe, its amorality, its unjudgmental accommodations, its fundamentalist adherence to the religion of cause and effect—but you don't. Not until someone gouges your eye out with the scalloped handle of a stainless steel spoon. They put the metal there, apply force, intention, and what must follow follows. What can the universe do about it? Nothing. The universe is compelled to supply effects on causal demand. You think in spite of all available evidence to the contrary the universe will draw the line at your eye, which has seen your whole precious waking life, but the universe is in no position to grant exceptions. The universe is the perfect ideologue. If this is a scalpel and this pressure then this is an optic nerve—cut. Language cooperates. Language astonishes with its fidelity: *my eye*. Disbelief keeps surging: How can it be your eye if they've forced it out? How can your eye suddenly be an object first and your eye second? How can the attachment between the words and the things endure? But your eye's part of the universe so obeys the universe's laws.

Together the universe and language radiate brilliant innocence. *They've gouged my eye out.* Your beautiful magician's eyes. And God has not yet said a word!

Harper said: I think that's about it, don't you? I don't think you want us to do that to your other eye, do you? And Augustus jackknifing against the cuffs had screamed from the tossing waves obscenities and pleas, whirled between horror and pain and desperation and disbelief but in spite of this with another part of himself already curled around the loss, the specific degradation, a thing done to you that can't be undone so that now whenever you say or think "I" or answer "me" it's with a concession to them and the miracle of brutality they performed. You can't believe the miracle—that a few small actions reveal the paltry *thing*ness of even your eye—but there it is, and the universe continues breathing normally because these are nothing but the effects of certain causes and God has not yet said a word. Nor will he. Or these are his words, the small actions, the eye, the screams, the blood and Harper's voice saying: I think that's about it, don't you? Either God speaks continuously or is nothing but silence.

The mustached guard had held Augustus's blood-slippery head back by the hair so that the screams jammed in his throat. The spoon's edge was placed at the corner of the remaining eye. Harper bent so close to Augustus's ear that when he spoke his voice entered with a tympanic tickle: Do you want to tell us what you know? And Augustus had bellowed yes through his bent throat and as soon as the guard's hand relaxed began giving up everything he had in disorderly sobbing chunks starting with Elise Merkete who even as he said her name was replayed in his head sitting up in her sleep and saying: Future generations will thank the elephant but he kept stalling and going back in searing misery and disbelief but they had done it, they had, a fire there now, a raging white heat in his head there was no going back you couldn't reverse it had happened it had gone misery was a kind of filth, facts were filthy with innocence because what was this other than a fact what was this other than something that was the case Wittgenstein said the world is everything that is the case and there no matter what he said or yielded now was the pain, something on an alien scale, beyond negotiation.

He'd passed out, not, he thought afterward, from the pain (though the last thing he remembered was white flame filling his head and the intimate wet creep of blood) but from exhaustion. The last big adrenaline-spend pulled him under. When he came around he found they'd moved him. He was on a bed, wrists and ankles secured in leather restraints, in a room with a medicinal smell. His clothes had been replaced with a hospital smock. Two other beds and high up on the opposite wall a narrow horizontal strip of barred frosted glass letting in what he believed was natural light. He wondered if he'd died. Wasn't this a likely afterlife? A deserted ward with the whiff of old antiseptic, the feeling of having been forgotten? But there was the pain, throughout his head but centered where his eye used to. Where his eye. Someone had applied a crude dressing. There was a furor under it, the nerves' deep grieving and frantic damage control. The word *socket* intruded and he fought back the urge to vomit.

Thirst repeatedly derailed all other thoughts. He lay on his back staring at the blank ceiling, oscillating between caring and not caring about himself. It was very hard not to care, but caring forced him to keep replaying the violation. Replaying the violation drew him again into searing rage and crippling self-pity, and into an asphyxiating panic that there was some way of getting back to before it had happened but he couldn't remember it. Horror was endlessly renewable. He knew the only solution was to stop caring but it was like turning your back on your own child and listening to its cries as you walked away. He went in and out of consciousness.

Eventually, Harper had come in alone and seated himself in the orange plastic chair next to the bed. He'd brought another bottle of Evian, at the sight of which Augustus lost everything but the need to drink. He swallowed two thirds before registering Harper's hand supporting his head, and even then found without much surprise that he didn't care, that a third option was to simply accept submission to and ownership by the other person. There were women who ended up in relationships with their rapists. Augustus saw it clearly: someone could put such a mark on you that it was easier to accept it as a brand of slavery than to spend the rest of your life trying to burn it off. He remembered his screaming and Harper's calm.

In the hours that followed he'd told Harper everything. An atmosphere of conciliation formed, as if the two of them were for the first time working together toward a common civilized goal. Augustus suffered flash-fires of conscience but they blazed and died in a moment, no longer than it took Harper to run a hand through his fair hair, or light a cigarette, or shift his weight from one buttock to the other. When he needed to use the bathroom Harper put the handcuffs back on and helped him to his feet. There was a surprisingly clean windowless latrine off the ward. Augustus could barely walk, had to sit down to pee. Lifting an arm for toilet paper made him dizzy. The handcuffs were utterly redundant. If someone had given him a gun he wouldn't have had the strength to raise it and pull the trigger.

There wasn't in the end that much to tell. Four people, starting with Elise Merkete. Four people who'd be arrested, eventually, then either framed, recruited or killed. It was a profound unburdening for Augustus, also a final measurement of himself: he'd found his limit, wasn't prepared to go through it again, no matter how short a time he had left. He had no increments; his capitulation was total. He didn't care what they did to Elise or anyone else as long as they left him alone. Harper made notes. Sometimes Augustus heard himself as if from a distance sobbing as he spoke, a weird adult version of childhood distress, the old familiar chopped, breath-catching delivery. Before he'd passed out he'd seen through the blood-blur his eyeball on the floor next to one of the stubbed Winstons and the beneficent hand pushed him under, let the dark water close over his head. The guard had done everything with a heavy silent determination, let out one chuckle of surprise when.

Harper's in fresh casuals looking as if he's just showered and shaved. "It's a beautiful concept," he says. "You borrow the operational structure from terrorism but leave out its commitment to killing innocent people. I take it you really don't know how it started?"

"No, I don't. As a rumor, a myth."

"No one person knows more than four others?"

"No."

"Built-in circuit break. For situations like this."

"For situations like this."

Augustus, adrift, has no idea what day it is or how long he's been here. The frosted glass is filled with gently growing light. That's all he knows, that it's the beginning of a day rather than the end. For perhaps the first time in his life the observation feels purely irrelevant. In love with Selina the weather was for them. It's getting light, she'd say, turning to him from the window. Naturally the getting light, or dark, or cold, or warm was addressed to them. Naturally they appreciated it. They appreciated all of it. In the Barcelona hotel she'd peeped between the scandalously closed curtains and said: The balcony's full of sun. He'd thought how the world had waited for them to come together again after all these years. Its fidelity caught in his chest, gave him a sort of panic so that he had to get up from the bed and go to Selina and put his arms around her.

"It would've been like one of those unexpected diseases that wipes out a species," Harper says. "Kooky bacterium blindsides the whole human race."

Not the whole human race, Augustus thinks, but can't be bothered to point this out. "What's in the drip?" he asks. Some time ago he woke up attached to an IV. He feels only mildly curious about it. They could be killing him or testing a new hallucinogen. Either's all right by him.

"Good stuff only," Harper says. "Antibiotics, painkillers. You're feeling them, right?"

"Seems like a waste."

"You know what the precious resource is around here?"

"What?"

"Conversation. You should see the guys I'm working with."

"Whereas?"

"Whereas you. Substance. Do you want more water?"

"Yes."

Harper's gone a long time but returns with a tray on which are two more bottles of Evian, a sliced peach and a small carton of plain yogurt. "Can you handle this yourself?"

"What?"

Harper gets the pillows from the other two beds, lifts Augustus (the cracked ribs take his breath, scrunch his face so the muscles around the missing eye contract and find their object gone) and slips them in behind him. Then he unbuckles the restraints. For the first time since his arrest Augustus has his hands free. A moment of dizzying liberty, then dissonance, because it reminds him what he's got to stop caring about. Since the loss of his eye he's moved a long way from investment in himself, but now the freedom of his hands undoes all his hard work, gives him great swaths of his life back, asks him if he isn't still a man, if he doesn't still expect to walk down a street or taste snow or swim in the ocean or drink coffee on a station platform or go to bed with a woman.

Harper puts the tray on Augustus's lap. "I'd go slow if I were you," he says. "It's been a while."

Augustus is weaker than he thought and the first peach slice is heavy with life. You pick a piece of fruit up and lift it to your mouth, requires immense care, slow, like a crane or derrick, reverence for the math. His tongue touches the baizy skin briefly then he bites into the sweet flesh and feels tears well and fall—and burn. Where the other eye. Tear ducts carry your heartbreak out into the world. Now burns. You'll feel better after a good cry.

"Doc's coming to see you," Harper says. "Ease that for you."

"Why am I still alive?"

"You're not."

"What?"

"I've told them you're dead."

"Why?"

"Because they wouldn't look favorably on you still being alive."

"But why *am* I still alive? You think there's something I haven't told you?"

"No. I just wanted to talk to you. Do you mind?"

Augustus swallows the remainder of the first slice. Takes the second. Strange to be eating knowing you're going to die. Some food will be the last food, the bon voyage cargo. Peaches. Yogurt. "What is this?" he says. "A script? I forgive you?"

"Curiosity only. I want to know what you held on to in there."

"What I let go of."

"Well it was a day and a night and a day."

"Is that all?"

"It's usually more than enough. I want to know how you do it without first principles. I mean I'm buying the absence of politics, the revenge story. You don't have religion, I think we established?"

"No, no religion."

"So I return to how it looks from my end: you accept there's no God, no right and wrong, no meaning, no purpose, no afterlife, no natural justice, no court of appeal, no glorious revolution—you accept all that?"

"Yes."

"From which it can't possibly matter if you just give up the information at the start. So we arrest your friends, torture them, execute them. Shut down the operation. So what? You must have been working under the assumption you weren't going to live anyway, so it's not as if you could've worried about wandering around for another thirty years feeling lousy about what you'd done. The body dies, consciousness dies, finito. No soul, no moral indigestion."

The peach is fibrous and juicy, the yogurt cold in his hot mouth. Anything from the old life's a temptation back into caring for himself, especially sensuous pleasure. Fleetingly he goes into it, the purity of the taste; a peach was a big deal in Harlem back then, his mother laughing because the skin's nap made him shudder and he said it felt like a bee. Eat it, dummy, it's delicious. He'd bitten into it with such caution—then the sweetness like nothing he'd ever tasted and his mother eating her half with her hand cupped under her chin.

He's ashamed to go to his memories disfigured. They'll recognize him—there's no doubt he's recognizable—but they'll pity him and he can't allow that because it'll release the flood of his pity for himself. *I never saw a wild thing sorry for itself.* He'd recited the poem to Cardillo, drunk, at one of the restaurateur's always excessive birthday dinners. *That's* the fucking beauty of animals, Gianni, he'd said. You look at those goddamn gazelles, they don't complain even when they're being eaten, just lie there blinking, maybe try to get up once in a while. You love animals? You've got to . . . I mean you should . . . But he'd had to abandon it because with the drunk's delay he'd realized where he was heading, to the accusation that Cardillo felt too sorry for *himself* the whole time. Cardillo, full of emotion, didn't see it, was still winded from the poem—Jesus that's right. Goddamn it, that's right.

"Habits," Augustus says. "I held on to habits."

Harper nods, takes a sip of water from the open bottle. "It's what it comes down to in the end," he says. "The durability of the habits. That sounds like one of those terrible titles in spite of which something becomes a best seller. Although presumably since you were going to kill Husain and crew you must have broken yourself of quite a few? They've been arrested, by the way."

"What?"

"Yesterday. Intelligence reaches saturation point. There wasn't anyone else the cells could offer up. Your information confirmed players and parameters. We could have picked Husain up two years ago. Didn't because by that time you were involved and we didn't know what the relationship was between your people and theirs. This Sentinel thing's been a headache for a long time."

"Is he here?"

"No. A legitimate facility. We want the world to know we've got him, obviously. War on terror. So in case you were thinking of running around here trying to find him, don't bother."

"Will you kill him?"

"Is that a question or a request?"

Augustus is in slight shock from the solid food. Go slow, Harper had advised, but after the first slice he hadn't. He's surprised how unmoved he is at the thought that Husain might be in the building. For a while in the interrogation one of the habits he'd held on to was the belief he must stay alive to kill Husain. But it hadn't proved, as Harper would say, durable. The truth was there was really only the one habit to sustain him—

and that had been broken in the end too, in a day and a night and a day.

"You're letting the Husain thing go," Harper says. "I get that."

"For the record, kill him. All of them."

"I'm not handling it but I'll do what I can."

"Why?"

"Why what?"

"Why do anything for me?"

"I told you, I'm an admirer. You're a lone operator, like me."

"You work for the government."

"Sure, but only strategically. For my needs. There are no values here."

"No habits?"

Harper takes a fresh pack of Winstons from his shirt pocket, tears off the cellophane. "Are you smoking?"

Augustus accepts a cigarette though he doesn't really want one. Vestigial health aesthetics say not when you're on a drip but he lets Harper light him up anyway. His hands whether he likes it or not can't get enough of their freedom.

"They dropped away when I was a teenager," Harper says. "I couldn't help it. It was, to quote Malkovitch in *Dangerous Liaisons*, beyond my control. The only one that stuck was curiosity, and I'm not sure that was a habit. Habits are acquired. I was born curious. Anyway aside from wine women and song only curiosity gets me out of bed in the morning. I realize the consensus is there's something wrong with me, but then what's the consensus other than collective habit?"

"You have the deficiency in feeling."

"I have the prodigious curiosity. I should've gone into science. Cosmology or genetics."

"Why didn't you?"

"Well there's all the grunt work before you get anywhere near the enigmas, but the truth is I need action, in-the-world action, flesh and blood and physical movement. I must be one of the few people still gets a little excited boarding a plane or a train. There's still *some*thing of a thrill getting behind the wheel of a car. Anyway I need the being in the game. I find I'm addicted to the times."

In spite of himself Augustus realizes he's looking for wrong notes when Harper speaks, anomalies, damage. But the calm alertness remains, the deep sanity. Why shouldn't it? There was only the one thing separating them and in thirty-six hours it was gone.

"You've got the life you want," Augustus says.

"Pretty much. Which means it's only a matter of time before dissatisfaction creeps in. As it is I feel like the dark prestige is beginning to fade."

"The dark prestige?"

"Of what I do. Of this element. It's becoming respectable, like pornography. The doctorate in DP or fisting's only a few years away. Ditto the master's degree in torture. Somewhat I blame the Abu Ghraib pictures. We needed to know we could do that, still do that. Otherwise why'd we photograph it?"

"We?"

"Collective consciousness. America—in fact the entire non-Islamic western world—is only just waking up to what its enemy wants. It's taken such a long time because what its enemy wants is so bizarre, so unreasonable. Its enemy wants to wipe it off the face of the earth, and has evolved a psychotic death cult to get the job done. You've got to love the jihadis' candor: 'We're not fighting so that you'll offer us something. We're fighting to eliminate you.' You know this. This is famous, Hezbollah. This is Hassan Massawi. Your man Husain's coming out with the same shit right now. You don't fight that with reason, you fight it with contempt and brutality. We needed to know we could count on ourselves to get down and dirty. The soldiers are the moral fingertips. We've got democracy and civil rights and women's studies and hug-a-homo day and fear's been creeping in we've turned sissy. There's the froth of outrage from the intelligentsia but the truth is the Abu Ghraib pictures were a relief: That's right, we're bad motherfuckers. Let the towel-heads know what they're dealing with. What was the real feeling for ordinary Americans when the photographs came out? Déjà vu, recognition, confirmation. Why did the MPs *take* the photos? Because everyone back home, in a collective surge of self-doubt, had asked them to. It's one of the reasons they look so happy. Look at Sabrina Harmon giving the thumbs-up over the dead body. Look at her smile. She's sending home the picture she knows they'll love. We get the news we need, the stories we're desperate to hear."

"I don't care about any of this," Augustus says, though as with much of what Harper's said he has to admit he's had similar thoughts himself. Newsreaders intoned their horror headlines as if mastering revulsion in order to deliver the facts—*the savagely mutilated body of a 23-year-old woman was found in a park in Queens early this morning. Stunned local police have admitted the victim had been dismembered and had its head partially severed* ... An invitation to righteous incredulity but also deep reassurance; the networks were happy to tell us all the worst things were happening in the world because they knew the worst things were already happening in our heads, and so did we. In Barcelona, between lovemaking and shameless assaults on room service he and Selina had watched snippets of Spanish television. She'd said: The sinisterness of newsreaders is now global. Jesus go back to that thing with the twin sisters.

"It's not just me," Harper says. "Other guys are feeling the dulling of the edge, the mainstream opening and letting us in."

"Maybe you should become pedophiles," Augustus says. "Not much prestige but it's dark." The morphine's wearing off. His body's pain centers are stirring. Conversation implies a future he refuses to imagine he has. A future he doesn't want.

"Fifteen, maybe, twenty years to mainstream for pedophiles," Harper says. "Obviously the law'll prosecute flesh-and-blood offenders but the conceptual horror's already gone. It's an inconvenience. We'll get these guys hooked up to something virtual. Another fifty to seventy-five years you've got the *Blade Runner* solution: genetically engineered kids who'll respond any way you want. Is it live or is it Memorex? You're going to see a shift in the pedophile demographic because initially only the superrich will be able to afford the product. It'll be an earning incentive for blue-collar child-molesters. Okay, here's the doc."

"The doc" is a small, stocky, hawk-faced man with nutmeg brown skin and close-cropped snow-white hair and mustache. Augustus reinvents him as a melancholy headwaiter in an Old Europe restaurant dying on its feet. These imaginings are involuntary, as if the loss of his normal eye's opened a third that springs parallel universe glimpses on him whether he wants them or not.

"What's the story, doc?" Harper says, after the doctor's taken a look under Augustus's dressing.

"Local anesthetic," the doctor says. Very slight eastern European accent. Polish, maybe. Croatian? An old reflex in Augustus sifts possibilities but after a moment peters out. It doesn't matter where the guy's from. It doesn't matter where they are.

"It's not going to win any awards," the doctor says.

"Long job?" Harper asks.

"Fifteen, twenty minutes after the local kicks in."

It takes, Augustus guesses, less time than that. After the injection they tape the remaining eye shut and he feels nothing. The smell of the doctor's latex gloves makes him queasy. Soon there's a new deftly applied dressing. The doctor's very careful removing the tape from the good eye. Augustus, sensing it in the man's touch, has to override the right it seems to give him to care for himself. This is a danger: the slightest humanity has the power to open the floodgates. When he's blinked sufficiently for clarity he watches the doctor removing the gloves and changing the drip. Harper's by the window talking on the phone. Without looking at him the doctor says, "I'll have another look at you later. May be able to do something for your feet." A moment later he's gone.

Augustus wakes in his clothes in the early hours with a thudding whiskey thirst. It's dark outside, silent now that the rain's stopped. He's had broken sleep, crowded dreams, violent starts awake. Too late with the disinfectant and dressings, he's pretty sure. The leg wounds are hot and busy. No doubt his temperature's up. No doubt the whiskey hasn't helped.

The girl, Morwenna, lies curled up asleep in a survival bag in front of the hearth, also fully clothed except for her shoes, with her sweater folded for a pillow. There's a short radius of warmth from the fire's embers but cold's retaken the rest of the room. He should put a couple of logs on but there's no way without waking her and he doesn't want that. With the help of his stick he goes barefoot to the sink and with great concentration manages to fill the tin mug and drink without her stirring. In fact now that he listens he can hear her snoring very lightly. He gathers his boots from beside the bed, goes quietly to the door, takes his coat and slips outside.

The air's cold and smells of waterlogged land. Darkness glimmers where pools and puddles have formed. He hurries into his coat and boots but it's obvious the walk down to the beach is out of the question. In these conditions he'll be over within a dozen paces. Instead he picks his way to the edge of what he thinks of as the front yard (though it's not demarcated by anything other than a few bits of junk and the remains of the barbed wire covered in brambles) and stops, leaning on his stick.

He's oscillating between deriding himself and giving himself up to the bare fact of having done it. Not that he's done anything. He wasn't aware of doing anything. The whiskey'd given him a comfortable indifference and there was another quarter bottle it turned out. Halfway through her mugful she started talking. The gun was for when Paulie finds her. He's like clairvoyant. Won't matter where you go I'll find you. She went to London when she was fifteen. Lucky in a way because if she hadn't met him she'd a gone on smack. Paulie's first rule is no smack. Catches you with needles you're in deep shite. Grass okay, coke, speed, E, acid, ketamine, fine. Smack you're in deep shite. It was good at first. You were like a princess.

Augustus had said: You don't need to tell me this. I don't need to know any of this. As soon as she'd started he'd felt gathering tiredness but at the same time noticed the absence of pity for her-self, the severance from ordinary self-care. Meanwhile through his own golden veil of whiskey the movie trailer voice (the by now presumably digitally generated mixture of honey and gravel full of American humanity's precariously balanced hope) kicks in with *Their lives couldn't have been further apart. Now, in a world of bleak beauty* . . . Harper had said: The truth is we can go into anything. The world really is our oyster. Here's Jesus and self-sacrifice, all the blood and the chalices and candles—maybe I should go into *that?* Stamp collecting, archaeology, particle physics. Or what about the Buddha and the dissolution of desire? Gardening. Rare books. Marxism. Husain and his crew, all these self-exploding terrorists—it's a laughable failure to make the next step after ni-hilism, which is just to find something and go into it. These guys blowing themselves up are like titanic crybabies: if we can't have God we don't want anything—and just in case, we don't want you to have anything either. It's supposed to be a profound dem-onstration of belief. It's the baldest demonstration of existential panic. The West's superiority's in its refusal to panic. It's in its ca-thedrals and Monty Python and psychotherapy and the Genome Project and the NFL and *The Catcher in the Rye.* You find something you like and go into it. What's a meaningless universe other than infinite opportunities to make meaning?

Augustus had felt like saying to the girl: It's okay, I can go into this. I can see the shape and I can go into it—but knew she wouldn't understand and he'd drain himself trying to explain. The bare bulb of the croft's overhead light had been on, which gave their drinking a stark feel. He'd said: What makes you think he'll find you all the way out here? And she'd said: He just will. You have to know him.

He's like that, he can do things. Augustus didn't doubt it, had felt the spring and stretch of clairvoyance in love and in the cell with Harper, in the Barcelona synchronicities, Selina, Elise Merkete.

He'd got up and gone to pee and in the freezing bathroom had his drunkenness brought home to him. In the old life of parties you went to pee and took stock, something of which remained because standing swaying over the bowl he found himself adding up and hypothesizing: runaway at fifteen so no proper parents presumably abusive and her in this case good intuition says I'm no danger dead in the male part but what other than the gun can she want she doesn't seem scared only tired.

When he'd gone back into the other room the light had been turned off and she wasn't at the table where he'd left her.

What's going on?

Don't put the light on.

What is this?

Here.

She moved to stand in front of him but he couldn't see more than a lump of darkness. He didn't think but reached back for the switch, which movement she must have discerned because she said, Don't put the light on, but he couldn't stop himself and felt a sudden panic at how many hours she'd been here already and even the beginning of anger as the light flicked on.

She covered her bare breasts and spun to get her back to him. It rushed him up through the whiskey. Neither of them said anything. He turned the light out and the darkness was an immediate relief.

I was gonnie say: if you let me stay here f'ra bit. You know? I don't mind. You weren't supposed to see.

Augustus had put his back against the wall and closed his eyes to the revolving room. For what seemed a long time neither of them moved. The fire's chirpy soliloquy continued.

Put your shirt back on.

He'd stepped outside to give her the now redundant privacy and sober himself with the cold. He heard her throwing up in the bathroom. When he went back in she was fully dressed, lying on the cot in the fetal position.

Sorry, she slurred.

It's okay.

I didn't make a mess.

Don't worry about it.

She shuddered. He'd been an idiot to let her drink so much. He sat down on the chair and rested his arms on the table. The bit of moving about without the stick had set his hip off.

Did he do that to you?

She didn't answer. Blinked a few times, slowly. He knew words became diseased. *He. That. You.* They were diseased for him too. Stupid to use them. He'd known anyway. Why ask and put her through it? One big bruise on her arm like a dark jellyfish.

Do you think you got it all up? he said.

She drew her knees closer to her. Shivered. Think so. I'll be all right 'n a minute. Sorry.

He'd got up and washed the tin mug, filled it with cold water, put it next to the cot. There were half a dozen logs left, enough till morning. The fire had made itself indispensable though he'd managed so long without it, all those days huddled next to the stove.

Eventually she'd said: major embarrassment.

Her voice was hoarse. He got up and poked the fire with the blade of an old file he'd found. *When I was fifteen.* Her body was dead to her, had been *made* dead to her, that was why she had no pity for it. If you let me stay here f'ra bit. Her breasts small and turgid as little water balloons, full of young womanhood. Something had got through to him. Not desire (there was nothing, a splinter of absence he curled around) but a sense of her body compelled by its youth to raging renewal, physical wealth so immense it could hemorrhage for decades without apparent decrease. Beauty hurts, Selina said, years ago, by being unable to help itself. The idiot fidelity of crocuses coming up every spring, unable to help themselves, clueless. So this girl's body, Augustus thought. Major embarrassment. She meant both his rejection and the marks of what had been done to her. By the clairvoyant Paulie whose rule was no smack and at first you were like a princess.

Don't take it personally, Augustus had said. I can't do anything like that.

How come?

Too old.

Get out.

He hesitated. Considered telling her he was gay. Knew he wouldn't be able to maintain it.

It's an injury. (He didn't know if this was true. There were very occasional morning erections, but the two or three times he'd tried to masturbate, he'd been unable to maintain them.)

Seriously?

Seriously.

What about your eye?

Same thing.

A strange little meditative time passed, neither of them speaking. The rain subsided to a faint exhalation. Augustus rolled another cigarette. She said she'd puke ("boke" was the word she used but he got it) again if she tried smoking just then. He poured himself the last of the Scotch and drank it quickly. Balanced between accepting and denying this was something he could go into he needed the booze to pitch him one way or another. After the interrogation, in the first dream-edged hours of survival he'd tried to get word to the compromised contacts. Two of them, Jacques Dertier and Elise Merkete, were already dead. Future generations will thank the elephant.

At last sneering slightly at himself he'd said: You can stay here tonight if you want.

She'd insisted on not having the cot. Got ma bevvie bag in there. He was flummoxed, then saw: bevvie bag was bivvie bag was bivouac bag was survival bag. Produced from the shoulder bag and unrolled. Also a soft clattering purse of toiletries that made her seem older. He listened to her brushing her teeth in the bathroom, wondered how many weeks or months she'd been lugging her minimal accoutrements around. Bus shelters and shopping malls and car parks and stations, the special exhaustion you get from being repeatedly moved on. She came out smelling of toothpaste and he went in, feeling as they crossed that he was giving himself over to corruption. In the bathroom he stretched his two-minute routine to ten, stood toothbrush in hand staring at the half boarded-up window. By the time he came out she was lying in her plastic bag by the fire. He got into bed. Watch that doesn't melt, he said. She said, Okay.

Now, after four hours of twitchy sleep and chiseled sobriety he stands at the bottom of his front yard thinking it all went too fast. His cynic's available, asking in a voice like Harper's whether she hadn't seen *his* scars that first morning with Maddoch. Don't put the light on. Which is an instruction to do the opposite. Young girls are always smarter than you think.

He doesn't care. This is something he can go into for a while whether she's ingenuous or arch. The conclusion doesn't matter. That feeling of corruption when he passed her on the way to the bathroom, what was it if not the acknowledgment that in spite of everything there remain traces of loneliness in his bloodstream?

Selina and Augustus got married in secret at City Hall, a brisk civic ceremony presided over dyspeptically by a registrar who looked like Edward G. Robinson. I can't deal with them freaking out right now, Selina said, "them" being her parents. I know we're going to have to go public sooner or later but I just want to get through the first trimester without having to duck crockery. It'll fuck the kid up. With an effort Augustus managed not to sulk about it. Pretty soon she was going to start showing, at which point the precious parents would have to accommodate the monstrous fact whether they liked it or not. Get that nigger brat out of here, his grandfather had said. No doubt they'd be hearing the like again. They'd made no other decisions. Selina was still taking classes at NYU though she'd established that deferring her final year wouldn't be a problem. Augustus too only had a year to go. With Selina's permission he'd taken his mother and Cardillo into his confidence. After their marriage Juliet had moved into the restaurateur's Upper East Side apartment. To everyone's surprise and Cardillo's chagrin she'd insisted he teach her the business, and within a year she was a familiar face to suppliers, chefs, waitstaff and regulars—not to mention Cardillo's connections, who had "an interest" in all six restaurants. I like working, she told Augustus. Who would've thought? All those years living like a slob. Jeez, I'm sorry I was such a lousy mom, kiddo. Yeah that's great, Augustus said. Just make sure you don't get *shot*. Augustus still gave Cardillo a hard time, but with an air of self-satire and an increasing understanding of how much his mother cared for her husband—The Comedy Husband as they referred to him. Cardillo didn't try too hard with Augustus but chose his moments. Her old man going to give you two trouble? he'd asked one night at the 14th Street restaurant. (A rare dinner foursome. Selina and Juliet had never been close but the imminent baby had inclined them to make an effort. Hence dinner together. The women were in the ladies' room.) Some, Augustus said. He's a big wheel. You know Northrop Aircraft? Cardillo wasn't impressed. You want this guy leaned on it's not going to matter who he works for. Augustus smiled, shook his head. I'm just sayin', Gianni said, he's a man, right? He likes his ankles better when he can walk on them, right? Am I right? Augustus couldn't keep a straight face. Neither could Cardillo. It was the way they played his Mafia connections, as if they were a harmless fantasy, indulged occasionally but never taken seriously. It was part of the man's charm, Augustus had come to see, the clownish front with behind it real power. Gianni, believe me, if we need to apply pressure you'll be the first to know—then when he saw Cardillo needed to know the offer was understood as genuine—I promise, seriously. I know we can count on you. I appreciate it. Here come the girls.

Money wasn't, immediately, a problem. Selina's father had cut off her allowance when it became obvious the relationship with

Augustus was more than just the latest stick to beat him with. This ought to have been devastating, but in fact Selina had for two years been diverting her father's stipend into antiwar organizations, literacy programs, Amnesty International and the Red Cross. Don't give me any credit, she said. I'm only doing it because there's other money. If I was busting my ass waiting tables these do-gooders wouldn't see a dime. The other money was a legacy from her grandmother she'd come into on turning eighteen. It wouldn't last forever but it would get them into an apartment and might tide them over until Augustus got a job. (He'd thought, vaguely, of becoming a journalist, but hadn't done much about it.) Cardillo and Juliet both spoke privately to Augustus, made it known they'd make sure all was well. I know your little witch thinks I'm a grifting old whore, Juliet said. But talk to her will you? Tell her we love her. We don't, but tell her anyway. If she wants to finish college this year Gianni and I will look after the kid. Talk to her.

Selina had moved out of the shared apartment into a second-floor studio on East 6th Street, which because neither Virginia nor her stuff was in it seemed palatial. There was a sitting area with a pull-out and a fireplace overlooked by two windows. A breakfast bar sectioned off the small white tiled kitchen. Overnight Selina had abandoned slovenliness. Augustus, astonished that he was legally entitled to do so, moved in with her. He did it in the low-profile manner he'd made an art form—unnecessarily, since the building was full of aspirant bohemians who, if they thought about it at all between performance verse and body collage, claimed it as a countercultural victory.

Pregnancy was rough on Selina. She threw up every morning,

went in and out of nausea all day, suffered headaches, insomnia, constipation. She and Augustus began referring to her breasts as the Grenades of Tenderness. He might forget and cup one—the result was what Selina described as "white light detonation." Naturally prohibition re-eroticized them. It's just as well, Selina said. You were beginning to take them for granted. It wasn't only her breasts; he was newly crazy for her. You're doing something, he said. You're doing something with your pheromones. Selina, whose libido had all but disappeared, said: Baby, let me make this unequivocally clear. I'd rather eat a leper's sock than have sex right now. I'll jerk you off and you can look at my boobs but it'll basically be a tedious act of charity. I don't knock charity, Augustus said, unzipping his pants. Holy mother of God I don't knock charity.

Then at around ten weeks Selina's mood changed. Abstracted silences and vicious lashings out. Nightmares woke her in a sweat. She wouldn't talk about them. Twice in the small hours Augustus found her sitting on the can in the brightly lit bathroom staring at the floor. Everything he did irritated her. The tedious acts of charity stopped. He absorbed it for a couple of weeks without complaint. Then one night much against his inclination they went to see a rerun of *Rosemary's Baby*, which they'd missed first time around. When they came out of the theater Selina said, Don't say anything. Especially don't say, *Wow, that was a hot idea.* They walked the eight blocks home in silence. When they got back to the apartment and it appeared she was ready to go the rest of the night without uttering a word, he said: What the fuck is wrong with you? She was at the sink with her back to him, had begun putting away the washed dishes without even taking her coat off. Oh nothing's wrong with me, she said, not turning to face him. Nothing at all. What could be wrong? I'm twenty-two and having a black man's baby and not graduating and throwing up the whole time and crucifying my fucking parents and killing my brother and wondering what it's going to be like trapped in a fucking apartment waiting for you all day and thinking it's only a matter of time before everything starts to feel Sylvia Plathish and something like a door handle or a lamp says yeah baby this is your life. Jesus fucking *Christ*.

Augustus stood still behind her with his hands full of useless life. The kitchen countertops were white Formica and the breakfast bar stools were stainless steel with pink vinyl cushions; everything shone. He thought again of how she'd gone at a stroke from mess to order. A baby arrived in a woman and she could do these things, snip off habits as if pruning a bush. He made himself keep his mouth shut.

Selina turned and moved past him, leaning away so as not to touch. She stood in the middle of the room for a few moments, then sat down on the edge of the bed. I had a letter from Michael, she said.

In the years that followed this was one of his abiding images of her, sitting hunched forward in her fawn woolen overcoat, hands thrust into its pockets, her face's confidence gone. Michael had gone back to Vietnam in January and written her a cri de coeur. Didn't she know she was what he carried between himself and death? She was lying to herself. The life—any life other than their life together—was a lie. He had power over her. That was the letter's refrain, that he had power over her. Augustus didn't like her voice's edge of fascination. Selina looked at the floor. He's not wrong you know, she said, quietly. He does have power over me. With him I don't ever have to be better than I am. He's like a palliative darkness. I don't think you know how much I disgust myself.

Augustus wanted to lie down. For the first time in the three years he'd been with her he wondered if he had what it took to keep her. One of her soul's voices never tired of telling her she was rotten, *stained with sin*, as she satirically put it. The cosmic fairy-tale world shivered under the real one with its appealing absolutes and paradoxes. We always know what the right thing to do is, she'd said. We *always* know.

I wrote back to him, Selina said, then looked up.

When?

If you could see your face.

What?

Full of doubt.

Yeah I guess I shouldn't have a shred of doubt.

He wanted to fight because there was something worse than fighting. It was in her eyes, the concession that there was no *point* in fighting, a look that said she'd resigned herself to the gulf between them.

I wrote back to him a while ago, Selina said. She lifted her toes, balanced on her boot heels, lowered them. He'll have had the letter by now.

She'd written and told Michael everything, that she was in love with Augustus, that they were secretly married, that she was having his child, that what had happened the summer she was fifteen would never happen again, that she loved him still in the wrong way, didn't blame him, felt the deep, awful connection, but was absolutely resolved on making a life, family and future with Augustus. There was a different love, she said, one that called you out of your weaknesses, like Christ commanding Lazarus to pick up his bed and come forth. In a life with him, Michael, too much of her would be stuck at fifteen. The morality was neither here nor there; it was that between them love would be a kind of stasis, a force against growth, a willful deafness to the call forward into uncertainty. He must find someone else, make an adventure of his own, let her be his sister once and for all.

That's why all this, Selina said, meaning the moods, the bad dreams, *Rosemary's Baby*.

They'd remained in the same places, her hunched forward on the edge of the bed, him standing behind the breakfast bar. Augustus had registered that the apartment's heating wasn't working properly—the studio was freezing.

I'm going to have a bath, Selina said. I'm sorry about everything. Tomorrow we'll go see my parents and tell them and they'll just have to deal with it or keel over dead if that suits them better. I'm sick of all this sneaking around. You should go have dinner. I'm not hungry. Just bring me back a maki roll from Tomoko.

They'd got through practically all of this without looking at each other, but now they did look, and she said: Assuming you still want to do all this. Assuming you still want me.

Later, Augustus would remember the bounce with which he went out that evening. A new bar had opened on the corner of Eighth Street and First. He went in and had a drink, chatted with the bartender, watched the band set up, exchanged smiles with a couple of white hippy girls at a corner table, all with an energized benevolence, an alert love for the ordinary world. It was five below outside. Sidewalks glimmered, he felt his shoulders packed with strength, thought goddamn it he should've boxed. He wasn't hungry either but stayed out an hour for the pleasure of going back. He kept seeing her in the bath, hair pinned up, face moist. You forgot the beauty. Then you watched her soaping her lifted leg. There was a flower stall open next to Tomoko. Realizing with a surge of panic that he'd never done it before he bought an armful to take home for her. Why hadn't he ever covered her with flowers? What was wrong with him? He was insane!

When he got back to the apartment she was naked on her knees throwing up into the toilet. The bath was full and quietly crackling with foam.

Tell me you didn't forget my maki roll, she said.

Augustus dumped the flowers and takeout in the kitchen and joined her on the bathroom floor.

I'd rub your back but I don't think you want hands this cold on you. Did you get in the tub yet?

While she lay in the bath Augustus found a vase for the flowers (given her pronouncement that she felt "like death" he didn't think it worth strewing them on the bed) and ate a few mouthfuls of sushi. The heat came on.

I don't want food, she called. But how about a peppermint tea?

He wondered where Michael was at that moment, pictured him in waterproofs under a dripping tarp rereading the letter. There's a love that calls you out of your weaknesses, like Christ commanding Lazarus. Assuming you still want to do all this. Yes, he wanted to do all this. Pouring her tea he realized (with, he thought, staggering belatedness) how much living with her evoked the best moments of living with his mother, and how awful that would sound if he told Selina. Juliet had been crazy and unreliable but she'd known how to make boiling a kettle or sending him down to the store or reading a dumb magazine an adventure. (He wasn't kind enough to his mother these days, he knew, had never forgiven her for being a woman beyond her motherhood. It was still shocking to consider that your mother when you were six or ten or fourteen was just as much in a phase of her life as you were in a phase of yours.)

Oh, Selina said, when she came out and saw the flowers, and for a moment Augustus thought he'd made a terrible mistake. But she swallowed, tried to blink away tears, failed. Sorry. It's my lady hormones. Don't surprise me with kindness like that. Sorry. She sniffed, had to go and get a Kleenex from the bathroom.

I had a twinge, she said, sipping her tea.

A twinge?

Like a cramp.

A period cramp?

Kind of. But it was just once, then I threw up and it was gone. I think it's from throwing up so much.

Around which hypothesis they knew not to leave too much silence.

Are you okay now?

Yeah, it was fleeting.

They had the flowers by the bed. Augustus confessed he didn't know the names of any of them, which she said made it an even sweeter gesture, as from a retarded person. These were irises, those crocuses, these big ones camellias, the red ones white ones and purple ones tulips. As a matter of fact, you uncanny man, tulips are my favorite flowers. As they were falling asleep she said: Do you love me? He held her close to him, hypersensitive to the femaleness of her, the softness and curve and swell. He was full of pride that his child was alive inside her, that she was his woman after all. He felt archetypal, simplified, needful of very little, though his modern self knew that wouldn't last, started already conjuring up diapers and job interviews. He wished they were cave people, felt a memory of another life, fire, meat, stone, darkness beyond the flames, the shape and warmth of her body there in his arms. It was a wonderful thing to be a man. Yes, I love you, he said.

In the night she had a violent dream, whimpered, flailed, and before Augustus could grab her, sideswiped the vase with such force it smashed against the wall. He had to shake her to wake her up, and when he did she curled into a ball with her back to him. No, I can't tell you. It was horrible. I'm sorry. He made her stay put while he cleaned up the broken glass. There was no other vase so he filled the sink and put the flowers in there. It was getting light when he got back into bed and put his arms around her. Sorry, she said again. He held her, pressed his nose into her nape, kissed the soft hair there, whispered: Shshsh. Everything's going to be all right.

At the tail end of a confused dream he heard her say: Baby, wake up. Wake *up*—then he was suddenly wide awake and it was fully light and his first thought was he'd missed a piece of glass and she'd cut herself. She was standing a few feet away, holding her abdomen. There was blood on her fingertips. For a dreamy moment he watched as she bent her left knee and touched herself between her legs and brought her hand away wet with more blood. The action had a ritual aspect, like a gesture in a Balinese dance. She looked up at him and said: It's going wrong.

Everything that happened in the hour after that was both blurred and studded with detail. Dialling 911 for the first time in his life a disinterested part of his brain registered it as a dreary rite of passage and wondered why start with a 9 since it took a precious second longer than a 1, why not 111? He spent an eternity impotently existing by the bed unable to do anything to alleviate the pain and the horror. She curled into the fetal position but kept having to move, make adjustments, none of which made any difference. He gave her a towel for between her legs in obedience to the instinct that says blood shouldn't just be allowed to run out of a person, brazenly. She clutched it there for a few moments but soon stopped bothering. He'd seen her cry before; he'd never seen her in misery. The face changed, revealed a version of the person you realized to your horror had always been there, waiting for the circumstances. The torment of being unable to do anything brought him to absurdity: he could laugh, smash crockery, do a little dance, jump through the window, maybe just calmly leave her and go to the bar for a drink. Helplessness yielded an exhaustive equalization: if there was nothing you could do you could do anything. There was a seed of hatred for the person who was doing this to you, rubbing your nose in your own uselessness. He imagined grabbing her and quickly breaking her neck. She couldn't look at him for more than a moment, her eyes moved away with disgust. He could see pain debunking her myth of him. She moaned low in her throat. You forgot we were animals.

The ambulance took her to Beth Israel. She was put on a gurney and wheeled into a very small examination room with a curtain and a huge angle-poise lamp. Augustus was allowed to sit on the room's one chair. A Polish nurse said a doctor would be there in a minute. Fifteen minutes. Twenty. Augustus had been high on relief when the ambulance appeared and two medics in peppermint green took charge. Then higher when they got to the hospital and she was taken in. Now, after twenty minutes of saying to himself, any second now, any second now, he was internally frantic again, at the edge of hallucination—then a doctor appeared and he got high on relief again. It wasn't until he was in the hall, where he'd been asked to wait, that he realized the whole time possibly since he first woke up and saw her standing there he'd been praying to God for her to be all right even if the baby dies she has to be all right in fact I'll make a deal take the kid if you want but leave her all right. If you really don't believe spit on it. Go on, right in Jesus's face.

He asked if I wanted to see it.

Augustus and Selina were in a cab on the way back to the apartment. They'd kept her in overnight. Augustus, having been told to go home and come back in the morning with clothes for her had in fact gone home, collected a bagful of things and returned to the hospital, where he'd spent the night in a waiting area chair. He'd wanted to call her parents but she'd said no. He knew what "it" was. But what was there to see at three months? He held her hand. The cab bounced over a welt in the road. When he'd stepped out of the hospital with her he'd thought: It's going to snow. Now sure enough the first flakes were falling. Selina said very quietly: It was a girl.

Storefronts were vivified. COFFEE & BAGELS. BREAKFAST SERVED. KEYS CUT. The cab stopped at a red light, overcoated pedestrians crossed, deep in their own details.

At least now I can graduate, Selina said.

Augustus realized he had his jaws clamped, forced himself to relax. He wanted to surround her, let her sleep in him for a long time. He thought of the place in her where the fetus had been now a little well of blood as when a tooth's first pulled and how she'd said: I had this twinge. The word "twinge" gave *him* a twinge somewhere, maybe his bladder.

It was about this big, Selina said, holding her thumb and index finger two inches apart.

Augustus knew he ought to be feeling some sort of grief but all he felt was throbbing relief that she was still alive, a person sitting next to him in a warm coat and scarf, Selina, with the little scar under her lip. The bleeding had seemed so bad. He'd thought he was watching her die. Now here she was with her hair tucked behind her ears, talking to him, his wife. God bless the sidewalks and the snow and cabs and everything he'd never take for granted again.

Her father was standing on their stoop when the cab pulled up. Oh my God, Selina said. I told you not to call them.

I didn't.

What?

I didn't call them. Augustus gave the driver his fare and rushed around the cab to get Selina's door but she was already out, standing at the bottom of the steps looking up at her father.

What is it?

Jack came down the steps and put his hands on her arms. He was a tall man and in the black overcoat looked monumental. His shirt cuffs were exactly the white of the snow. Selina had her fists clenched against her chest. She laughed, once, then shook her head, no, then said: No. She tried to get out of his grip but he pulled her close to him. She held her head away from him, writhed in precisely the way she would have when she was a little girl. She stopped and looked at him and there was his implacable face, at which point Augustus knew her father had come to tell her Michael was dead.

It's the second week of December and Calansay's under heavy snow. Trees are intricate with it. The stream's frozen. Indoors Augustus and Morwenna feel the new weight on the roof. The morning after the first fall they couldn't get out either door. She had to climb through the window in his boots and scrape away at the drift with anything she could find. Later in the afternoon Maddoch sent the boy over with a shovel.

Augustus's leg wounds are healing. Marle's GP, Goyle, came out to see to them a week ago, apparently at the connivance of the Maddochs. Antibiotic injection, sutures, fresh dressings, drugs. This might sound like a stupid question but did you *want* to have these amputated? Augustus had submitted, head hot and confused. There'd been a danger of collapse into something when he felt the care in Goyle's hands but it passed. We'll send you a practice registration form, the doctor said. If you've not had that hip X-rayed I can arrange for it. Augustus had observed Goyle noting conditions in the croft. Plenty of fluids and stay off the booze.

You've got to keep the dressing dry. Flannel wash or a plastic bag round it. Health visitor'll come out to look at it in a couple of days. Meantime no jitterbugging. Morwenna had leaned against the chimney breast and watched everything.

A routine's established itself. Augustus wakes early, washes, dresses (or rather adds to the clothes he's slept in) and steps over her to light the fire. In the first few days she'd wake with a start, shocked, face pouchy, hair full of static, and sit up in the bivvy bag, blinking, a look of complete bewilderment that sometimes took an hour to fade. But by the end of the first week her animal self had adapted: now at the sound of Augustus stirring she struggles awake, moves her legs so he can get to the fire, then falls asleep again. He makes instant coffee, rolls a smoke, takes his stick and goes outside to look at the weather. She wakes up much later, has trouble summoning the will to leave her plastic cocoon and the fire's warmth, to concede it's another day. If they're low on supplies he gives her money and she goes into Marle. Otherwise she stays by the fire with *Hello!* and *OK!* and *Cosmopolitan* and *Elle*. He's made her buy clothes against the cold, a fleece, jeans, a woolen hat, a pair of hiking boots. Cash. (Marle inferred the obvious transactional relationship but Maddoch—bizarrely as if his own honor was at stake—put the idea down. 'S'no like that. Lassie's had a tough time of it an Mr. Rose is helping her out. There's nothin like that goin on. 'Sides which, fella can hardly *walk*. He doesnie need to walk, Ade McCrea in Costcutter said. He just needs to lie back and enjoy!) They eat the same tinned junk diet, more or less, though lately she's been coming back with a few fresh things, bananas, tomatoes, a cauliflower, carrots, zucchini they call courgettes here. The only thing she can cook is chili, which done by her is vegetables, tinned tomatoes and excessive chili powder. Mrs. Maddoch, aghast at the amount of Heinz she knows they're consuming, has sent down with the logs a cooking pot, a sharp knife, a colander, a set of tea towels. Also once or twice, a winter vegetable pie. Bit late for housewarmin' Maddoch had said when he brought them, peering around Augustus in the doorway to see if the girl's presence had domesticated the croft.

It hasn't. She's not interested in what the place looks like. Its existence between her and the outside world is enough. Not being moved on is enough. Paulie's the dark matter her talk surrounds. Augustus doesn't need the details—or so he thought, until after she mentioned being in hospital for the second time and he said, Why didn't you go to the police? and she'd looked surprised and said, Did I not say? Paulie's a copper. Plainclothes.

The snow sanctions postponement. There are questions (all resolvable into one: What is he doing?) but this unexpected beauty pushes them aside. He's used to city snow, the hush after the first big fall, someone opens a canned drink a block away and it sounds so close—this is different. Clear days look enameled, white land and turquoise sky. Dull afternoons are moody daguerreotypes. He might be on an alien planet. Aesthetic amnesia dictates big things are every time almost new: snow, thunder, moonlight, cloud-shadows, frost, constellations. He's twice struggled up the hill, leg plastic-bag-wrapped, to get the bigger view and both times felt close to final dissolution. The first time the blue of the sky invited it. He wouldn't have been surprised to see his atoms trickling upward, could've sat down and let himself go. The second time the same effect from dusk light on the sea. The water was a peach-tinted mercury he was convinced offered a portal to oblivion. For a moment he felt sure this was a great gift humanity had yet to discover, the ability to gently volunteer oneself into nonexistence. Harper had said we were antsy for the next paradigm shift. What if it was this, the knack of dying peacefully? Experimentally, Augustus had lain down in the snow and waited. But there was interference. He remembered the small pleasure he'd experienced when Morwenna had pulled the new woolen cap down snug on her head. Which memory called up his inner Harper. We see this. The obvious script is she gives him the will to live. Harrowing but uplifting. You're working with this—otherwise why let her in? So the woolen hat, the flicker of fatherliness. There's a lost child back there after all. And a fifteen-year-old's maidenhead blasted to the devil. O Rose, thou art well, or at least trying to get better. The flip-side script is you do something horrible to her, true to the universe's grotesque equalizations and benign indifference. It's the familiar story: for better or worse all that stands between you and the void is the durability of the habits. And yes that is snow melting through the calves of your jeans. The senses are the most durable of the habits. We see this. You know this is true.

So the moment had been lost. He'd got up, stood for a while watching the water, conscious of his flesh knitting where the sutures itched, then with great difficulty in the failing light inched and slithered back down the hill.

Out of boredom, he knows, she asks him about his life or tells him about hers.

"What's a proxy?"

"Someone who stands in for you when you're not there."

"And that's what this Darlene does?"

The truth is Darlene could've cleared out by now for all he

knows. He hasn't spoken to her since coming to Calansay. I want someone who can run the show, he told his lawyer. Make all the decisions. I draw a salary. I'm out of it. That's all. Cardillo left six restaurants to Juliet, in which the mob had what amounted to a 50 percent stake. She made a deal, signed four of the restaurants over completely, kept two for herself. When she died in 1983 she had two more of her own places up and running. Augustus inherited.

"So you stopped being a journalist?"

"I became a restaurateur."

It sounds, he realizes, like the result of deliberation. But by the time of Juliet's death it was simply that he couldn't stand what he was doing. El Salvador had made him sick, not with its corpses or its corruption or its crash course in U.S. moral bankruptcy, but by his own apathy. He didn't, in the end, care. *Fuoco dentro di te*, Juliet had said, the fire inside you. It means you're going to do something big in life. Fire, yes, but since he'd had (and lost) love it wouldn't burn in anything else. Love was the big thing. This was his deformity. His theorist rationalized it down to racial liminality, the rootlessness of being neither one thing nor the other, an inconvenient mix of black and white, ghetto and academe, no home in Faith thanks to Reason and no faith in Reason thanks to History, so where *would* he find shelter if not in love?—but he'd spent enough time with Selina to suspect himself. He was just like millions of others, a lazy selfish coward. The Golden Years of protest and argument at the end of the sixties—who or what had it all been for? the soldiers? the Vietnamese? the Peace Movement? the principles of justice? It had been for Selina, which was to say it had been for himself.

After Michael's death it took less than a week for Selina to end things with Augustus. Superstition feasted on her: she'd killed her brother. She kept saying: It's no use, it's no use. But there was love. He'd be endlessly patient and gentle. There was love. Yet the gentler he was the stonier she became. In the end she said: You don't understand. I can't *fuck* you any more. What I *see*. Thirteen years later he was still hollow from the loss. On a tip he went with a photographer to La Rancheria to look at the remains of an Atlacatl Battalion raid: a woman, a man, a boy and girl of maybe ten and twelve, all decapitated. There was the usual unreality, the mildly surprising availability of laughter or dreamy dislocation. This was normal. But also a sudden grasp of his abiding delusion, that all his experience would one day be shared with Selina. He moved through his life haunted not by the past but by the future. He disgusted himself, though as with all such seizures of the soul it passed. The photographer took shot after shot, Augustus made notes, they were both inured. But he knew he had to get out. The death squads were murdering hundreds every month and governing his experience of it was the image of a time when he'd tell Selina all about it. The belief was that his life was still for her. He was an offense, a retardation. He lingered for a couple of months. Then came the message that Juliet was in the hospital.

"Costcutter fella says there's gonnie be more snow tonight," Morwenna says. It's evening. They've eaten canned kippers on toast, potato chips, a bar of Cadbury's Fruit and Nut chocolate. "Another foot they're sayin."

The forecast's a momentary relief to Augustus, who's in no hurry to discover the consequences of his recent choices. Momentary because delusory. This is the twenty-first century: if the consequences want him snow's not going to stop them.

"Bring it on," he says. He knows she's glad of the weather for the same reason he is. You open the door and day after day the white landscape says the lockdown's still in place. Nothing's required. Questions are about what to eat, when to put another log on the fire, whether you want a cigarette. Under its roof's frozen pelt the croft sits in a stillness that says this time is finite but pure. Relish it, each second.

"Time for a wee dram?" she says.

"Sure."

"For the cold, you know, for the cold," in a falsetto she says is an imitation of a bag lady she knew in London. As of her last trip to the village there are two plastic tumblers with "CALANSAY" printed on them. Since the disastrous drinking session she adds water to her whiskey.

"D'you not miss it just now, New York?"

"Just now?"

"Well anytime. But I mean, Christmas. Must be great at Christmas there. All the skyscrapers lit up."

"I can't say I miss it," Augustus says. "I haven't lived there for quite a while." After quitting journalism he'd resided almost twenty years in Manhattan (in what used to be Cardillo's apartment) running the restaurants without ever regaining the Selina-era feeling of having his teeth in life's throat. His days had shape, content, challenge, conflict, no soul. No *passione per la vita*, as Juliet would've said, no *fuoco*. Naturally there were flings, affairs (two less fierce versions of love, which for the women involved *were* the fierce version—therefore wreckage) but as his thirties gave way to his forties he began to be aware of a constant mild nausea at . . . (he pictured himself sitting opposite a shrink and having to come up with what was bothering him) . . . well, *every-thing*. He did nothing extraordinary, ran the business, watched TV, read the newspaper, surfed the Web, bought a new coat every now and then, dated women—black, brown, white—consumed pornography, smoked, met friends for dinner, dreamed, honed anecdotes, got minor ailments. He had a life. He had the sort of life meant by the phrase "get a *life*." But year on year the silt thickened. The meta-nausea was knowing the nausea wouldn't lead to anything. There was no revolution gestating, no psychic crash or religious conversion in the offing. He'd live with it, but this was what it would be like, a state of tolerable vapidity overlaid with entertainment and fucking. It was nothing. It was the deal. He was the protagonist in a million creative writing class short stories, one more quiet sufferer lost in the American Dream. He took antidepressants and managed the restaurants perfectly well. A TV ad he'd seen countless times would suddenly irritate him— Have it your way at Burger King—and if he stayed with it irritation became disgust and if he stayed too long with that despair. You saw how, incredibly, you became someone who ought to avoid reflection. The unexamined life is not worth living. The examined life was not worth bearing. He supposed he should devote himself to macrobiotics or feng shui or Led Zeppelin memorabilia. People said of shows like *Seinfeld*, it's a religion, and thought they were speaking figuratively.

"Oh aye Barcelona, I forget," she says. "D'you speak Spanish then?"

"Yes."

"How d'you say: Hello, my name's Morwenna?"

"Buenos días, me llamo Morwenna."

She repeats it, solemnly. Meeyarmmo Morwenna. Then a sad smile that says she'll never remember it. Or have cause to use it. Her experience is like this, bits of paper blowing past her, she grasps one for a moment, starts to look, then it's snatched by the wind and gone.

In the small hours something wakes Augustus, though the room's silent—or rather bears the not quite silence of falling snow. Huge flakes descend like an angelic invasion. He lies still and watches, lets the repetition take him. Is it that each snowflake's unique? Something about fractals. Mandelbrot? Either way he's aware of entering this drowse to fend off the question of the girl and the future. The future's in the vicinity, a perpetual threat. He used to have a recurring dream of himself and a wolf trapped in the apartment building on 128th Street. He never actually saw it, but it was there, a presence. The dream was one of knowing that sooner or later he'd open a door or round a stairwell and there it would be. The future's like this, a padding predator. Sooner or later.

Morwenna sniffs, suddenly, with a rattle of mucus and a swallow that says otherwise silent crying. The snow light will show her face wet with tears if he looks down from the cot, so he keeps still, fixes his eyes on the drifting flakes, lets them take him again, like counting sheep.

It's dusk when Augustus wakes up. He's wet himself in his sleep but since he's once again in the restraints there's nothing he can do but lie in it. Thinking of Joyce: *When you wet the bed first it is warm then it gets cold.* He'd dreamed he was back in his Manhattan apartment. The whole front of the building had been blown off so that his sitting room fourteen floors up was open to the elements. Bit by bit, starting with light things—pencils, socks, papers—the contents of his home were being sucked out and carried away on a wind that spiraled up into the sky. He'd held on for as long as he could, but eventually, clinging to the arm of his sofa, he'd followed the rest of his possessions irresistibly up into the freezing darkness above the city.

The door unlocks and Harper comes in with a Styrofoam cup and something wrapped in a paper napkin. Another change of clothes: combat trousers, pale T-shirt and light canvas bomber jacket, a getup that convinces Augustus he's leaving, maybe even tonight. Augustus's model now is that the existing thing gets replaced by something worse. Better the devil you know.

"You awake?"

"Yes."

"Do you want this?"

He lets Augustus out of the hand restraints and gives him what he's brought, tepid sweet coffee and some kind of savory pastry. Augustus tastes mincemeat, thyme, potato, peas. The coffee allowed to go tepid so there'd be no point throwing it in Harper's face. Does Harper still think he's capable of doing something like that? If the coffee had been scalding would the idea of using it have occurred? Augustus concludes it wouldn't. They've retained the notion of his potential for autonomous action. He's let it go. You let things go so there's less to care for.

"Something I never asked you," Harper says. "Were you ever tempted?"

"Tempted?"

"By the whole thing: Husain. The peace of submission. The alleviation of the burden."

Augustus remembers the early days of paranoia, when he was so afraid of exposure he stuck to the prayer times even if he was alone in his apartment, even *fajr* and *isha*. Ritual wears away reason. Mere repetition's enough to wear it away, much quicker than you'd think. *Allahu Akbar! Allahu Akbar! Allahu Akbar! Allahu Akbar!* It wasn't long before he *was* in a kind of madness addressing God, dreamily asking for strength to do what he knew must be done. Need breeds faith, the need for vengeance no less than the need for consolation or love. Sometimes he'd get up for *fajr*, imagining hurrying straight back to bed afterward, but end up on his prayer mat for hours.

"I had a contained disease of belief going on," he said. "A thing between myself and the Mystery I knew wasn't there. But I'd have got it anywhere, the church, Transcendental Meditation, kabbalah, the Hare Krishna, probably just by sitting down and staring at myself in the mirror or repeating the word 'moron' for several hours a day. You can let yourself be led by it knowing it's nothing. It's reason using faith to get a job done."

"But Husain himself? The group?"

"Different species. I was never tempted by that."

There's a gentle elation about Harper just now. He's lit up by something inside. Augustus wonders if *he's* tempted by it, supposes according to the law of antithetical attraction he must be: All extremists risk conversion by their opposites, and what is Harper if not an extremist of flexibility?

"I'm not tempted," Harper says, reading Augustus's one eye,

"but I'm fascinated by its success. I don't mean the success of its alleged goals, I mean the success it's had in simply mesmerizing the West. Liberal relativists say nothing's black and white. Fanatics reply by blowing them up. How do the liberal relativists respond? Broadly, by sitting around saying, 'Wow, I guess those guys really don't agree with us. That's kind of amazing.' It's like a superfeminist sitting there coyly transfixed by a guy with an enormous cock saying I'm going to rape you, cunt. And that's not mentioning the superfeminist who sits there thinking it must be something she's *done*. The Chomskyites and bleeding hearts took 9/11 as an opportunity to educate the world about America's atrocities. As if it's ever going to be anything other than choosing your atrocities. What's wrong with people?"

For the first time Harper seems slightly rattled. There's the surface incredulity—What's wrong with people?—but beneath, an irritation.

"It's a death wish," Augustus says. "And a vacuum where the big things we believed in used to be. Hard to care about a way of life when your way of life is lifestyles. Also there's envy: the fundamentalists might be crazy but they're not anorexics or credit card junkies. They don't know the peculiar despair of trying to project their individuality through a personalized cell phone jacket." He's finished the pastry but still nurses the coffee, stone cold now.

"Death wish is right," Harper says. He gets up, takes the smokes out of his top pocket, lights two and hands one to Augustus. The room's dark but for a wedge of light from the latrine. Harper, on his feet, moves about the room aimlessly, as if merely stretching his legs.

"Or maybe less a death wish than a wish for the possibility of ending. We've lost the biblical myths of Ending. Since the end of the cold war we've lost our myth of man-made ending, too, nuclear Armageddon. It used to be a remote consolation that the sun would die one day but now we know we'll have cleared off by then, galactically emigrated or built a replacement that'll last forever. Crucially, we didn't get the cataclysm we were promised at the millennium. Y2K was supposed to punish our investment in science and technology. Planes were supposed to drop out of the sky and a new survivalist order emerge. But absolutely nothing happened. We were disappointed. Jesus, are we just going to keep *going*? Isn't anything going to *stop* us? Granted there's the prospect of environmental meltdown but we don't really believe we won't be able to deal with it. So, depressingly, we're going on. It's time to look at the future again. What's that going to be like? What's all the *new* science going to mean? Nothing new. Genetic engineering, space travel, bioweaponry, cyberspace—it'll all pass through the same matrix of human power and human accident and human desire, wear man's smudge and share man's smell, and if history's any guide the future will deeply resemble the past. We've come within a hairbreadth of losing the myth of a secular End of Days. But wait! Into the disappointment has walked apocalyptic anti-reason in the shape of a medievally misogynistic death cult that simply doesn't want anything from us other than our destruction. Our thanatotic glands are juicing. We don't want them to go, we want them to stay! We *love* these guys! Maybe they'll wipe us out!"

Harper stops talking (and walking) as if suddenly embarrassed by how long he's *been* talking, or by the uncharacteristic emotion he's worked up. It's surprised Augustus, and since it's something he hasn't seen in Harper before, brought a draft of fear. Harper tosses the cigarette butt and stubs it out.

"I have to do something," he says. "I have to execute you."

One lunchtime in the summer of 2002 Augustus stood at a kiosk on the broad central reservation of Las Ramblas, the tree-lined main thoroughfare in Barcelona. He'd just bought a pack of Marlboro Lights and was tearing off the cellophane.

"Oh my God," Selina said.

There was a bar right there with outdoor sunshaded tables and ICE COLD CERVEZA, also a ponytail-flicking young waitress he'd liked the look of from the kiosk now reduced to a nonentity. The sunshades were blue-and-white check. Leaf shadows twittered on the asphalt.

There was no pretense. The question from the second they looked at each other was whether this was going to be something, everything, do all the damage it could. Both of them supposed marriages, kids, an edifice of love and loyalty but at once felt their right to challenge it.

"I don't like this layout," Augustus said.

"What, the traffic on either side?"

"There's a feeling of being marooned in the middle of a lava flow."

He was ashamed of his twenty years of bearable misery. All the days and weeks of nothing in particular like a mountain of unrecyclable rubbish. He thought of the credentials he'd be lining up for anyone other than Selina. Affluence, polyglotism, El Salvador, the restaurants, the Upper East Side, the house in Vermont, *characters*. Naturally the usefully exotic mix of his blood.

"You look exactly as you should," she said. "I think I do too."

"We both have those faces that keep their look. Actually you look like someone for whom something this big is still small. But then you always looked like that."

"This isn't small. Trust me."

"What is this?"

"It was weird. I saw you from across the street and thought, My God that's Augustus—then immediately annihilated the idea, but slowly kept walking toward you waiting for it not to be you. But it is you."

Unchanged mutual transparency made it easy and difficult. They stabbed awkwardly for the immediately relevant information, for parameters, for what room they might have to maneuver. He was on vacation, so was she as of yesterday but here with work, charity, international, too complicated, later. Their hotels were five blocks apart. It was as if they had only the time it took to drink one beer to decide. And it was too big a decision to be made with anything other than blind instinct. Either that or toss a coin. They both felt this. There was a silence.

"Well?" Selina said.

They went to his hotel because it was nearer. In fact it was also more luxurious. Floor-to-ceiling drapes (which she closed) and a sun-trap French-windowed balcony. There was a Bose music system and a marbled en suite and air conditioning.

When he put his hands on her waist she had a moment of hesitation, tensed slightly, then relaxed.

Afterward they lay side by side on the bed. What Augustus wanted to say was: Whatever your life is leave it and be mine. He imagined himself saying this looking not at her but at the ceiling, then closing his eyes and waiting for life or death.

"I don't think I'm going to get away with just saying 'Well?' again, am I?" Selina said.

"I'll tell you something," Augustus said. "I have a house in Vermont. In this house are many books. Probably four or five thousand. Over the years I've had a repeated fantasy of you staying at the house when I'm not there. You're lost and you chance on it, like Goldilocks. In fact that's part of it, you coming out of the woods and seeing the house. It *is* near woods, by the way. You don't know who the place belongs to but you know it's perfectly safe and you can stay as long as you like. You know sometime the owner will show up, but not for quite a while, and anyway the thought pleasantly intrigues you. You feel calm, private and secure, and spend a long quiet season there reading whichever books take your fancy."

"Then you come home?"

"No. It's not a reunion fantasy. The pleasure's in the image of you reading the books and making yourself incrementally at home in the house. I can't tell you how often I run this footage. It gives me incredible peace and delight."

The city, obliterated by their lovemaking, was returning. With it the world, time, consequences, the dreadful larger context.

"What sort of damage are we looking at?" Selina said.

Augustus felt the bliss begin to drain. What was the point of being given this if it was only going to be this? You think you're out of the habit of looking for the point.

"For me, none," he said. "I've been saving myself for this."

"Okay."

"I'm serious. There's no one. Not even a cat you'd have to win over."

"Well," she said. "That's quite something."

"Your turn." No wedding ring but that didn't mean anything. She'd get up from the bed, start dressing. He wouldn't be able to move. The universe's lights would go out again. His life, a bearable dull dream before, would become a searing boredom. The racket of emptiness would build, intrude, deafen, drive him to something.

"Am I really to believe there's no one?" she said.

"Yes."

"What about exes?"

"What about them?"

"Ex-wives."

"Nil. Other than you, obviously."

"Children?"

"No."

A pause. Children? Mothers asked the question with smug musicality. She hadn't. She didn't have any. He realized he'd known it when they were having sex just now. There was something guilty and plaintive in the fucking of older childless women, a shame or sadness or fury at the cunt's thwarted teleology. At the thought he felt the old reflex outrage that she should have to suffer anything, but also a surge of excitement: No children was another potential obstacle removed.

"Put me out of my misery will you?" he said.

"I'm not with anyone."

He didn't move.

"And as the superb condition of my body must have already made clear I don't have any children either."

He had a vision of them on a talk show, beaming, exuding indiscriminate generosity, a host saying in the mock-incredulous let-me-get-this-straight way *And after thirty-two years. You guys mmmeet again* ... while the caption read: SWEETER SECOND TIME AROUND: WE MET AFTER MORE THAN THREE DECADES—AND WE'RE STILL CRAZY ABOUT EACH OTHER!!!

"You know what this means, don't you?" he said.

"What?"

"We can call room service."

"I want a Long Island Iced Tea."

Selina's father died of a heart attack two years after Michael was killed. Her mother, Meredith, now seventy-eight, lived in a huge apartment on the Upper West Side. She'd decided to be interested in art, and in the years since Jack's death had made herself a presence on the New York scene. "There's a gallery in SoHo," Selina said. "She's on various boards. We became friends. Christ knows how many lovers she's had over the years. There was a terrible phase of young guys. She's over it. Currently there are three beaux, a banker and two art dealers she makes a hobby out of tormenting. This is way better than the food at my hotel, by the way." They'd ordered up champagne and tapas and were eating off the tray on the bed. Neither of them had quite accepted all that had just happened. As the minutes went by Augustus felt himself tensing for derailment. They daren't look fully at each other, as if the trick to prolonging this was to keep a part of themselves in disbelief. He thought of the decapitated family at La Rancheria, all the places he'd carried her with him and now here she was. (What had Michael written?

Don't you know you're what I carry between myself and death?) Being with her made him want to go back to every opportunity he'd had for doing the right thing and this time do it, unreservedly, so there'd be a better man to offer her now. As it was he kept catching inner glimpses of the mass of life he'd wasted. Hours and days and years of nothing being spectacularly wrong, long sessions of wondering whether to buy a new car or extend one of the restaurant dining rooms. Sundays spent doing nothing in the apartment, not even reading, dully yielding to television's inanities. He'd alight on a sport he wasn't remotely interested in then arbitrarily invest in the fortunes of one competitor or team. *I've been saving myself for this.* It was a lie. He'd been wasting himself. Now she was here again it was as if he'd just been told he had only a short time to live. That was the deal: the later in life love came the more clearly you saw the distance between you and your death. He was fifty-five. Maybe twenty more years, maybe not even that. Juliet after all was only three years older than this when she died. Before he could stop himself (surely this would hex it what was he fucking insane?) he vowed inwardly that if he was given this chance with Selina then not a single moment, by God not one single *second*—

"You've always been in my dreams," she said. "In the mornings they'd say: What did you dream about? I'd have to make something up."

"You've always been in mine too."

"It's a sad thing, the number of people still dreaming of their lost lovers. Think of it, all over the world, night after night."

"Once I dreamed about Stevie and the Vaseline and woke myself up laughing."

Selina laughed now, remembering. They'd babysat one night for a couple of friends from Harry's, Laura and Jeff, whose regular sitter had let them down and whose son, Stevie, was not quite two. Augustus and Selina had been paranoid he was going to fall out of a window or spontaneously combust, but Laura and Jeff said he'd be fine if they put him in his rocking horse chair with some toys. This they did, and Stevie was content. For a while they remained anxious, but when it became obvious the kid wasn't going to give them any trouble they relaxed and turned on the TV. They probably only took their eyes off him for five minutes. When Selina next looked down at him she gave a cry.

"He looked so pleasantly surprised," she said now, laughing. "As if he'd just accidentally discovered something wonderful."

"Well he had," Augustus said.

Stevie had found himself within reach of an open economy-size jar of Vaseline and applied the entire contents to his head and face. One long twist of the stuff came off his nose like a ski jump.

"I dreamed about it a few years back," Augustus said. "Woke up laughing my goddamned head off. I can't tell you how crushed I was when I realized it was just a dream." The feel of Selina laughing under his hands gave him a surge of panic because it was so clearly one of the things that would make the thought of death bearable and what would he do now if it was taken away?

Jack left her enough money so she didn't have to work. "I became a volunteer. Worthy organizations. The ethics option. Turns out I've got a talent for troubleshooting. Now I work pro bono as a consultant telling charities what's wrong with them and how they could be raising more money. I've got quite a reputation. You surprise yourself."

It was evening. They'd had too much sex. Selina was in the bath, up to her neck in foam. Augustus, slightly faint, sat in the open doorway leaning against the jamb. They'd opened the drapes to find dusk, smoke-blue sky, the city stirring, people heading to restaurants and bars.

"But you left Manhattan."

"I couldn't stand the prospect of bumping into you. I moved to San Francisco that same year, finished my degree at Berkeley eventually." Eventually because for two years after Michael was killed she lived in "a manageable hell." "I'd been waiting my whole life to find out what the worst of myself was. Michael's death gave me the chance. I won't bore you with the details. Some people need to go to the dogs sooner or later. I was one of them. You want the details, I know."

"Of course."

"Well you can have them later. Let's not spoil this. I don't have HIV, by the way."

Which condition the details he was to get later might be expected to have left her with. He had a clear image of her in a cold sweat getting sodomized by a pockmarked Latino drug dealer in a toilet cubicle, her hair swinging, a look of miserable concentration on her moist face.

"Good," he said. "Neither do I. As far as I know."

They lay in each other's arms in the dark and listened to the nightlife through the open French windows. Augustus felt the muscles of his face at peace. Here after all these years was the reverence for the immediate world, the sounds of drinkers and diners, beeping traffic, teenagers and their scooters. The kids here rode crazily, the girls never fearing for their bare legs, the boys with sunglasses and cigarettes. It was terrible to see beautiful young people when you were old. But now he had her it didn't matter. Now he could bless the little bastards.

She didn't have children because she couldn't. During the manageable hell she'd got pregnant and had an abortion. You can have an infection without even knowing. Later it turns out your fallopian tubes are ruined. Scar tissue. Blockage. "We tried for four years," Selina told him. "Did five IVF treatment cycles, spent thousands of dollars, became wraiths. Eventually I accepted defeat. Punishment for the abortion. God's only consistency's in his vindictiveness." "We" were Selina and now ex-husband Louis, a San Francisco lawyer she met after Berkeley. She'd loved him, but without mythic force. "You know what I mean," she said. "You and I could've sat down with Tristan and Isolde and held up our heads. It wasn't like that with Louis. He was a good, smart, subtle, compassionate man but he didn't call to anything essential in me. He's so well put together I didn't even ruin him. Now he's married to a nice smart well-put-together interior designer, with two grown-up kids."

They made love again just before dawn. Afterward he kissed her shoulders and hands and midriff and knees and shins and feet, Thank you, thank you. He'd sensed the strength she'd called on to haul her sexuality out from under the weight of infertility. In his experience childlessness in women either warped into a dedication to self-hating sexual expertise or formed a subsonic noise of sadness and loss. There was sadness here but forced to one side to accommodate a hard-won space for desire. It was typical of her that she'd refused to let it be killed in her. Augustus remembered how he used to imagine her soul—something like a yolk of pure light in God's hands—getting its portion of courage before birth, God smiling and on a whim putting in three four five times the amount.

She slept on her left side and he slid in behind her as if thirty-two years hadn't passed. They drifted in and out of consciousness, in Augustus's case because he was afraid he'd wake up to find it had been a dream. It made him probe the ether for his mother's ghost for the first time in years, evoked her voice saying: Well, I hope you're happy now, kiddo. Yes, Mom, I'm happy. Suddenly he realized how lucky he'd been in Juliet, what a force of nature she'd been. Cardillo had said to him once: Women like your mother, Gus, there's a tiny—I mean *tiny* handful in every generation. You got one you don't need heaven. Heaven can go to hell. You got one, I know. Selina's an elegant firework. Augustus had felt his heart open to the restaurateur when he said that, could've hugged him. Lying in bed with Selina now he wished he'd been kinder to the man who had been, albeit briefly, the closest thing to a father he'd ever had.

"I suppose we should go out," Selina said.

They'd ordered breakfast in the room. Augustus in boxers and bathrobe stood at the open windows drinking a cup of coffee and looking out. Another hot day of milky blue sky and the streets' baked odors. He was torn between fear and angelic well-being. Now he had all this joy and patience and appetite and gentleness he wanted to use it.

"Well," he said, "that does offer the prospect of sunlight on your arms and legs."

"Not what they used to be, the preservative powers of barrenness notwithstanding. I think if we are going out I should paint my nails."

But for a long time they lay together on the bed. "I read an article about Calley recently," Selina said. "You remember him, the My Lai guy?"

"Yeah. He got life, right? Must be out by now."

"He was out after three and a half years, and most of that was house arrest with booze and his girlfriend. Being the only soldier convicted must have seemed shit luck at the time but it bought him a huge amount of sympathy. Nixon started angling to get him out practically as soon as the sentence was read. Anyway he married into a wealthy jeweler's family in Georgia and by all accounts had a pretty pleasant life. He looks like Colonel Sanders now. It made me think of you. *Porphyria's Lover* and God not saying a word."

"Whereas the things that remind me of you are: tulips, affectionate horses, French toast, silver birch, the smell of snow . . ."

"Are we really to be given this?" she said. "So late in the day?"

"Yes. God's got a romantic streak it turns out."

"If this is his doing I might consider giving the old bastard another chance. How do you feel about ordering up a couple of Long Island Iced Teas, by the way?"

"Fine, but I think you might be an alcoholic."

"I thought everyone was. Aren't you?"

"Well if you put it like that."

The maid knocked and Selina said, *"Por favor vuelve más tarde,"* and there in her voice in the foreign language were the thirty-two years, every one of them his enemy. It made him want to fuck her but they were both too sore. At last, sometime after noon, they got up, dressed and went out.

They were too tired to go sightseeing.

"What we do is, I do a little light shopping and you suggest places we can interrupt that for a consumable treat."

"You try things on and I come in and mess about with you in the changing room."

"Okay, but remember, I want nail polish and a bag. One of those great leather satchels I keep seeing everywhere."

They were moving into a phase of realism. When he'd first turned and seen her standing there he'd entered a dream state. You found yourself living through what you believed impossible, perhaps the way hypnotized people observed themselves behaving out of character. That phase had required very little of them, as if they were being gently choreographed by invisible forces—otherwise how was it they'd moved from the Ramblas bar to his hotel with such quiescence? Then immediately after the intimacy he'd dropped into a state of self-protecting pessimism: invisible forces loved cruel pranks; they were waiting for him to start believing a life with her was possible—that they were really to be given this after all these years—to maximize the pleasure of whisking it away from him at the last minute. Gotcha! She'd felt it too, he could tell, the suspicion that they'd met like this only because some power had decided they hadn't suffered enough the first time around. They'd have been less skeptical had one or both of them been encumbered with a spouse or children; at least then there'd be pains and losses before the reward. As it was the absence of obstacles presented a deal too good to be true. But yesterday had passed, a day and a night. He'd fallen asleep with her in his arms (his happiness on the edge of anger because he'd been forced to live thirty-two years without it) and woken up with her beside him, golden warm living Selina whose spirit for him renewed and revivified the world, and now here they were in a second day and God had not yet said a word.

So to this latest phase, terrifying in a different way. Now when they looked at each other it was with a tense mutual concession that pessimism was starting to give way to hope. He put his hand on the nape of her neck under her hot hair and she gently touched his hip and these gestures were tentative claims on the future. However unlikely, the facts remained: they were free and still in love.

"How come you never tried to contact me?" he asked her. They were having espressos and whiskey at a café in the Barrio Gótico, again with outside tables. She'd bought nail polish the color of dried blood and was applying a coat to her fingernails. He loved the older version of her skin, the way the veins showed on the backs of her hands. In the hotel he'd crossed her wrists above her head and kissed her underarms and felt the skin there looser than it used to be. The perceptible aging turned him on, gave a rousing strangeness to her familiar mouth, cunt, nipples, anus. He imagined her other lovers, hunted and absorbed with every inch of himself her body's troubled enrichment—but also its prosaic history of coughs and sneezes, all the times she'd brushed her teeth or eaten ice cream or menstruated or taken a shit, even the abortion and the vague darkness of the manageable hell. He wanted it all. Her flesh testified, wearily but with resolve and hunger and every time he thought of this he wanted to go inside her or go deeper, break her spine with fucking because the thirty-two years of all this were a source of desire and rage.

"I was scared," she said. "I would've been an affliction to anyone. I *was* an affliction. Selfish enough to fuck up other people's lives but not yours. I thought you'd be with someone anyway. Plus you tell yourself the world's just not like that. You don't just pick up the phone after ten years."

He thought about this for a moment. After the surreality of their rapid divorce, he'd never tried to contact her either. And yet not a single day in thirty-two years had passed without his thinking of her, even if only for a moment.

"You know how it is for me, don't you?" he said. In lieu of saying: You know I'm still in love with you, don't you? He could see from her face she understood. Using the word "love" was a risk neither of them wanted to take. But she kept her blue eyes steadily on his and said:

"It's the same for me."

"Really?"

"You felt it."

"You look like your mother."

"I know. If you want to see what I'll look like at seventy-eight I can arrange it."

"Would I still have sex with your mother?"

"Probably. But probably not if she wasn't my mother. *Your* mother'll be turning in her grave by now."

"I discussed it with her when you were asleep. She said she hoped I was happy now."

"I can imagine. The way you say that to a kid who's finally broken the toy."

They had to keep veering away from it. After the café they wandered without a map, zigzagged loosely around Las Ramblas, found themselves outside the Picasso museum, didn't go in. The as yet unpurchased leather satchel was becoming mythic. Augustus had been here for a week in the roving numbness that had been his state for twenty years and the city had said nothing to him. If he'd noticed anything it was the presence of global brands, the McDonald's, the Starbucks, the Subways, the same relentless high-resolution inanity of television and advertising, the universal logos—Coca-Cola, Nike, Nokia, Microsoft, Motorola—that no matter where you were had found a purchase, a place from which to add their portion to the world hymn of corporate homogeneity. But now with Selina suddenly he was in *Spain*. History glimmered, Moors, Visigoths, Columbus, Torquemada, Isabella, Pizarro, Goya's witches, Franco's fascists, bulls' blood in the dust and all the primped matadors with their womanish behinds still at it in the twenty-first century with pics and swords. This was her doing; she was what she'd always been: his license to belong, to take an interest, to make a claim for a share in the world.

"I'm struggling to not say things," he said to her. They were in a little empty church just off the Carrer de Pi. She'd said: Come on it'll be nice and cold in here. Just for a few minutes. In the vestibule they'd dipped their fingers in the font and crossed themselves with an unexpected sadness for the child selves they'd betrayed.

"I know," she said. "But it seems absurd to say them."

"Answer me one thing."

"What?"

Augustus couldn't remember the last time he'd been in a church—then could, of course: his mother's funeral. Juliet had specified a full Catholic Mass.

"Do you want more of this?"

She looked at him. This. Us.

"Yes," she said.

"A lot more?"

"Yes."

He could see the sixth station of the Via Crucis over her shoulder, a sub-Giotto relief with blue sky and gold leaf halos. *Verónica enjuaga la cara sagrada*, Veronica wipes the sacred face. He tried to remember what the seventh station was. Couldn't.

"Do you want more?" she said.

"What do you think?"

"A lot more?"

"Yes."

"Okay. That's good."

"Now show me your knockers."

Which was for the past, one of the things they used to do. She gave one quick glance to check the place was still empty then just in the way she'd always done with a look of bored impunity lifted her shirt. He bent and kissed her breasts through the lace of her bra, felt her breathing and was suddenly so full of tenderness for her there was no gesture he could make that would sufficiently honor it. This was the sweet panic. He straightened and she lowered her shirt, stared at him with the dead-eyed queenly self-containment that was part of the role.

"You'll be returning the favor later," she said. "In the restaurant. And I won't want any argument. Waiter or no waiter the wang comes out."

He sat in a pew at the back while she walked a slow circuit of the church. Thirty-two hours had passed since they met. Cosmologists had time doing all sorts of things you couldn't believe when you heard it, but here was proof. Twenty years collapsed in on its own emptiness, became a finger snap. Thirty-two hours held times within time, private ages you consumed without the clock's knowledge. What had they had? A day and a night and a day. Nothing.

It was just after eight when they left the church. The lamplit streets were warm and busy. (Until now Augustus had been Americanly baffled at how bad so many European cities smelled. In Barcelona as in Rome as in Marseille as in Athens there was a ubiquitous double act of blocked drains and ammoniacal cleaner that could hit you like a karate chop to the gullet. The sidewalks frequently stank of urine and dog shit. Now—how not?—the reek was honest and human, a celebration of messy life.) They walked up to the pedestrianized Avenida Portal de l'Angel, halfheartedly perusing restaurant menus along the way.

"Let's go and see something dumb," Selina said. They'd stopped outside a theater showing American movies.

"That's not going to be hard. Look at the selection."

"Oh wait. El Corte Inglés. I should go here." Opposite the movie theater was a large department store.

"For the Satchel."

"For the Satchel. I can feel it. You choose a movie and get tickets. I'll meet you back here in ten minutes. Fifteen minutes. Pick the dumbest one."

Yes. You let her go briefly for the pleasure of her coming toward you out of the crowd. Revenge on all those times you thought it was her but it wasn't.

"Hey."

She turned. "What?"

There was nothing he could say that wouldn't have the sound of tempting fate. She saw it.

"Don't go anywhere," she said.

He watched her and she turned back several times to see him watching her. A few yards from the store, turning back from giving him another look, she walked straight into a litter bin, stumbled and almost fell over. It looked like a finely tuned bit of slapstick, but it was an accident. Immediately she turned again, laughing, waving him back. He was laughing too. It's okay, she mouthed. I'm fine. I'm fine. There was an old guy selling flowers there next to her and *he* was laughing, one arm extended to her as if steadying her aura. Augustus watched her exchange a few words with him. The bin had left a smudge on her skirt. She brushed at it a couple of times, gave up, waved to him, grinning, then turned and went into the store.

"I have to execute you."

Augustus, still holding the Styrofoam cup, feels how far he's traveled from the wanting-to-die of the interrogations. That wasn't a wish to die but a wish to stop suffering. It was just that he couldn't imagine anything other than death with the power to grant it. Since they took his eye he's worked hard (or so he'd thought) at not caring, letting the fragments of self swirl but not cohere. Now, when Harper steps into the latrine's wedge of light with a gun in his right hand the fragments rush back together and there's nothing he can do but yield to the fear that he really is going to die right now and the hope that somehow he isn't.

Your hands are free. The brain can't help it. The brain's compelled to throw in whatever might be useful. He has no strength, no weapons, nowhere to go. Harper moves out of the light then stops again. "I'm finding it difficult," he says.

If you're not in extreme pain you don't want to die. You're a disfigured prisoner who could be shot any time but you want life right up until the end. Light still comes and goes in the frosted glass. There's still a cigarette, cold coffee, disgorged memories. There's still speculation and the margin of anesthetic bliss just before sleep. The blanket still feels good around you. There remains your poor body asking if it's still a deal between you.

"Children who don't have rules and boundaries become hyperactive and irritable," Harper says. "This is the current thinking. They want dos and don'ts, discipline, parameters. Without restraints their own potential's like vertigo."

For a surreal moment (although all these moments are surreal) Augustus thinks Harper's about to start talking about his *own* childhood, with what would be laughable belatedness begin looking for explanations in his distant past. But no. It's an analogy.

"I find myself irritable," Harper says. "It's the freedom. Like wealth or sex or cocaine. This is a basic wisdom I'm only just acquiring: too much of what you want leads to irritation, an impatience with yourself. I'm often late in my insights."

Augustus is alert with every cell. All aspects of himself have pooled resources to make sure he doesn't say or do anything that will nudge Harper from holding the trigger to pulling it. He's rushing up an incline that will end in a sheer drop into the great empty answer, that there's nothing beyond this life. The last moments' urgent message is that they are the last moments, precious bright beautiful granules of time, but the last. You want time to sift them, to raise them up to the light, to enjoy them, but they're all the time you have. In El Corte Inglés Selina was one of the people nearest the blast. Despite what had been done to her body her face was wholly recognizable. At the morgue Meredith had insisted on seeing her daughter's remains, though Augustus had offered to go in alone. There was Selina's face, one large cut in an almost perfect diagonal from left to right but otherwise absolutely her. The little silver scar under her bottom lip testified, as if this was what it had come into her life for. He remembered the footage he'd imagined, her running, laughing with the glass jar of nickels and pennies across a green lawn in warm sunshine, the trip, the smash, the hot pain and shocking taste of her own blood. She'd told him it was the first time the world shifted for her, showed her it could open under her feet or block out the sun. She'd said, I was such a little monster, I was *outraged* that the world would suddenly turn on me like that. On *me*, its darling, its *point*. Augustus had stood next to Meredith and felt rather than seen the old woman taking in the wrongness of the shape under the white sheet, the declivities and gaps, a landscape of terrible absences. He'd thought of horror movie corpses, shark attack victims, afterward told himself it would have been better to see everything, to leave his imagination nothing to work with. Outside the building in Barcelona's crisp morning sunlight Meredith had said: Your generation's weighed down with all this idiotic chatter about what to do about these maniacs. This slew of tolerance, it's like the sewers have ruptured and no one's noticed they're swimming in shit. Don't you know wretched stupid ignorant evil when you see it? My daughter was a force of beauty in the world and now . . . She'd been unable to finish, fractured against the word "beauty." Augustus had said nothing, watched her turn and get into the waiting car. After she'd gone he'd stood on the steps smoking a cigarette, remembering Juliet telling him that in heaven people who'd lost limbs would have them back again, the blind would be able to see, the crippled to walk, the deaf to hear. The wrongness of Selina's shape under the death sheet was giant, an error he couldn't imagine the universe—the mere continued existence of things—failing to put right. There must be a heaven because there *couldn't* be only the hell of such subtraction. It wasn't that he couldn't bear never seeing her again, it was that he couldn't bear her never being herself again.

Now, as Harper moves closer with the raised gun pointed directly at his head and the speed of these last moments makes him think of atoms in a particle accelerator, he knows it was both, that the dumb belief in being with her again has never entirely gone, that it takes the genuine imminence of death to blow away the last cobwebs of habit. The Gospels talked of Jesus in the final moment of the Passion "giving up his spirit." This is what he should do now, consign himself with whatever grace to whatever power—except there is no grace and there is no power, only his consciousness desperately grabbing every detail and even now, even *now* rifling every file for a strategy, something, anything that will make Harper—

"The truth is," Harper says, "I don't think I'll be doing this much longer. It's become boring. As I said, I'm susceptible to boredom. My curiosity's been shifting away. I think the guys who can keep going with this year after year are secretly waiting for God, for comeuppance. As trajectories toward belief go it's pretty radical but still . . ." He chuckles. "In the end it's because they want faith. Do you remember that scene in *Cool Hand Luke*? Paul Newman in the rain shouting up into the sky for God to do whatever it takes—love me, hate me, kill me, anything, just let me know you're up there! Same thing with these guys. Faith by provocation."

Augustus feels stretched, as if his consciousness is a length of elastic, one end fixed to the here and now, the other pulling into the space where the afterlife should be, straining for the faintest sign of his mother, Selina, Cardillo, even poor Harry the bartender who died, painfully, of lung cancer back in the early nineties, anyone from history's billions of dead who can say yes, there's something, don't panic, it's not the end.

"It's not impossible I'll become a saint," Harper says. "Morality, like the planet, is round. I've traveled so far from virtue I must be very close to reaching it again, and from the other side this time, the *inside* I like to think. It's like, there's this girl I've been seeing. She's insatiably curious too, but only in the sack. We spent probably three or four months doing all the perversions, as many as we could think of, pretty much everything. You know what we do now, what we've arrived at? Penetrative sex, naked, in the dark, usually in the missionary position. Kissing. We do a lot of kissing, like teenagers."

"Mr. Harper?"

Unseen and unheard by Augustus and Harper, the doctor has

come in and is standing in the shadows. Harper, having started at the voice, laughs. "Jeez, doc, you scared the shit out of me."

Augustus has just time to begin willing the doctor to mean somehow *not death*, just that, no details but a gush of raw need, before something extraordinary happens.

At the sound—the discharge of a single shot from a silencered handgun—Augustus becomes weirdly aware of his mouth, his whole face locked in a grimace. He's wondered what getting shot would feel like, imagined the entry line white-hot, searing, a smell of burned flesh and the bullet's instant raging dictatorship in a smashed bone or punctured organ. Whatever he's imagined it's not this warm numbness and heightened consciousness of his face and scalp, his face and scalp pulled in terror. There's no pain, only an acute awareness of his particular dimensions, where his fingernails and hairs and lips meet empty space. He hears himself making small sounds, then is somehow deafened by the sight of Harper (who's dropped his weapon) raising with peculiar slow care both hands to a darkly bleeding wound in his throat, swallowing, hugely, lifting one leg in a bizarre loss of balance. Augustus finds himself sitting up. He's unfastened the first of the leg restraints. The doctor steps out of the shadow with his right hand raised, holding a silencered gun at the level of Harper's face. Harper drops to one knee, still swallowing as if struggling to get a lump of food down, his hands and shirt dark with blood. The doctor fires again, missing completely, then a third time straight into Harper's forehead. The shots sound as they do on television but crisper, with in the bare-walled room a little resonance.

Augustus goes on with the second leg restraint while the doctor checks Harper's pulse. They move together in silence, as if all this has been rehearsed, Augustus with compressed urgency, the doctor with the same professional calm Augustus sensed during the surgery on his eye.

"Is he dead?"

"Yes. Get into his clothes, quick."

"Are you Sentinel?"

"What? No. Move fast if you want out of here."

Despite everything it's agony for Augustus to stand. His feet send violent signals as soon as he puts weight on them. For a second he thinks he's going to pass out, has to grab the bed until he can make room for the pain. His ribs knife his heart getting the hospital gown off and Harper's clothes on. The Timberland boots are a size too big but he slides his screaming feet into them. He helps the doctor roll Harper's body under the bed. Questions swarm but he asks none. He keeps the bigger part of himself in disbelief. He hasn't accepted Harper's dead, will never move or speak again. Nonetheless there's this moment of his appearing to be dead. The room's dark space and wedge of light from the latrine are sympathetic, suddenly, as if they've been waiting for this too.

"Agree to do exactly as I say or I'll shoot you myself," the doctor says, quietly.

"Whatever you say," Augustus says.

The doctor goes out of the room and returns with a gurney. On it, an unzipped body bag. "Hurry up," he says. "Get in. Once you're in, don't move at all. You move, we both die. Understand? No matter what, you don't move."

Augustus gets up and slides into the bag. The doctor zips it not quite completely closed. Within seconds the heat's stifling, but they're on the move. Augustus's memory is innocently trying to make a connection, some game they must have played as kids in Harlem, a shopping cart . . . The gurney goes bone-shakingly over something, a cable maybe. Augustus has no idea of the place's layout but they seem to move unaccosted for hours. In reality maybe two minutes. Then a man's voice asking in Moroccan Arabic: Which one? And the doctor replying: The American. Who's on duty in C-Block?

Augustus doesn't catch the reply. Doors slam. They move down a slight incline. Morocco? Which means if he can get to the safe house in Rabat—but no. It's compromised. He probably gave Harper the address. More doors, cell doors by the sound, steel bolts sliding. Sweat trickles down the left side of his face. Several men's voices away to his left and the sound of a television or radio. Two more sets of doors. The heat of the bag's like the inside of a boxing glove.

Then, suddenly, the smell of outside. Dust and petrol and concrete and wild thyme. A rougher surface under the gurney's wheels. They stop. Augustus desperately wants to move his head, to see if he can catch a glimpse of the world through the gap in the zip, but you move, we both die.

He keeps still, decodes the sounds: a van door opening. Do you want any help? No, I can manage. Again Moroccan Arabic. Every moment now is incredible, his time is an incredible blooming into mystery.

The doctor's reply has been ignored because the other male voice says suddenly close to Augustus's head in Arabic: Got a cigarette, doc? Augustus closes his eyes, imagining the zipper being pulled down, the fresh air against his face. If the guard opens the bag and looks in he won't be able to pretend death. Something will give him away.

But of course the guard doesn't open the bag. Why would he? Instead between him and the doctor Augustus feels himself lifted briefly and deposited on a firm cushioned surface. He smells antiseptic. An ambulance? Someone fastens straps across him. The doctor says, in Arabic: Three left. Take these. I've got a fresh pack. Thanks. See you tomorrow. Augustus expects *Inshallah.* If Allah wills it. It's what he'd say, what it's become second nature to say, in his pidgin Arabic, but the door slams and one set of footsteps recedes. The driver door opens, closes, the vehicle rocks slightly.

"Don't move or speak until I tell you," the doctor says. All Augustus's hard work toward not caring about anything has been wiped out. How much time since he gave them his contacts? Future generations will thank the elephant. Please God please God please God but he knows it's been days. He remembers falling asleep with his head in Elise's lap in the hotel room in Barcelona, the clean denim smell of her jeans. If you still feel this way in a month, call me on this number. Can this really be his life? Is there really a series of moments reaching all the way back to East Harlem, the first roachy apartment, Clarence hitting him in the face, his mother's fingernails on his bare back, his monumental grandfather saying get that nigger brat out of here?

Checkpoint. Lights revolving, Augustus thinks. A brief pause. Then through. The doctor's been driving slowly but now speeds up. They're traveling uphill.

The explosion, when it comes, hammers on the walls of the ambulance. Augustus in the boxing-glove heat of the bag jackknifes but is held by the straps. A second detonation, louder than the first, seems to lift the vehicle's back wheels off the ground. Augustus struggles but his arms are pinned. He twists his head but the tiny gap in the zip shows only darkness. He hears the driver door open and close, feels the doctor's jump down. The back doors open. The doctor unzips the bag and unfastens the straps. "You're out," he says. "You'll want to see this."

Augustus wriggles out of the bag, crashes to his knees and looks back.

The camp, the detention center, the prison (he's never thought of it as anything other than "the place" or "in here") is ablaze. Cumulus-thick smoke expands in what looks like time lapse spasms. Cicadas, silenced by the explosion, are starting up again. There are no sirens, no sounds or signs of movement. Only the oranged darkness and convulsing smoke.

"We have to move," the doctor says. "Get back in."

"Who are you?"

"No one. It's personal. Not you. Him."

"Harper?"

"Yes. Get in or I'll leave you here."

They switch from the ambulance to a Peugeot and from that to a two-seater van that belongs to a drain cleaning company. "I don't have a plan for you," the doctor says. "You can't come with me. I can give you medicine and some cash but that's it."

"Where are you going?"

"I can take you as far as Rabat. Then we separate."

"Why did you—"

"He hurt someone close to me."

"The other prisoners?"

"That's on my conscience. They were dead anyway. See if there's any money in his pockets. Can you walk?"

"I need a phone. You have a cell phone?"

Augustus calls the numbers. No answer from Elise. No answer from Jacques Dertier. He gets through to Marie, has time only to tell her they're all compromised, get underground—before the battery dies.

"Rabat's no use to me," Augustus says. "I need an out."

"A what?"

"I need the means to get out. I have to get to a phone. Where are we?"

The next filling station is closed but has a phone on the forecourt. Augustus calls Darlene collect in New York.

It takes him a moment, hearing her voice (and what he believes is the background noise of one of his restaurants) to find his own. His throat knots as Darlene, hearing nothing, says Hello? a second time, with calculated impatience. Nothing's changed. Darlene's a Manhattanite. Her meter's running. You're wasting her time. In two seconds a whole way of life he left behind is brought to the other end of a phone. Somehow he manages to speak—and in speaking remembers why he picked her for this job in the first place. "Darlene, it's Augustus. I need you to listen very carefully and do exactly as I tell you. This is an emergency, a matter of life and death. Do you understand?"

It takes a long time, even with Darlene's unnatural composure and efficiency. Waiting for her call back he rests his head against the metal plate behind the phone. The doctor sits with the van door open, smoking a cigarette. The man's reservoir's empty. Augustus understands: Certain actions use up your last power without you realizing it was all you had left. No doubt there's a plane ticket, a plan, an out. But it's just as likely that if Augustus doesn't rouse him he'll simply sit here in the drain cleaners' van and wait for the security forces to pick him up. *He hurt someone close to me.* This is the risk the Harpers run, the Husains. Provoke someone into being prepared to die as long as you die too and you're never safe again.

Darlene calls back. She can be in Casablanca at five-thirty tomorrow afternoon, Delta to Paris, Air France to Morocco.

On a blue-skied afternoon four days before Christmas Augustus stands on the hill in the snow, thinking of something Selina said in the hotel room just before dawn. The two of them had been lying on the bed, unstrung from too much sex and alcohol, drifting in and out of conversation. I used to think it was just the kids today who were infatuated with emptiness, Selina had said, but it's bigger than that. I've got friends, smart, educated, grown-up people, who suddenly find the alleged fakeness and corruption of everything exhilarating. Why is that? After a pause, she'd slurred: I don't expect you to answer that, by the way. I know I've fucked you practically to death. Augustus had kissed her knees and said, I think I've got at least one more in me. What do you say, white girl? Then he'd fallen asleep.

They never went back to the subject, but he knows what he'd say to her now: They find the alleged fakeness and corruption of everything exhilarating because it frees them from having to do anything about it. If the world's a lost cause you're at liberty to think of nothing but your own pleasure. Cynicism licenses hedonism. He'd sensed this drift in his last years in Manhattan, a cold delight in the unmasked bankruptcy of everything, the entire human project. Harper had been right about the millennium. The failure of the world to end, or at least suffer a transformation, had forced the species into a status report. The status report in the West was that the Enlightenment had failed, or rather had succeeded in leading us to its logical extremity, nihilism. Augustus had subscribed to it himself, living his life of new overcoats and casual sex and consumer preferences and movies and continual irritation. If he thinks back to the time just before he met Selina in Barcelona he remembers feeling constantly tired, not physically, but, underlyingly, of everything. He was a good example: it took the millennium, the great Non-Ending and the willingness of time to go on indefinitely to make the whole western world realize how tired it was of itself, its ways, its projects, its values, its beliefs. This also is the tired franchise, Harper had said, the Future. Exhaustion was everywhere, some of it manic, some of it urbane, some of it brutish, but all nausea at the prospect of Carrying On. He supposes, though he's too far gone from the world to check, that optimists will regard the rise of Islamism as a blessing in disguise. It'll take the threatened destruction of Enlightenment values to remind us they're perhaps not so laughably shitty after all, spawn a humanist renaissance, produce a new Leonardo Da Vinci or Shakespeare, wake the West up to what it's got and what it stands to lose. It's just the latest version of absolute certainty, Selina had said, when channel-surfing had turned up footage of self-proclaimed jihadis burning a U.S. flag and firing automatic weapons into the air. Absolute certainty beyond the need for conversation. Beyond *tolerance* of conversation. I'm against absolute certainty everywhere except in pure mathematics. It had reminded Augustus of Juliet's version of the Crucifixion, in which a great, heartbreaking meal was made of Jesus's moment of doubt: My God, my God, why hast thou forsaken me? Can you imagine what horrible agony that must have been for poor Jesus? Juliet would ask, rhetorically. To think that after all he'd been through, all that suffering, his father had abandoned him? In later years she and Augustus laughed at how she could bring him to tears with this performance—but the meaning of the story stayed with him. Doubt was written in. Doubt, sanctioned by Christ himself, was human. God had a soft spot for doubt. But the yelling and gun-waving young men in the news footage admitted no doubt. They looked as if doubt was punishable by death.

Augustus's eye waters as he lets the memory dissolve. The air's a purged element between the snow and the blue sky, offers a dizzying clarity, suggests ghosts—or else he's going mildly nuts. Several times lately coming out of a reverie he's seen—or half-seen, or imagined, or glimpsed with the eye that's no longer there—Selina or Juliet or Harper whisking away just a moment before he can get a perceptual grip. Initially he explained it as his own doing, an effort to put something into the world worth staying alive for. But if he's honest he must admit that while he's thought of himself since his escape as a man waiting to die, he's never more than fleetingly considered actually killing himself. It was a shock to realize this and it came with a feeling of failure. How could what he's been through have been that bad if he's still here? Colloquially he knows this would be the will to live. But that rings false, too. It's really that since his escape he's been convinced that if he just hangs around for a while the world will do him the favor of finishing him off. On the one hand he knows he's entitled to end his own life; on the other, when he contemplates the practicalities, the how and the where and the when, an invisible collective headed by Juliet (but somehow including himself) weighs in with withering scorn. *Absurd melodrama.* Incredibly, this is the judgment: yes, you can have your eye gouged out, be reduced to a whimpering baby, beg for mercy, offer up your friends to save yourself—but still, it's absurd melodrama to let all that drive you to kill yourself. Perhaps that's what the will to live really is, the intimation that suicide's bad art.

Morwenna was still asleep when he left the croft. These mornings when he gets up he wakes her and she takes his place on the camp-bed, sometimes completing the maneuver without once opening her eyes. She sleeps for hours. Epic cellular recouping is going on. The jellyfish bruise has faded. Augustus keeps asking himself what he's going to do when the snow melts. The thought of spring, blowing apple blossom or shivering forget-me-nots—or worse, summer, warmth enough to sit with your bare feet in the sun, brings him to a rolling boil of panic so rapidly that he has to move, create the distraction of physical challenge to calm himself. He turns and starts down the hill for the croft.

He's lucky. First in that it's his habit to move quietly and second in that he hears the unfamiliar voice while he's still outside.

"Look at the fucking *state* of this place. How can you stand it?"

"Don't wreck it, Paulie, please."

"Jesus Christ it's a *shit*-hole."

Augustus keeps very still, surprised in the detached part of himself at how you forget this level of alertness, this hypersensitivity of skin and hair. The body, as he's learned, supplies effects on causal demand. Adrenaline rushes to the sites of action. There in his knees is the feeling of pooled weakness that is in fact sprung readiness.

The question is: the front door or the back door? He can see himself doing it, one hand holding the gun steady at just below chest height, the other flinging the door open. The front door involves a step up. The back door involves creeping and ducking two windows. And in any case it's irrational to suppose that just because it's the back door he'll have his back to it. He. Him. Paulie, whose rule is no smack and at first it's like you're a princess.

Augustus shifts the weight to his good leg. The gun's a thing of humming sentience against his chest, sensing proximal destiny, the call to its function. Even without relinquishing the stick he should be able to get a good grip on the—

Suddenly the door flies open. Augustus doesn't have much time to take Paulie in—registers artfully chopped dark hair, bony good looks, maroon leather jacket—before he's grabbed by his coat collar and yanked stumbling over the threshold into the croft. The stick gets away from him and he crashes to his knees.

Morwenna's on her side on the floor, struggling to get up. Her mouth's bleeding. She's got one elbow under her but keeps the other arm wrapped around her abdomen.

"Oh this is great, this is. Please tell me this rancid old coon's not sticking it in you?"

Which means he doesn't know about the gun. If he did that would come first. That's the ace. Absolutely everything from here must be designed around that. You're a rancid old coon who doesn't have a gun.

"Don't hurt him, Paulie, please."

"Because if he has you're going to douche with fucking Domestos. Jesus Christ."

"He hasnie touched me," Morwenna gasps, still trying to get onto her knees. "Honest to God, he hasn't. Juss don't hurt him, don't—"

Augustus on all fours senses the kick coming but can't move fast enough and Morwenna's scream synchronizes perfectly with all the breath leaving his body as if it's the scream that's pulled it out of him.

"Like that, you mean?" Paulie says.

"Paulie don't I'll do anythin you want I'll come back with you anythin you want juss don't hurt—"

"Or like this?"

The boots are steel-capped and this one goes hard and sharp into the side of Augustus's left leg. He can't scream, since his breath's gone, can't make a sound. He feels his face wide-eyed, open-mouthed and deep reflex curling him fetally though he mustn't, *must not* let the gun clunk or fall out of his pocket and through the pain is asking himself which grades of British police carry firearms, she said plainclothes, didn't she? Which means what? Yes? In any case he'll have to assume a gun or maybe more than one. But Jesus for a few seconds just a few seconds he's got to get air into his lungs. He can absorb violence to preserve the gun's secrecy but not so much that he'll be incapable of using it.

Morwenna, weeping, says, "Stop it, stop it, stop it—"

"Shut up!" Paulie turns and kicks her in the ribs and when she doubles up, the back. "Shut up you stupid. Fucking. Cunt. I can't believe you've dragged me all the way up here to find you gobbling a fucking darkie granddad and living in a fucking chicken coop. What's the matter with you? I mean seriously, what is the matter with you?" He addresses an invisible presence, his like-minded guardian angel: "You try'n instil a bit of class in these girls, a bit of savoir faire. What do you get? Aged niggers and fucking outbuildings."

Augustus twists to see Morwenna hunched on her side with her back to him, her arms covering her head, silently sobbing. Through all this the fire shimmies and snaps softly around two almost consumed logs, the window shows clear blue sky that makes him think of the empty Technicolor sky of *Soldier Blue.*

"Why do you make me do this? And Jesus Christ woman look at your *hair.* You've let yourself go. I don't like to say it but you've let yourself go and you look like a *shopping bag.* When we get back first thing you're getting is a makeover. That hair is a criminal offense. Christ Almighty."

There's a little conflict going on in Paulie, Augustus knows. Prudence says get in, grab the girl, get out. But this self's cramped and ravenous. Here's an opportunity for expansive play.

Morwenna coughs, chokes, retches. Tries to get up onto her elbows. Can't.

"I told you I'd find you," Paulie says. "Why didn't you—why doesn't anyone ever take me at my word? Did I tell you I'd find you or not? Eh?"

Morwenna nods. Augustus is within reach of his stick, but there's no point yet: he'll need both hands for the gun. He's managed to take a breath.

"Did you tell him? Did you tell him I'd find you? And he didn't believe you, did he? Took it with a pinch of salt, didn't he? You failed to convey my uncanniness. I'm not surprised. We're living in skeptical times." He takes a step toward Augustus, notices the nearness of the stick, bends and picks it up himself. Augustus is lying in an approximation of the recovery position, left arm and left knee bent. The gun under him presses his lowest rib. Paulie rests the tip of the walking stick on Augustus's neck and applies light pressure. "Been filling the aged nigger head with fabulous tales of tribulation, has she?"

Hardwiring says there must be something that will defuse the aggression. Find out how you're provoking your aggressor and stop doing it. But not here. Augustus knows the type. What provokes Paulie is Paulie's existence. His existence fills him with fear. He needs the radical distraction of your suffering. When he gets it it's not sufficient, which brings his existence back, and thus fear, and thus the need for radical distraction, and thus your suffering, and so on. Like all cruelty, even the nuanced, it's a failure of nerve and imagination, nerve because facing the fear requires courage, imagination because making someone suffer requires nothing but will. A child can do it, a moron. Paulie's the single psyche version, in fact (Augustus could laugh if he had breath) of Husain and his crew. The collective realization these guys share, Harper had said, is that where God and faith and the soul should be in fact is Nothing. Simply Nothing with a capital N. They can't hack it. They don't have the imagination to hack Nothing. It terrifies them, this Nothing. They have to make it into something. So they turn religion into politics, prayers into bombs. Now they've got something. Now they've got a shitload of insulation between themselves and Nothing: historical grievances, training camps, weapons, targets. Now they can relax. Now there's a point. Thank fuck, because for a moment back there they were staring into the void. What fundamentalists from the Inquisition to Al-Qaeda share isn't faith, it's faithlessness. The real war on terror's being waged in the arena of their own terrified hearts.

Another two breaths. Since for the moment Augustus can't speak he's spared the trouble of choosing what to say. A blessing: anything you say to Paulie is grist for the provocation mill. Unfortunately so is your silence, which lets the sound of his existence back in. Augustus closes his eyes, mentally rehearses the maneuver with the gun. He needs Paulie to return his attention to Morwenna for a moment but wonders how much more the girl can take. She's very still. A rib's most likely gone.

"Aged Sambo," Paulie says, tapping Augustus's neck with the stick. "I'm addressing myself to you. Have you put dew on this lily? Have you interfered with her in a Biblical fashion? Come on, speak up."

Augustus shakes his head: no. There's a certain type of firework that wriggles up into the sky with a movement like swimming sperm. This is how he pictures the pain's signals from his belly up into his throat. His left leg's dead but is going to have to be made to bear weight. There isn't time to let it come back to life.

"No? How come? Not your type?"

"Leave him alone, Paulie, he's not well."

"What, aside from being old and black with a gammy leg and B.O. you mean?"

"He just lets me stay here. He doesn't know antythin. Let's juss go, please. I'll do what you want. Whatever you say."

Paulie removes the stick from Augustus's neck and leans on it with both hands, feet apart, as if he's about to start a Fred Astaire dance routine. "Hear that?" he says. "She really doesn't want you hurt. Fatherly, is it? Grandfatherly. What about if I just cut one of his ears off, Mor?"

"No!"

"Both ears then."

"Leave him out of it! He's an *old man* for fuck's sake."

"Old people depress me like nothing else. Come here."

Paulie turns and with pretend dependence on the stick hobbles to Morwenna. "Get up. He's been in there I'll whiff it in a jiffy. The Paulie Costain nose never lies. Come on, get up."

"Please let's just *go*."

He whacks her buttocks with the stick. "Get *up* I said, I think."

Augustus very slowly rolls onto his back, gasping. Paulie sits on the upturned crate watching Morwenna getting to her feet, an incremental business, stopped by pain, interrogated, let go at an odd angle. The rib or ribs on her right side definitely. She holds them to prevent full expansion when she breathes in. The right leg doesn't want any weight on it either.

"Come here."

Augustus won't get another chance and in any case doesn't want to see this. There's no calculating. You reach into the pocket and hope it doesn't coincide with his glance. And if he has a gun he'll be the part of the world that does you the favor of finishing you.

The possibility enriches Augustus. Isn't this what he's been waiting for? *Yeah, yeah,* the Juliet-headed collective says, *to be or not to be. Very grand. Get over yourself, kiddo, it's a long time dead.* This is so clear in his head he fears Paulie will have heard it. He could laugh if breathing weren't such a challenge.

"Come here up close. Fuck are you wearing trousers for? What did I tell you about trousers? Lesbo combat trousers at that."

The fit of a gun's grip in your hand is of the deep geometry. That first time with Selina when he went inside her they looked at each other, shocked. Essential recognition. Marriages mutated into war or drifted into sadness because the physical match was minutely off. The effect like a watch losing a minute a day.

Augustus releases the safety with no clear idea of what he's going to do.

"Correction," Paulie says. "First thing when you get back is a fucking *shave*, woman. Jesus—"

"Don't move."

Augustus is lying on his belly with the gun gripped in both hands, pointed at Paulie. As a kid you were always on your belly with an imaginary gun, desperately outnumbered. Two little hot spots of pain in your elbows, maybe the beginnings of an erection.

"Don't move at all. Morwenna, pull up your pants and come over here behind me."

Possibly there was a time when the reversal would have been satisfying, but seeing Paulie's face drain does nothing for Augustus now. On the other hand the gun's introduced a verbal economy that reminds him of Harper and for the first time in a long time he feels as if he's reentered reality. Extraordinary the way a gun pares objects and purges space.

"You must be out of your mind," Paulie says.

"Morwenna," Augustus says. "Pants up. Get behind me."

Morwenna reaches down—stops, jolted, wraps her left arm around the right ribs, manages to get her underwear and trousers up. She backs, limping, rib-holding, keeping out of Augustus's line until he's between her and Paulie.

"Good. Now, Paulie, drop my walking stick. Just drop it on the floor. Go ahead."

"Do you know who I am?"

"Drop the walking stick."

To get upright he's going to have to suffer. Weight on the left hip, bend the right knee to get it under, then elbows, keeping the gun trained. The firework pains are still shooting, crazily.

Paulie drops the walking stick. Augustus knows if he continues giving instructions from the floor Paulie will try some move that works on television but in real life has disastrous consequences. As it is Augustus can see him growing bolder by the second, his aura tensing for masculine action. It irritates him. Paulie, suddenly, irritates him profoundly—and from Paulie his irritation without warning reveals itself as huge, exhaustive, touching everything from the Godless blue sky to the tongue pimple he's been nibbling for days, but fueled by the fact of his own continuance, the wearying business of not having died when he should have. You think you'll die but you don't. Life is the most durable of the habits, the most shameless and tasteless. This is the ghoulish aspect of doctors, who see only a challenge, monstrously premature babies wired, tubed, warmed and electrified into viability. In stories the will to live is something flamy and noble. For him, now, it's animal and revolting, at best farcical. He thinks of postpartum women weirdly compelled to eat their placentas, feels a kinship. Or dogs who must return to their vomit. The will to live isn't in the soul it's in the entrails, the mucous membranes, the blood and glands, the teeth. You're still a man. Don't make me take that away from you. But it was taken away. It went with the sound of his own voice, pleading then giving up all the information. He doesn't think of himself as a man anymore. He's a leftover, a freak who should have died but didn't and now for weeks, months, has been trying to swallow the simple fact that he's still here. *Waiting to die* was his inner answer to Calansay's question. It might as well have been *waiting to come back to life*. For the first time his racial ambiguity's resonantly apposite. Turns out it's been his lifelong training in being neither one thing nor the other, neither dead nor reconciled to life. His habits of narrative—dilemma, choice, action, resolution—are still wretchedly alive, like mutilated animals who can't shut up, who should be put down, who won't ever die of natural causes. Otherwise why—the voice asking this is a conflation: his own, Selina's, Juliet's, Harper's, possibly the disinterested subsonic interrogation of snow, rocks, sea, sky—did you tell her she could stay? From where he is right now, on the floor pointing a gun at a policeman, the core of his irritation is a binary star, laughter and disgust.

"You're not going to fucking—"

He pulls the trigger.

Deafening. Literally. For a moment the shot wipes out sound. Paulie, hit in the left ankle, jackknifes and pitches forward off the crate to the floor reaching for the wound. Augustus takes this underwater opportunity to wrestle himself up onto his knees, then using the edge of the camp-bed for support, onto his feet. He's aware of Morwenna frozen behind him. Paulie's face is crimped with pain and disbelief. Also misery and injustice. The water drops and sound surges back in, Paulie's incredulous gasps and the shot's echo bouncing off the croft's walls.

"I'LL KILL YOU YOU FUCKING CUNT! Oh God oh *God* you fucking cunt Jesus fucking Christ." The last word degenerates into a gargle as Paulie gripping his ankle doubles up, shuddering.

Slowly, because he can't move quickly, comically, because the left leg remains dead, Augustus gets to his stick and picks it up. The familiar transfer of weight's a relief. He stands over Paulie.

"Take your jacket off."

"What?"

"Take your jacket off."

Paulie in pinched shock merely looks at Augustus. With a force and accuracy that surprises everyone, especially himself, Augustus reverses the stick and whacks Paulie on the head with the heavy end. Paulie screams, throws up an arm to protect himself, then in an access of rage lunges at Augustus, screaming: You fucking black cunt I'll fucking kill you I'll fucking kill you I'll fucking—

It's a close thing, a second's blurred calculation, but Augustus doesn't fire. She's an accessory. The machinations of dull justice will follow. Which means what? This is the labored business of being involved with someone. He should never have said she could stay. But again why did he if not for something like this?

He hits Paulie ferocious blows in rapid succession. The stick's not cudgel enough to knock him out but it hurts, can't be withstood. Paulie takes a shot on the right hand that breaks a bone (Augustus believes he hears it) and with a scream curls up on the floor, crying and repeating: *Black bastard... black... bastard.*

"Take your jacket off."

"I'm not fucking armed!" Paulie screams. This rage is the satanic toddler's who for once is telling the truth.

"Take it off or I'll shoot you in the other foot." Augustus is thinking this would have been less of a problem in summer. Getting away in this weather's going to be an ordeal. Practicalities, the first buzzing outriders of the swarm, are starting to arrive. You don't get any concessions. Which thought makes him laugh, quietly. Lame one-eyed leftover no longer a man freak. Vigilante restaurateur.

Paulie struggles out of his jacket.

"Throw it to the girl."

Paulie tosses the jacket. "I'll find you, Mor. I'll find you and—"

Augustus whacks the broken hand with his stick and Paulie spasms in silence as if he's been electrocuted. He can't, Augustus sees, get past the outrage, can't accept the power relationship's been reversed. It's a mental block. Harper wouldn't have had it. Harper understood power aside from himself, a neutral tool that serves anyone who acquires it.

"Go through the pockets," Augustus says to Morwenna. She's very calm, holding her ribs, saddened by her satisfaction in this, underneath it angry that he's turned her into someone who can take such satisfaction. Augustus can imagine how she fell in love, what Paulie can be to a fifteen-year-old runaway with his diver's wristwatch and quick decisions and casual knowledge of everything and all the people who know him and smile when he walks in. He needs you to love him first, the foxy glamorous ease of him. He has to make you his princess. That's the whole point.

Wallet. Police ID. Cuffs. Two mobile phones. Condoms. Camel filters. Lighter. Change. Keys. Notebook.

"Over to the stove," Augustus tells Paulie. "Move. I know how much that hand hurts but I'll hit it again, as hard as I can. Move. Morwenna, the handcuffs."

Paulie, dragging himself backward to the stove, starts laughing. This, Augustus knows he's meant to infer, is Paulie enjoying the certainty of his future revenge. This is Paulie *tickled pink* by letting these two have their moment. A gesture of vital self-comfort.

"Facedown on the floor," Augustus says. "Left hand on the leg of the stove. You don't need me to spell this out."

Paulie, still chuckling, complies. Augustus kneels on his neck. There's the option of giving the gun to Morwenna for a moment but he doesn't like it. Better to struggle one-handed himself. He knows cuffs, of course. In any case Paulie's past trying something.

"Okay, sit up."

Augustus helps him get his back to the stove, legs stretched out in front of him. From here he can reach the logs and toss them on the fire. Enough for maybe a day. Then cold. Augustus checks how much blood to make sure it's not an artery.

"We should get going," he says to Morwenna. "Warm clothes, no more than you can carry in your shoulder bag."

"He'll find me," she whispers.

"Not this time."

She closes her eyes. Replaying the worst of it, Augustus assumes, the footage, the episodes. He doesn't want to know. She'll have to tell someone, eventually, but he'd rather it wasn't him. "Come on, let's get out of here. How much money in the wallet? Might as well have that, right?"

While Morwenna stuffs clothes into the shoulder bag Augustus builds up the fire, making sure Paulie gets to see his wallet, ID, condoms and notebook going into the flames. The two cell phones and car keys go into Augustus's coat pocket.

Morwenna's ready, but stands staring at Paulie. Augustus wishes he could shoot him for her, since there's blood on his hands already and nothing will happen to him after he's dead (though habit imagines a bulge in the ether even as he thinks it—and where or what is the invisible collective he's been in confab with? Just him, he tells himself. Juliet, Selina, Harper—it's all him); but Paulie dead will do her more harm than Paulie alive. Paulie dead will set the unpredictable Law in motion. He has no faith in the Law.

"You're a piece of shit," Morwenna says to Paulie. Augustus worries she's going to kick him or spit on him, hopes not because such things go awkwardly and you end up with aesthetic horror and disgust with yourself and the inadequacy of the act. But she turns her back on him and goes to the door.

"I'll be out in a minute," Augustus tells her, quietly. "Just want to make things secure here. Wait for me outside."

When Morwenna closes the door behind her Augustus lights one of the Camels and drops the lighter and pack in Paulie's lap. Paulie has difficulty with the damaged hand but manages eventually. Augustus pulls the one chair up and sits down.

"You have to understand something," he says. "If it was just me I'd shoot you. Point-blank, in the face, the mouth, the back of the head. Right now you'd be looking at death. Actually I think you've worked that out. Your instincts are fine and you know the sound of a liar. You've got the nose for character, you've got the psychology."

"Who the fuck *are* you?"

"No one important. A rancid old coon who turned out to have a gun."

"You can't fucking leave me here like this."

"Don't waste time, just listen. If you come after us, I'll kill you. No hesitation. I'll kill you. Look at me, closely. Understand: I'll kill you because I'm not afraid to die. Do you see this? Look at me. Do you see it?"

Paulie doesn't want to look at Augustus in the way Augustus wants to be looked at, but when their eyes meet for a moment Augustus feels the rejuvenating purity, sees Paulie, knows Paulie sees him. Nothing's had this quality since the night of his escape. This is the only version of himself that feels familiar, as if he's briefly sober in an epic of drunkenness. "She's told me everything," he says. "And within the next twenty-four hours my lawyers will have the same information. Which will remain inert, unless anything happens to me or the girl, anything at all, the slightest suspicion you're trying to reach us. In which case an investigation will begin. Look at me."

"Get fucked."

Augustus stamps on the broken hand and keeps his foot there. Paulie screams and twists against the cuff, his feet slither in the little pool of blood.

"Okay okay please, fuck, please—"

Augustus presses harder. Paulie's scream turns to silence, face scrunched, bearing the unbearable.

"You feel that force there on your hand? That's the world. The story of the world is the story of force. It's just some people are better at applying it than others."

Augustus stands, releases Paulie's hand. There's an almost full bottle of Glenfiddich on the table. Augustus sets it down within the policeman's reach. "The farmer or his boy'll be down. Maybe a couple of days." He feels tired, suddenly, remembers the doctor sitting in the drain cleaners' van on the dead forecourt, door open, smoking. You never know what you've got in the tank. Halfway through a sentence it's empty. The doc, as far as he knows, got his flight out of Casablanca, but it's hard to believe there was a life for him. He hopes he made it somewhere like Mexico, got absorbed into a small town or village, has a doorway he can sit in watching the dust swirl in the sunlight. Romantic fantasy. The old man will have drifted into vagrancy. Sores and sour clothes. He was already at the end of himself at the gas station.

Augustus pauses at the door, takes a last look at the room it seems he's seeing for the first time. The fire blazes in the hearth. He has no conclusions. This all feels, approximately, like an accident. Life's dervish mass spins erratically and sometimes snags you on a spur. It might have come nowhere near him had he not let the girl in, or a dozen times near-missed and passed by in the night. But he concedes he did let the girl in. This is the source of his weariness now, the thought that all along the living part of him has been meticulously plotting, that the dead part has had no control over it. Not an accident. A setup. A sting.

He has no resolution. Inertia nuzzles and he knows it'll offer itself at every step from here out and up the hill, into Marle, onto the ferry, the mainland and beyond. He isn't fortified. Already the reactive momentum's spent, adrenaline on the ebb. In fact he regrets what he's done, or rather resents how unthinkingly he's done it. No qualms about Paulie, but a feeling of being shystered by spontaneity, carried away by impulse. Art would demand an epiphany (quiet admission or Carlylean *Yea*) a realization that life's worth living. He doesn't have any of that, only the rueful feeling of having hoodwinked himself into action. Absurd action, moreover. Paulie handcuffed to the stove looks like a life-size ventriloquist's dummy. Yet the man has a childhood, dreams, memories, a history. There are moments you glimpse everyone's cluttered uniqueness, the endless particularity that requires so much effort, too much effort. The thought of the long trudge with Morwenna (who, back in the world of demand and exigency will be different, possibly irritating, at the very least more talkative) exhausts him where he stands, brings the brutal realization that he doesn't have to stick with her, owes her nothing, could shoot *her* in the head and consign her body to the sea. And yet God has not said a word!

Oh come off it.

Not God but the self-conjured cabal of ghosts says this—Juliet, Selina, Cardillo, Elise—all the good dead or all the bits of him their living fashioned. At his center is what Harper helped him find, the solitary eye that sees the void and the darkling plain, that knows the dead don't speak, that no one's keeping score, that earth receives the bodies of the evil and the good with null equalizing silence. This is his center, to which he'll go when his time comes. He supposes until then the ghosts prove his pleasure in remembering them. He could put a bullet in the girl's brain, cut off her head, gouge out her heart and wolf it down—but it would spoil his pleasure in remembering the ones he loved. There's nothing necessary about this. The presence or absence of love in a life is purely contingent, which if it points to a grand narrative points to one of spectacular natural injustice. But the fact remains that contingently, he, Augustus Rose, had these people, had that love, takes this pleasure in remembering. Contingently, he's doomed to live under the rule of certain durable habits.

There's nothing more to say to Paulie. The policeman will either come after them or not. That's out of Augustus's hands now. If he wants a project it's getting the girl away. Again the thought leaves him leaden. Even the struggle up the hill seems beyond him, though he's made it a dozen times at least since the snow.

Heaving against sleepiness, Augustus opens the door, steps out and pulls it shut behind him.

Morwenna's waiting for him at the bottom of the hill, woolen-hatted, scarved, hands in the leather jacket pockets, shoulder bag bulging. The rib's keeping her from straightening up properly. Now he's outside Augustus feels wide awake, horribly alive to the difficulties crowding ahead. Remember to toss the phones into the sea. That's the least of it. The car key on Paulie's bunch is for an Audi. With luck you find that where the track comes off the lane. If not there won't be many Audis in the ferry car park. No choice but to take it and switch on the mainland. It occurs to him Morwenna isn't likely to have a passport. Her look over the scarf says she's not sure how or if this has changed things between them, what he might want from her, what he might do. It gives him a small pleasure (as when he noticed Selina's broken silver chain and knew he could spare her its loss) to know she's got nothing to fear from him, since he's made his decision, since the habits, thus far, have endured.

"What happened?"

"Nothing. I told him not to come after us. He'll be stuck there for a while anyway." He holds up the Audi key. "We may have transportation." It's just striking him that he'll never see Calansay again. He feels the need for a gesture of acknowledgment, but it passes.

"It's up to you," Augustus says, "but if you want, I can help you for a while."

Morwenna's nostrils are raw. The last hour's left her eyes bright. Her lip's split and swollen.

"Thanks," she says—and suddenly tears well and fall. Augustus understands: not because she's suffered but because he's helping her. When you're a child people's cruelty makes you cry. When you're an adult it's their kindness. Seeing her making this shift he feels ancient, flimsy as a paper lantern, for just a second or two wholly not up to the job.

"Sorry," she says. "Sorry."

"It's all right. It's okay. We better get going, though."

But she can't, for a moment. Things have caught up with her. She goes down on her knees and vomits in the snow. No stopping the effect on her ribs. In solidarity rather than because there's anything he can do Augustus gets down on one knee next to her, puts his hand gently in the small of her back. The sky above the snowline is deep blue. You can see how people lie down in snow to die and eventually it feels warm.

"I'm all right," she says after a little while. "Juss needed to do that. Sorry."

They get by ridiculous degrees to their feet. "Here," Augustus says. "Take these." Ibuprofen. Four left in the bottle in his pocket. Morwenna swallows two with a mouthful of snow. Augustus is thinking of New York. He has a vivid mental picture of Darlene sitting at the window table in Ferrara, drinking a double espresso and looking over the numbers Maguire the accountant's run for her on a possible new purchase, a prime spot on Third Avenue and 7th Street. You find something you like and go into it.

A few paces ahead of him Morwenna slips, but recovers her balance. She stops for a moment, adjusts the shoulder bag, looks back at him.

Acknowledgments

I'm indebted to a collection of essays, *Abu Ghraib: The Politics of Torture* (North Atlantic Books, Berkeley, 2004), for diverse illuminations of this very old and very new phenomenon. In particular, "Breakdown in the Gray Room: Recent Turns in the Image War," a transcript of the lecture by David Levi Strauss, first given at the Los Angeles Times Media Center, June 17, 2004; "Abu Ghraib and the Magic of Images" by Charles Stein; "Feminism's Assumptions Upended" by Barbara Ehrenreich; and "Abu Ghraib: A Howl" by Richard Grossinger.

Augustus's version of the arrest and treatment of Johnson Hinton derives from Malcolm X's account in *The Autobiography of Malcolm X* (Malcolm X with the assistance of Alex Haley, Penguin Classics, Penguin Books, London, 2001).

Selina's story of her accidental ingestion of the ant belongs to Andrea Freeman, who has very kindly lent it to me.

Many thanks to my agents, Jonny Geller in London and Jane Gelfman in New York, for keeping the faith, and to my editor at Ecco, Abigail Holstein, who brought to this book immediate understanding, fierce enthusiasm, and consistently sound judgment. I am much in her debt.

For editorial guardianship during the writing of this novel, and for patience with my delays, thanks to Millicent Bennett. For tactical support and an incisive first read, I'm grateful to Paige Simpson. For Italian and Spanish language help, I salute Mike Loteryman, Eva Vives, and Nicola Harwood.

Last but not least, thanks to Kim Teasdale, for being cheerful first thing in the morning, and for gently forcing me to experience the world outdoors every now and again.